Somewhere in Southeast Asia

Frank Lucas entered a natural cavern the size of an airplane hangar. A general of the Chinese Kuomintang examined Frank's papers, studied him for a moment, and said, "How would you get it into the States?"

"What do you care?"

"Who do you work for in there?"

Again, Frank replied, "What do you care?"

"Who are you, really?" the general asked.

"It says right there. Frank Lucas."

"I mean, who do you *represent*?"

"Me."

"You think you're going to take a hundred kilos of heroin into the U.S. and you don't work for anyone? Someone is going to *allow* that?"

Frank shrugged.

"After this first purchase, if you're not killed by Marseilles importers—or their people in the States—then what?"

"Then there'd be more. On a regular basis. Though I'd rather not have to drag my ass all the way up here every time. . . ."

AMERICAN GANGSTER

UNIVERSAL PICTURES AND IMAGINE ENTERTAINMENT PRESENT IN ASSOCIATION WITH RELATIVITY MEDIA A BRIAN GRAZER PRODUCTION IN ASSOCIATION WITH SCOTT FREE PRODUCTIONS A RIDLEY SCOTT FILM DENZEL WASHINGTON RUSSELL CROWE "AMERICAN GANGSTER" CHIWETEL EJIOFOR CUBA GOODING, JR. JOSH BROLIN TED LEVINE ARMAND ASSANTE JOHN ORTIZ JOHN HAWKES RZA MUSIC BY MARC STREITENFELD COSTUME DESIGNER JANTY YATES CO-PRODUCER JONATHAN FILLEY

EDITOR PIETRO SCALIA ACE PRODUCTION DESIGNER ARTHUR MAX DIRECTOR OF PHOTOGRAPHY HARRIS SAVIDES ASC EXECUTIVE PRODUCERS NICHOLAS PILEGGI STEVEN ZAILLIAN BRANKO LUSTIG JIM WHITAKER MICHAEL COSTIGAN PRODUCED BY BRIAN GRAZER RIDLEY SCOTT WRITTEN BY STEVEN ZAILLIAN DIRECTED BY RIDLEY SCOTT A UNIVERSAL PICTURE © 2007 UNIVERSAL STUDIOS

NOVEMBER 2007

www.universalpictures.com

IMAGINE SCOTT FREE

R RESTRICTED UNDER 17 REQUIRES ACCOMPANYING PARENT OR ADULT GUARDIAN VIOLENCE, PERVASIVE DRUG CONTENT AND LANGUAGE, NUDITY AND SEXUALITY

UNIVERSAL

AMERICAN GANGSTER

A NOVELIZATION

BY

Max Allan Collins

•

Based on the motion picture screenplay by

Steven Zaillian

TOR®

A TOM DOHERTY ASSOCIATES BOOK • NEW YORK

This is a work of fiction. All of the characters, organizations, and events portrayed in this novel are either products of the author's imagination or are used fictitiously.

AMERICAN GANGSTER

Copyright © 2007 by Universal Studios, LLLP. American Gangster is a trademark and copyright of Universal Studios. All rights reserved.

Edited by James Frenkel

A Tor Book
Published by Tom Doherty Associates, LLC
175 Fifth Avenue
New York, NY 10010

www.tor.com

Tor® is a registered trademark of Tom Doherty Associates, LLC.

ISBN-13: 978-0-7653-5901-8
ISBN-10: 0-7653-5901-4

First Edition: October 2007

Printed in the United States of America

0 9 8 7 6 5 4 3 2 1

"Anyone is capable of anything."

CHESTER HIMES

"Tell those bastards that Eliot Ness can't be bought."

ELIOT NESS

"There is no peace, saith the Lord, for the wicked."

ISAIAH 48:22

AMERICAN GANGSTER

1. Tru Blue

Two days before Thanksgiving 1970, Frank Lucas had things to do for Bumpy Johnson. As usual.

On that cold sunny afternoon, Frank's first stop was a funky little jazz club, one of those basement joints where cigarette smoke and spilled-liquor smell passed for atmosphere, and volume from the combo on the postage-stamp stage stood in for talent.

The bartender who glanced up warily from polishing glasses knew that Frank's businesslike, businessman demeanor was deceiving. With his tailored charcoal suit and crisply knotted tie, Frank was as tall and handsome and confident as Sidney Poitier, if not as dark. He had left his topcoat in the waiting Lincoln Town Car, desiring freedom of movement.

Without seeming to rush, Frank strode to a back booth where four black dudes with terrible taste in attire looked up with lidded eyes and sneering expressions, unhappy to be interrupted in their private talk of business that they no doubt felt was none of Frank's, or his boss Bumpy's.

They were wrong, and Frank told them so, or tried, as the din of music made it hard for them to get his words. The men leaned forward to hear better and Frank took a revolver from his pocket and shot them in their respective heads.

This they heard.

And Frank was gone before anyone had time to scream.

His next stop was 116th Street where he oversaw Bumpy's annual Thanksgiving turkey toss. Frank, like everybody in Harlem, thought of his boss as "Bumpy," though Frank (even as close as the two men were) always paid him the respect of "Mr. Johnson" when they spoke.

Bumpy would stand up there in the flatbed truck, a benign king dispensing freshly butchered turkeys like benedictions, and poor folk in their tattered clothes would crowd around and grin up at him gratefully and an elegantly attired Bumpy would grin right back.

Frank had no idea how old Bumpy Johnson was, though everybody knew he'd been around forever, the Robin Hood of Harlem who stood up to Dutch Schultz himself back in Prohibition days. So, hell, by any yardstick the old boy was elderly, and yet up there pitching turkeys to the crowd, he looked sturdy as Woody Strode.

And as rich as God, in that cashmere topcoat and silk scarf and those leather gloves, his head of Brillo-gray hair bare. As far as Frank was concerned, this man *was* God; Jesus Christ Himself never saved anybody better than Bumpy had Frank.

Frank had come up from North Carolina already a career criminal, and started indiscriminately ripping off everything and everybody from jewelry stores to crap games. Some of those crap games had included Harlem gangsters and, Frank now knew, such recklessness would have caught up with him . . . if Bumpy Johnson hadn't caught up with him first.

Frank had been hustling at Lump's Pool Room on 134th Street, taking chumps for eight ball. A tall duded-up motherfucker called Icepick took the bait, displaying a choke-a-horse roll of bills. And Frank—having no idea this was a stone killer who freelanced to the Mafia—decided that Icepick's roll was going to be his, whether at the pool table or with a gun in an alley.

Icepick wanted to shoot a thousand-dollar game of pool, but Frank only had a hundred dollars, which prompted Icepick to wonder aloud what kind of goddamn punk goes around with nothin' but a lousy C-note on his skinny ass.

Frank was seconds away from saying he really did have a thousand after all, ready to reach for his piece when a Bourbon-smooth voice from behind asked him: "Son, can you *beat* this boy?"

Frank turned and saw a black man the likes of which he'd never seen: close to six foot, dark-complected, in a gray suit sharper than a serpent's tooth and a maroon tie and camel's-hair overcoat with a flower in the lapel, a Homburg perched jauntily on a big noggin. Looked like he walked out of an ad in *Esquire*.

"I can shoot pool with anybody on the planet, mister."

"Then how about I back you. Fifty-fifty split?"

"Cool."

Suddenly Icepick was as twitchy as a flea on a skillet. "Bumpy, man—you *know* I don't never bet 'gainst *you.*"

But this Bumpy character paid Icepick no heed, just thundered, "Rack 'em up!"

As Bumpy watched silently, the two players rolled for the break, Frank took it, and crushed the dude. Icepick never got off a damn shot. Took his beating, paid up and slunk off.

Afterward, Bumpy told Frank to come along with him, and Frank didn't argue. Soon they were in a chauffeured Caddy, and Bumpy directed them straight to the best men's clothing store on Lenox Avenue, where the benefactor picked out for his new charge the nicest suits, slacks, ties, you name it.

For six months, Frank slept in the front room of Bumpy's place. And everybody in Harlem, including men he'd robbed, from the jeweler to various hoodlums, started paying seventeen-year-old Frank Lucas respect.

Why Bumpy had taken Frank under his wing like that Frank never knew and sure as hell never asked; but the older man must have seen potential in the kid from North Carolina. Bumpy personally showed Frank the ropes, from figuring the vig to doing the collections. And everybody in Harlem paid Bumpy Johnson. The protection racket was the foundation of Bumpy's business.

Now, twenty years later, Frank was still at Bumpy's

side—his driver and bodyguard and collector and pro-
tégé. The turkeys tossed, the two men—with Bumpy
leading his loyal German shepherd on its leash—were
walking toward the Wells Restaurant when the nattily
attired older gangster paused and pointed. His leather-
gloved finger indicated a vast wall of TVs playing in
the expanse that was the window of the latest of these
discount emporiums popping up everywhere, like
plastic-and-metal mushrooms.

"*This* is the problem," Bumpy said.

Frank wasn't sure what his boss meant—did he
mean the Vietnam War? The image playing on all of
the screens showed soldiers in the jungles of that distant land. You could hear the whisper of gunfire
through the glass.

"This," Bumpy said, shaking his head woefully, "is
what's wrong with America."

Frank nodded, still not sure he was getting it. Poli-
tics wasn't something either of them talked much.

"It's gotten so big," the sonorous voice was inton-
ing, "you can't find your way."

Then Bumpy led both his watchdogs on, human and
canine, a Red Sea of pedestrians parting—whether out
of respect or fear, what did it matter?—and the two
men approached the entrance to the big discount store.

Again Bumpy paused.

"Where's the corner grocery? It's a supermarket now.
What happened to that funky old candy store? Mc-
Donald's is squatting on its ruins. And *this* place. . . ."

Bumpy indicated the yawning chasm of a store with
its endless aisles and towering stacks of merchandise.

A few customers wandered within, as if lost in an overseas airport, with no sales clerks to guide them.

"Where's the pride of ownership, a warehouse like this?" Bumpy demanded. "Where's people waiting on people? Does anybody *work* here?"

Frank did not know the term "rhetorical question," but he knew one when he heard one, and didn't reply. They were walking again, slowly, and now Bumpy was indicating a display window filled with Japanese stereo components.

"What right do they have, cutting out the suppliers, pushing all the middlemen out, buying direct from the manufacturer? Sony this, Toshiba that, all them slant-eyed sons of bitches putting Americans out of work! We fought a war for *that*?"

Bumpy stopped again, TVs replaced by cameras. His eyes widened, his nostrils flared.

"What's an honest businessman like me supposed to do with a goddamn place like *this*, Frank?"

Now Frank wasn't sure—maybe he *was* supposed to answer. . . .

Bumpy shook his head in sheer frustration. "Who the hell am I supposed to ask for—the assistant manager? How do you collect from a goddamn octopus that won't show you his fuckin' head?"

Frank nodded. The protection racket was definitely going out of style, though he had never expressed this opinion out loud.

Bumpy stared back at the window of cameras. Again he pointed.

"*That's* the problem, Frank. Eyes looking at you, but

no faces. That's the way it is, now: you can't even find a heart to stick the knife in."

Bumpy was still returning the cameras' stare when his jaw went slack and his expression turned fearful.

Which shocked Frank, who did not shock easily. Thing was, in all these years, Frank Lucas had never seen Bumpy Johnson look afraid.

Now, astonishingly, the big man dropped to his knees, as if praying to this church of consumerism. Both Frank and the German shepherd stared down at their master in disbelief.

Then Frank was on his knees, too, asking, "What is it, Mr. Johnson? *Bumpy!*"

Hand splayed on the breast of the cashmere topcoat, Bumpy looked at Frank but remained slack-jawed, no words coming out, though the eyes pleaded.

Frank heard a voice yelling, "*Somebody call an ambulance!*"

It was his own voice.

He scrambled to the entrance of the cavernous discount store and yelled those words again, but the place seemed empty, the echo of his cry for help having a hollow ring, blending in with Muzak and cash registers ringing up sales that Bumpy would never see his piece of.

Frank threw a desperate glance at Bumpy, whose tear-filled eyes were on him.

And finally Bumpy managed to speak: "Forget it, Frank. Nobody's in charge."

As usual, Bumpy was right, even with his last words.

* * *

On the day of Bumpy's funeral, the media was waiting outside the Lenox Terrace apartment house,
recording the parade of limousines and the mourners
who emerged from them, family and friends, of
course, but also celebrities and politicians. This enormous crowd, mostly Harlemites, called for cops on
horseback to maintain order; for a protection racketeer, Bumpy was beloved.

And in certain unmarked cars, FBI agents snapped
pictures with their long-lensed cameras, their focus on
the Italian gangsters coming to pay their respects, capo
Dominic Cattano in particular. The black criminals
were beneath their interest, though when Nicky Barnes
in his tinted Gucci glasses stepped from his white
Bentley, to pose happily for anybody with a camera,
the feds felt obligated to snap a few of this attention-
craving drug dealer.

The live coverage played on a television in the Johnson apartment, though no one was really watching.

*"The passing of Ellsworth 'Bumpy' Johnson has
brought together a who's who of mourners on this chilly
afternoon. The Governor has come down. The Mayor of
New York and the Chief of Police and Commissioner
join sports and entertainment luminaries . . . "*

In a corner of Bumpy Johnson's well-appointed garden apartment, Frank Lucas was sitting on a couch,
half-listening to this March of Time obituary. Nearby
but not right next to where Frank sat, Bumpy's loyal

German shepherd perched, watching all these intruders as suspiciously as Frank.

"*According to the eulogies*," a male reporter down among the crowd below was saying, "*Bumpy Johnson was a great man, a giving man, a man of the people. But no one chose to include in their remembrances the word most often associated with Johnson: gangster.*"

Frank rose, went to the TV, switched it off and returned to his couch. This had been his boss's private sanctuary, with its carved-ivory chess table and bookcase of leather-bound Shakespeare and a stereo console with a record collection running from classical music to Henry Mancini, no jazz or R & B at all. Frank was among the few to regularly hang out here with the boss.

Now the sanctuary had been invaded, on the pretense of respect. Among the vultures were the self-styled Superfly Nicky Barnes with his ever-present crew of ass-kissers, and that thug Tango Black, a big bald-headed bastard known to be quick for a man his size. Right now Tango was quick to scavenge food and booze at this catered wake.

Vulgar men in vulgar clothes, Frank thought. Ironic that the two Cosa Nostra types at the wet bar—elegant, hawkishly handsome Cattano, who Bumpy did business with, and his accountant-like minion, Rossi—were among the most truly respectful mourners here. While Tango and Nicky Barnes sloshed down the booze, Cattano sipped white wine. Class.

Taking the liberty of plopping himself down next to

Frank was an anonymously respectable-looking white guy in a dark suit suitable for a mortician or banker. He was in fact the latter, with Chemical Bank in the Bronx.

"How you doing, Frank?"

"All right."

"Terrible loss."

Frank nodded.

The banker risked a small smile. "How are you . . . otherwise? Things okay financially?"

The banker was obviously wondering whether Frank had been appointed by Bumpy as his successor. But he didn't reply: this was neither the time nor the place. The banker's lack of tact, however, didn't irritate him as much as seeing that waste of skin Tango Black plonk a watery glass filled with melting ice on the edge of Bumpy's antique inlaid chess table.

The banker was pressing on: "Did Bumpy set anything up for you?"

"Excuse me."

Frank got up and crossed to the chess table and picked up the glass and set it on a coaster.

Tango, noticing this, grinned at Frank and said, "Hey, while you're at it, Frank, I could use an ashtray."

Frank reached into his jacket. Tango frowned a little; so did the German shepherd, watching his master's friend ever closely. His revolver in its shoulder holster was revealed, but what Frank was going for was his handkerchief, which he used to dry the condensation Tango's spent drink glass had left.

Then, from a drawer of the chess table, Frank took an ashtray and held it out toward Tango.

The big man looked at Frank, at the ashtray and back at Frank; finally, unsure of whether this was a genuine response to his sarcastic comment or some kind of challenge, Tango wandered off to scavenge more free eats.

When Frank returned to the couch, the banker was gone, but Charlie Williams had taken his place. Charlie, an older player in the dope game, was an affable guy, stand-up all the way, and Bumpy had thought well of him.

Charlie had an almond-shaped face emphasized by a receding hairline and a mustache a shade lighter than his dark hair. "You going to be all right, Frank?"

"Yeah."

"You don't like havin' all these people walkin' around in here, do you? Sniffin' around is more like it."

"No I don't."

Charlie patted Frank's shoulder. "Listen, knowing Bumpy, he prob'ly never told you, but he made me promise . . . anything ever happened to him? I'd make sure you didn't go without."

Frank gave Charlie a smile, his first one today. "I'll be fine, Charlie." Then he turned away and stared into the mourners, making them a blur in his vision. "Half the people here owed Bumpy money. If they think I'm gonna forget to collect, they're dead wrong."

Charlie chuckled. Patted Frank's shoulder. "That's the spirit. Go get 'em, son."

Getting up with a nod and a smile, Charlie ambled off. Cattano's man Rossi, a mustached blocky character with shark's eyes, trundled over like a tank. His eyes asked Frank if it was okay to sit down. Frank's eyes said yes.

Rossi said, "Unseemly to do business here, Frank."

"Right."

"But life goes on."

"It does."

"Thought you'd wanna know you can pick up the stuff at the club tomorrow."

"Morning okay?"

Rossi nodded. "Ten?"

"Ten."

2. Could Be Fatal

Richard "Richie" Roberts knew what fear was.

This afternoon, for example, he and his partner Javy Rivera were about to serve a subpoena on a low-level wise guy, Vinnie Campizi, and wise guys, of any level, were potentially dangerous. At this very moment, Richie was lugging a sledgehammer as he and Javy headed across a street busy enough to take some doing, but also the kind of thoroughfare where no driver paid any heed to a couple fullback-size jay-walkers in leather jackets and jeans, one of whom was hefting a sledgehammer.

The seedy hourly rate motel they were heading toward was close enough to the waterfront that you could see the jagged teeth of the Harlem skyline on the other side, just beyond the George Washington Bridge. This was the kind of fleabag where you got rolled and not just in the hay, where catching a dose of the clap was getting off easy. Bad things happened behind those closed doors, but none of it, after all these years on the force, added up to fear for Richie Roberts.

Fear for Richie Roberts was walking to the gallows that was a blackboard at the front of his night-school law class, a fluorescent-lit dungeon where he existed in cold-sweat dread of hearing his name called. "Fuck you, pig!" from a PCP-addled perp held nothing like the threat of hearing his professor say, "Mr. Roberts— give us *U.S. vs. Meade* . . . subject, issues, what the determination was, and what it means to us today."

Fear for Richie was turning to face classmates, all of whom were at least a decade younger than him, every one of them knowing more than he did, and exposing the inadequacies of his thinking and self-expression.

Sledgehammer gripped in one hand, Richie—dark blond, boyish—was explaining to Javy: "They took surveys. It's scientific."

Javy, a pair of sunglasses surrounded by long hair, muttonchop sideburns and a thick mustache, said, "Yeah, right, it's in the *Enquirer*, it's gotta be true."

"No, it is," Richie insisted. "Number one fear of most people? Isn't dying, dying's easy—it's public speaking. They get sick, physically ill—puke their guts out."

Javy's eyebrows rose over the sunglasses. "So, naturally, this is what you want to do for a living. Get up in front of people."

"Naw, it's the law I'm interested in. We're at the bottom of the food chain, Javy—there's more control up top."

"More control than swinging a sledge?"

They were headed toward the motel office; seemed there was a VACANCY. There'd soon be another.

"Anyway," Richie said, "I don't like being that way—afraid to stand up in front of people. It's stupid. I wanna beat it."

They went into the office.

A portable TV on a shelf was playing another news report about that dead black gangster, Bumpy Johnson. *Christ*, Richie thought, *the old bastard was getting more play in New York than Martin Luther King.*

The clerk was in his thirties and needed a shave; his sleepy expression woke up a little at the sight of the sledgehammer. "Hey! What the fuck you guys think—"

Javy flashed his New Jersey detective's shield; he dug the subpoena out of his pocket and flashed it, too, though the clerk was already convinced.

About to go back out, Richie caught the clerk's eyes. He gestured with the sledgehammer. "No wake-up calls, now."

"No! Do what you gotta do, guys. No skin off my dick."

The two plainclothes Prosecutor's Office cops kept on the sidewalk under the overhang, close to the doors of the motel rooms. They walked with the deliberation and lack of concern of mailmen.

Javy waved the subpoena. "So who's gonna do this?"

Richie snatched it. "Campizi knows me; he'll take it from me. I've known him since high school."

"How the fuck many wise guys you know, anyway?"

"How many wise guys went to high school in New Jersey?"

Javy smirked. "Well, this is not your fuckin' class reunion, Rich. Just throw the damn thing in there—he doesn't have to take it. That's good service."

"You takin' law classes, too, Jav?"

"Well, if you're serving the moke, at least give me the sledge."

Richie handed it off.

They stopped at Campizi's motel room door. Their snitch said Campizi had been shacked up with a Puerto Rican hooker, and Richie and Javy, staked out across the way, had seen a female of that description exiting the motel lot in a nice new Trans Am convertible that indicated Campizi wasn't her only well-heeled client.

Javy knocked.

The door opened slowly, just the length of the night-latch chain, revealing the balding, pot-bellied, mustached Campizi in a T-shirt, slacks and bare feet.

Richie raised the subpoena and was about to say something friendly to his old classmate when Campizi's eyes golfballed and Javy yelled, "*Throw it in!*"

Richie flung the damn papers in, but his hand was in the crack of the door just as Campizi slammed the damn thing.

"*Fuck!*" Richie wailed, his palm wedged in there, and an ominous *click* told him the little bastard had thrown the dead bolt. He threw his shoulder into the wood as best he could, which trapped as he was didn't exactly give him a running start.

Then something, other side of the door, clamped down on his captured fingers. . . .

The prick was *biting* him! Fucking finger food!

"Jesus Christ," Richie said, watching blood run down the door frame. "Do it, Javy, do it!"

"Get *down*, Rich!"

Richie did his best to comply, and the big iron head of the hammer flew past him and shattered the door to splinters, relieving the pressure on Richie's hand, and then both cops were shoving through, taking what was left of the door with them, right off its damn hinges.

Campizi did a pop-eyed take and scrambled for the bathroom; it would have been funny as hell if Richie's hand and fingers weren't a smashed bloody mess. Slamming himself inside, Campizi said, "Fuck you, guys!"

This door was by comparison a hollow nothing to smash through, and two swings of the sledge made matchsticks of it. Bloody mitt or not, Richie took the honors, heading into the cubicle where Campizi was half out of the bathroom window, and grabbing him, flinging him into the shower stall like a little rag doll, plastic shower curtain going down like Janet Leigh dying in *Psycho*, smearing the thing with blood, some of it Campizi's, some Richie's.

Richie started in giving him a goddamn good left-handed thrashing, and was just getting into it when Javy yanked him away from the cowering T-shirted fetus.

Javy grinned at Richie and said, "So this is easier than night school?"

The rage left Richie, and he laughed. But the throbbing pain hung on.

Richie's discomfort eased, however, when the paramedic who tended to his bloodied hand on their ambulance ride turned out to be female and brunette and friendly.

A male paramedic was tending to Campizi, whose bloody face was pinched with contrition. "Swear to God, Richie, I didn't know it was you! Would I slam a door on your hand? Knowingly?"

Richie was off the little fold-down seat, startling the brunette paramedic as he lunged for Campizi and smacked him, yelling, "Would you bite my fingers knowingly, you prick? *Shit!*"

The latter expletive reflected the burst of pain Richie felt, having instinctively used his right hand, the injured one, to batter Campizi.

Both paramedics pulled Richie away.

Campizi, who hadn't been hurt by the blow as much as Richie himself, gestured with two hands, placatingly. "Richie, Richie . . . for old times' sake, we gotta work this out."

Richie glowered. "Now I need a fuckin' rabies shot."

"What can we do, Richie? You don't wanna do this, beat on your old pal. What can I give you?"

Richie's eyes tightened in interest.

"Who do you want?" Campizi asked. "Who can I give you, make this right? How about . . . Big Sal's bookie? No? Not big enough? Maybe you want Newsboy's accountant? Yeah? I'll *give* him to you. No problem."

Richie studied his old classmate, and his irritation receded. A policy ring accountant wouldn't be a bad bust at that.

His hand was almost fully bandaged now. He smiled in thanks to the brunette.

"Is it still throbbing?" she asked.

"Is what still throbbing?" he asked.

She smiled back at him.

At least he was getting something out of having his hand squashed—a policy ring accountant and a woman in uniform.

Not a bad night's work.

The next afternoon, in Newark, Richie sat with Javy and Campizi in an unmarked car, their for-shit Plymouth, across from a closed social club.

Not entirely closed: a nondescript guy in a rumpled suit came out of the front carrying a grocery bag. The sight of this unprepossessing character was enough to send Campizi, in the backseat, diving for the floor.

"That's him," Campizi said.

"Him" was J. J. Levinson, accountant for policy king "Newsboy" Moriarty. Right now the accountant was putting his grocery bag in the trunk of a dark blue

Buick Century. Clearly unaware he was being watched, the accountant climbed in behind the wheel and rolled off into light traffic.

This was only the accountant's first stop. He picked up another grocery bag to stow in his trunk at a scrap metal yard. Around dusk he came out of a bar with another bag.

Richie craned from behind the wheel to speak to the ducked-down Campizi. "All right. We're even. Get lost."

Campizi's smile couldn't have been sicker. "You're the best, Richie."

"Let's not say good-bye, Vinnie. Let's just say get the fuck out."

Campizi opened the door onto the sidewalk and all but crawled away.

Then Richie and Javy were following the accountant's Buick as dusk flirted with night. Apparently the bar had been the accountant's last pickup, because the guy swung into a parking lot—an attendant on duty, but self-park—and left his car locked up to take another one in a nearby stall.

As the accountant got behind the wheel, Javy asked, "We gonna stay with him, or the car?"

Not much time to think about these two options. . . .

Richie said, "Let's see who comes for the car."

By seven that night, a lot of people had come for a lot of cars; in fact, only the abandoned Buick remained, the detectives' Plymouth parked across the way.

"Let's get a warrant," Richie said.

"Okay. Want me to call it in?"

"Sure."

Five minutes later, Javy got in on the rider's side and took a can of Coke from a small bag, from which he then extracted his own Styrofoam cup of coffee.

"Think we got made?" Javy asked.

Richie, tapping the wheel impatiently with his bandaged hand, asked, "You didn't forget to call for the warrant, did you?"

"Yeah. I got all confused buying coffee and Coke." Javy shook his head.

Richie craned to look behind him. "Well, where are they?"

"Christ, Rich, I just called about a minute ago. Will you relax?"

They watched an attendant lock up. They listened to the electric buzz of street lamps whose yellowish glow painted the car and its occupants like jaundice victims. Richie checked his watch.

"Fuck waiting," he said. "Hell, we saw him with the slips."

Javy blinked at his partner. "You saw policy slips? You saw grocery bags is what you saw. And you don't know what the hell is in 'em."

Richie scowled. "Yes I do, and so do you. Don't give me that bullshit—"

"What's your rush? Half an hour tops, warrant'll be here."

Now Richie leveled with his partner. "Look. Javy— I got school."

"Then this is your lucky night."

"What is?"

"This is. You won't have to get up in front of your

fellow students and shit your pants—'cause you're cutting class."

Richie said nothing, tapping the wheel gently with the bandaged hand.

Javy sipped his coffee. "You know what you were saying before? About puking in front of people, you're so scared? Money's gonna take that bad feeling away."

"Money."

"The money you'll make as a rich lawyer, jerk. Take that sick feeling clean away."

"Not when it's less money."

Javy frowned. "Less money than what, man?"

"Less than I make now."

Javy grinned and waved this ridiculous assertion away. "Come on, Rich—no lawyer on earth makes less than a cop."

"They do if they're in the Prosecutor's Office. Three thousand less per annum than us lowly dicks."

Javy had a pole-axed expression. "You gotta be fuckin' kiddin' me."

"I wish I were." Richie checked his watch. Class started in half an hour. "Fuck this shit."

"Richie . . ."

Richie got out of the Plymouth, unlocked the trunk and reached in for a Slimjim and bolt cutters. In seconds he was across the street, snapping through the gate chain, and going on in, striding toward the accountant's car. Javy uneasily followed, looking both ways when he crossed the street like a good little kid.

Richie tripped the passenger door lock, popped the

trunk release and came back around to search it, telling his partner, "Check inside the vehicle."

"Might as well," Javy said, meaning any damage to the case was already done. He crawled inside and started looking under the seats; he was checking the glove compartment when Richie called out to him.

Javy came around and found Richie staring into the trunk like he'd found a body inside.

But it wasn't a body, it was the grocery bags, spilling their contents, which were not policy slips, rather stacks of green cash, rubber-banded together, more money than either man had ever seen.

"That's a lot of groceries," Javy said.

Richie didn't disagree.

He closed the trunk, and wandered back to their Plymouth, Javy following. They sat in the car under the buzzing street lamp in the sickly yellow light and said nothing for what seemed forever and was maybe a minute.

"This isn't a couple of bucks we're talking about," Richie said.

"Sure it is."

Richie looked at his partner; his partner looked back at him and shrugged.

"Same thing," Javy said. "In principle."

Richie frowned. "What kind of principle is it we're talking about? Maybe you should spell it."

Javy's tone was half friendly, half conspiratorial. "Look, Richie—a cop who turns in this kind of money sends one message and one message only: that he'll turn in other cops who *do* take money."

Richie shook his head. "It just says *we* don't take money."

Javy shook his head, too, but more forcefully. "No. No. You can't lie to me, and you can't lie to yourself— we turn this money in, we'll be outcasts. Fuckin' lepers on the department."

Richie tasted his tongue; he didn't much like it. "Sounds like we're fucked either way."

Javy's eyes glittered in the yellow light. "Not if we *keep* it. Only if we *don't*. We turn it in, we're fucked, you're right, one hundred percent. But if we hang onto it? Man, no way are we fucked."

Richie's reply was more to himself than his partner: "Yes we are."

Javy's eyes and nostrils flared. "Goddamn it, Rich! Did we ask for this? Or were we just doing our damn job? Did we put a gun to some guy's head and say, 'Give us your money?' No, it fell in our laps, and we *can't* turn it in, Rich. Cops *kill* cops they can't trust."

The two men sat in silence, looking at each other, and into the night, and at each other.

Finally Javy said, "You're gonna turn it in, aren't you, Rich?"

"Yes."

"Damn. Goddamn."

At a police station in Newark, a police captain counted stacks of money on a desk in the bullpen while Richie and Javy sat alone in a corner like bad boys outside the principal's office. Uniformed and plainclothes cops had gathered to watch this amazing, and soon to be legendary, inventory.

Their boss in the Prosecutor's Office, Lou Toback—a rangy brown-haired man with icy blue eyes and a perpetually wry expression—ambled in to observe. Toback wore a nice pastel sportcoat and tie appropriate not to work but rather the night out that had just been interrupted by this emergency.

"How much?" he asked Richie without looking at him.

"Nine hundred and eighty thousand."

Now Toback glanced toward his detectives, an eyebrow arched. "What happened to the rest?"

"Not funny," Richie said quietly.

"I know," Toback said.

Toback took in the glum expression of his two men, the "heroes" who had turned over almost a million dollars of unmarked bills, and then he went quietly to the side of the captain counting the bills.

Smiling, with a hand on the captain's shoulder, almost whispering, Toback said, "Are you out of your fucking mind, counting this in front of everybody? Take this shit into a room. Now."

Richie was close enough to hear; so was Javy.

And Richie sighed and flicked a glance at his partner, an admission that said: *You are so right.*

We are fucked.

3. Taster's Choice

At ten, the morning after Bumpy's funeral, in a little bar on Pleasant Avenue in East Harlem, uptown's Little Italy, Frank walked in to find a middle-aged bartender mopping up the floor, chairs on tables and a single table with no chairs on it, two chairs around it and on top several fat yellow baggies.

Stocky little Rossi, in a white shirt and dark tie, emerged from the darkness, gestured to the table as if the dope were a waiting meal, and the two men sat.

"You have any idea, Frank, what we have to deal with?"

Frank wasn't sure which sense of the word "deal" Rossi was talking about; so he just said, "No."

"These SIU cops, these *princes* of the city," Rossi said, each word a bitter seed he spat out, "they strut around in their leather jackets like movie stars. Are they cops? Are they gangsters? Who the fuck knows."

SIU stood for Special Investigations Unit.

"They can waltz into a property room," Rossi was saying, "and flash their gold shields and just sign out 'evidence.' You know what kind of evidence I'm talkin' about."

"This kind," Frank said, nodding to the dope.

Rossi grunted something that was almost a laugh. "Insult to injury, this is the fuckin' *French Connection* dope. The *same* dope Popeye Doyle and Sonny Grasso took off *us!*"

In his mind's eye Frank could see it: *he could see the detectives entering a warehouse with a suitcase of evidence and grocery bags of other goodies. They take the half-kilo bags of uncut heroin from the suitcase, and then from the grocery bags comes a Pyrex mixing bowl, flour sifter, boxes of milk sugar, latex kitchen gloves, a medical scale and yellow baggies.*

They peel off the black-and-green evidence tape, then they transfer the heroin to numerous yellow baggies, just a smidge compared to the bigger amount of lactose that cuts the heroin to next to nothing.

"They seize it," Ross went on, nearly raving, "arrest everybody, whack it up and sell it back to us. Our fuckin' dope. They been living off it for years, these New York pricks."

"Fuckin' crooks," Frank said blandly.

"They basically control the market with this shit. What the fuck has happened to the world, Frank?"

"Down the crapper."

Shaking his head, Rossi rose and went over to the bar and made them two espressos. The bartender turned on the high-perched TV and a news report began playing, Walter Cronkite droning on about the heroin problem—not here in the USA, but over in Vietnam, among the GIs.

Rossi returned with the small steaming cups and both men sipped.

Finally Rossi said, "Sad about Bumpy. Took God to kill him, bullets couldn't do it."

Frank nodded, sipped some more. He liked the strong hot beverage; the smell of it up his nostrils was as good as the taste.

"Things are never gonna be the same in Harlem," Rossi said, "without the Bump. Girls, clubs, music, all cheaper and louder. . . . Before, you walk down the street, nobody bothers you, 'cause Bumpy's making sure they don't. . . . How bad is it out there now?"

Frank shrugged. "Guys taking down crap games, cops rousting honest crooks, dealers shooting dealers."

"Jesus Christ."

"Chaos. Every asshole for himself."

Rossi, eyes wide, shook his head. "Who can live like that? There has to be fuckin' order, Frank. I mean no offense, but this would never happen with us Italians. More important to us wops, more than any one man's life? Order. A semblance of goddamn fuckin' order."

Frank didn't disagree.

Soon Frank and the heroin were back in Harlem, where he caught a late breakfast at his favorite diner. He ate alone, as was his custom, in a window booth, and when the attractive, middle-aged waitress, Charlene, offered a refill, he risked a second coffee despite the espresso he'd already had.

"But that's the last one, Charlene. Thank you."

She beamed at him. "All right with me, Frank, if you stay all day. But I wouldn't. It's nice outside."

"Then maybe I'll just have to go for a walk." He gave her the smile that he knew was the best thing he owned. "Just 'cause you said so."

She loved hearing that, ambling off a happy woman.

Frank was just pouring some sugar in his coffee when someone tapped on the window. He looked up and saw two army guys in uniform; one of them was a Harlem kid he knew, Willie Something. From the look in Willie's eyes, Frank knew what he wanted.

What the hell. Support the boys. Wasn't he heading over there, anyway?

Before long Frank was leading them up the stairs of the corner building where Red Top, a lanky good-looking chick with a trademark ruby-tinged 'do, kept her apartment. She was Frank's girlfriend, when he felt like it, but mostly she was his cutter, and that's what she was doing right now—sitting in her slinky pantsuit smoking at a worktable arrayed with her drug-cutting apparatus. They could hear Aretha Franklin singing "Respect" on the stereo playing in the living room.

Red Top gave each of the servicemen, sitting across from her, a packet. "On the house for our men in uniform."

"Why thank you, sugar," Willie said, "that's real kind."

"Don't thank me," she said, and smiled but her eyes were cold. "Thank Frank."

Willie looked at Frank gratefully but Frank nodded his "You're welcome" before the kid could even say the words.

While the servicemen cooked up their dope, the old acquaintances chatted, Frank asking Willie, "How's Nate? You see him lately?"

"Hell, I see him all the time. The dude is here, there and everywhere."

"That right?"

"Oh, yeah. He's in good shape. Great shape. Got himself his own club now."

"Oh. He *is* doing good, then. Where, Saigon?"

Willie shook his head. "Bangkok. That's where all the serious R & R goes down."

The other GI, who Frank didn't know, said, "I don't suppose Nate'll *ever* come home. Not till the rest of us do, anyway. Maybe not even then."

As the GIs prepared to shoot up, Frank offered some advice. "Better boot it a couple times, fellas. These cops keep cutting it, selling it, cutting it. . . ."

"I don't mean no offense, my brother," Willie said, as he shot the stuff into a vein, "'cause the price is right and all that. But since I got home? I find the shit over here is . . . shit. But the shit in Nam? It is way, way, way, way, way. . . ."

But Willie didn't finish, nodding off before he could.

Still, Willie may have been the one with the needle, but Frank got the point.

Good shit in Vietnam.

He would file that away, like he filed away all information, for when it would come in handy.

And it would.

Within his circle, in his private life and for that matter his business dealings, Frank Lucas considered himself a moral man.

Matters of right and wrong, in any larger sense—social or religious—were defined by the world he'd been born into, a white man's world. Dope being sold to black people was a reality that wasn't going anywhere; better another black man be in charge. Killing people who needed killing was strictly business—those yellow people getting killed over in Vietnam by boys both black and white made less sense to Frank than removing a business rival or a personal threat by violence.

Frank hadn't invented the world where money ruled, but if he was going to live in it, by God, he was going to have at least his share. The kind of money he wanted to make in legitimate business would have meant Wall Street, if you called that legitimate. And he knew he couldn't get a fucking janitor job on Wall Street.

As far as Frank was concerned, white men had sent him down the criminal road, had given him no choice, really, not since that day when he was six and the Ku Klux Klan came to his family's shack and killed his cousin, Obadiah.

Obie had been twelve and had committed the crime of looking at a white girl funny—"reckless eyeballing," they called it down South. Five rednecks grabbed his cousin, tied the terrified Obie up and shoved a shotgun in his mouth and blew his head apart. Right there on the front porch, Frank watching through the window.

With Obadiah gone, Frank was the oldest child and, needing to put food on the table, he became a prodigy of crime, at first stealing chickens and pigs, soon graduating to mugging drunks with a rock outside the local whorehouse, there in La Grange, North Carolina. By the time he was the age Obie'd been, when that shotgun blew his head away, Frank was on a chain gang in Tennessee. At fourteen he was shacked up with a lady bootlegger in Kentucky. At sixteen he decided to try going straight, took a trucking job, but sleeping with the owner's daughter led to his dismissal. Well, what really led to his dismissal was hitting the owner, a beer-belly bruiser called Big Bill, alongside the head with a piece of pipe. When Big Bill didn't pay up the hundred bucks Frank was owed, the young man took four hundred instead and set the front office on fire.

His mother had advised him to hightail, which he had, to New York, where he'd found his way from Penn Station to 114th Street and a world of black people—Harlem USA, where Bumpy Johnson had come into his life.

Frank didn't consider himself a violent man. He was willing to respond in self-defense, when need be, and he would do violence when business called for it. He took no pleasure in fists, knives or guns, and did not seek such foolishness out.

But foolishness did sometimes seek him out.

For example, on a cold clear morning a week after Bumpy's burial, Frank was sitting eating breakfast in his favorite diner, minding his own business, eating his damn eggs, reading the sports section. He hadn't given ten seconds' thought to Tango Black since he'd seen the bald thug scrounging food and drink at Bumpy's wake.

So when Tango and a bodyguard as big as he was came strutting into the diner, heading Frank's way, Frank didn't bother looking up from his paper. Tango was all in black, including a black leather jacket that said the dude was trying to be Shaft, only Shaft wouldn't have worn all that gold jewelry.

But when Tango planted himself next to Frank's booth, Frank knew foolishness had arrived. Still, he did not bother to look up at the man. He had enough on his mind, reading the paper and forking his eggs at the same time.

"Didn't you see the jar, Frank?" Tango rumbled. He glanced back at his boy and they exchanged school-kid grins. "I think he walked right past it. . . . Did you walk right past my jar, Frank?"

Frank already knew that there was no jar in question, not really. This was Tango being clever. Poetic. Frank ate a bite of eggs, not caring to comment on Tango's poetry.

Finally Tango plopped himself down across from Frank. The big man was smiling but not really happy. "The *money* jar, Frank. On the corner. What I got to do, put a damn sign on it?"

Frank gestured to his mouth, indicating he might

answer if he weren't busy chewing. Tango waited with surprising patience for Frank to swallow, which he did, but his guest got an irritated look when Frank's next move was to reach for his cup of coffee, and wash the bite down.

With quiet menace, Tango said, "Bumpy don't own 116th Street no more, Frank, in case you didn't notice. Bumpy don't own *no* real estate in Harlem no more, in point of actual fact. I'm the new landlord and the lease is twenty percent."

Frank, dabbing at his mouth with a paper napkin, gave Tango a skeptical look.

Tango's eyes widened and he gestured with open hands. "Don't like the tariff? Then don't sell no more dope, Frank. Try gettin' a real fuckin' job. Need one? I could use a driver, drive *me* around, open *my* door, like you done for Bumpy. Remember, Frank? Yessuh, no-suh, where to suh, right away, Massa Johnson suh."

Halfway through the speech—even before the most insulting part—Tango was a dead man. Of course, Tango didn't know that. And Frank would let Tango walk around a while. But Tango was already a ghost, just getting an early start on haunting Harlem.

Coolly, Frank said, "Twenty percent, huh?"

The big bald head bobbed up and down. "Offa every dollar. Every vig, every truckload, every girl, every damn ounce. You pay your tribute like anybody else, Frank. You put it in the goddamn *jar*."

Gently smiling, Frank shook his head. "You're a businessman, Tango. So you understand business."

"That's what we're talkin' about here. Business."

"But twenty percent's my profit margin. If I'm giving that to you, then what am I working for? I'm not looking for a hobby." Frank shrugged. "You hit me, everyone you know, for twenty percent, you put us *all* out of business. Which puts *you* out of business."

Tango displayed a yard of white teeth. "Then you'll just have to work harder, Frank. Raise your prices and shit."

Frank shook his head as he reached for the check. "There are reasonable ways to make money, Tango . . . and then there's this way. Bumpy never took twenty percent."

"Bumpy's fuckin' dead."

Frank studied Tango's dark eyes and the hard, determined cast of his jaw. This was a stubborn man and a stupid man. Also dangerous. But mostly stupid.

Taking out his money clip, Frank peeled off a five to cover the check; then he peeled off a one, and flipped it over in front of Tango.

"There you go," Frank said. "Your twenty percent."

Frank got up and went out. He could feel Tango's eyes on him, but he wasn't really concerned. He knew what he would do about this problem; he just had to pick the right moment.

Sitting in his apartment, which was nicely but not ostentatiously furnished mostly in shades of brown, Frank leaned back in a comfortable chair with a pencil in one hand and a spiral pad in the other.

On the yellow paper he did the math—for a guy who never graced a schoolroom door, he was a whiz at it. Just for the hell of it, he worked out what it would cost to accommodate Tango. After all, Frank had no desire to work the protection racket, which had been fine in days of Bumpy Johnson and Dutch Schultz and Al fucking Capone, but today it was a dying game to be sure.

And there was just no way.

After he paid the Italian suppliers, and Red Top and everybody else who worked for him, Frank would be a goddamn pauper. This shit *would* be his hobby. . . .

His first instinct, even though it had been tinged by an emotional response to Tango's disrespect for Bumpy, had been correct. Tango had to go.

But inadvertently Tango had opened Frank's eyes to a basic problem in the supply-and-demand scheme of things. Frank was working on way too slim a margin. The dope trade, for all the money that rolled in, was a pie getting cut up too many ways; and then there were those crooked fucking cops who were squeezing the goombahs by the nuts.

Something had to change.

And Frank had to change it.

Throughout his life Frank had developed a method of dealing with tight situations. He was not an impulse buyer in the showroom of life; he liked to mull, and mold his options.

He'd been known to lock himself in a hotel room, shut off the phone, yank down the blinds, take room service and just think. Isolation helped him get a clear view, he could look back over the past, backtrack five years if need be and think about everything he'd done and everyone he'd encountered and everything he'd heard, and search every nook and cranny of his memory for information and answers.

This time, however, he did not check himself into a room; instead he took the German shepherd he'd inherited from Bumpy out on the beach at Coney Island, and together man and beast had walked under a bleak gray-blue sky along a beach where seagulls fought for scraps in the sand. This time of year the place was all but deserted, a handful of screaming kids riding a roller coaster barely competing with the sound of surf rolling in and gulls cawing as they circled to provide a mostly soothing soundtrack for his thoughts.

Frank and Bumpy and, for that matter, the dog had often come here and walked and talked.

Bumpy had never come right out and said that some day Frank would take his place, if not in the protection business then in the black world that was Harlem. But the older man would dispense advice, without really saying why he was offering it or indicating what Frank was to do with it.

Drifting over the waves and into his thoughts came the memory of Bumpy's resonant voice: "*A leader is like a shepherd, Frank. He sends the fast, nimble sheep out front, and the others follow. And the shepherd? He walks quietly behind. Watching. Guiding.*"

Where the tide rolled in, Frank picked up a stick that seemed perfect for the dog to fetch. He hurled it and the animal went scampering after it. Gulls cawed hungrily. Kids screamed happily.

"*Now the shepherd, he has a stick, a cane, a staff . . . and you know he'll use it if he has to.*"

The dog brought the stick back and, as he threw it again, Frank pictured Bumpy on a day when he'd done the same thing.

"*But most of the time, the shepherd doesn't have to use that stick. He can move the whole herd, quietly. With skill. With brains. And with the force of his own personality.*"

On days like this, Frank and Bumpy would have ended up at the hot dog stand, where Bumpy would buy a naked pup for his German shepherd to gulp down, while the boss and his number one man would chomp at condiment-laden hot dogs like two more kids at Coney Island.

And Bumpy would dispense wisdom with relish, hot dog or otherwise, though the memory of his mentor's words were more recent, not given at Coney Island but in front of the electronics store window where Bumpy had died.

"*What right do they have, cutting out the suppliers, pushing all the middlemen out, buying direct from the manufacturer? Putting Americans out of work! This is the way it is now, Frank.*"

There on that bleak beach, Frank's mind assembled scraps of information and bits and pieces of advice into what he knew at once was a bold new plan.

Bumpy had been right: things had changed, cutting out the middlemen was a fact of life, the way it was now . . . and the little boy who'd seen the white men blow his cousin's brains out of his skull knew that you couldn't change the way things were. You had to accept the world as it was and work within it.

And make the world work for you.

If he were really to be white-boy rich someday, Frank would first have to cut out the Italians, whatever risk that might entail. No more picking up packages from Rossi or the like. Fuck that shit—Frank would get his own supply.

The voice of that soldier kid, Willie, sitting at Red Top's table, pushed out Bumpy Johnson's in Frank's mind: *Good shit in Vietnam.*

This war, this stupid war, had turned a lot of kids, black and white, into casual druggies and a good number into outright junkies. Right now Vietnam was full of GIs getting strung out, and shit good enough to string out GIs was good enough for Frank to sell stateside. Sell, hell—he'd make a killing.

So it was that Frank Lucas went from Coney Island to a doctor's office in Harlem where he took a series of shots, not the least of which was to prevent malaria. Then he went to a photography shop for a picture to take with him to the post office, where it was stapled to a passport application.

From there Frank went to the Chemical Bank in the Bronx where the banker he'd seen at Bumpy's wake watched, at Frank's invitation, as Frank emptied packet after packet of cash from a safety deposit box into a briefcase.

One packet Frank slipped into the banker's jacket pocket.

"Get yourself a new suit," Frank said with a wisp of

a smile. Then he added: "*Now's* a good time to talk business."

In an office arrayed with the portraits of dignified white bankers going back fifty years or more, the banker typed out a Chemical Bank check for Frank Lucas in the amount of $400,000.

"You're not nervous," the banker said, "traveling alone to Southeast Asia?"

"No."

"Well, I would be."

Frank took the check, folded it to fit in his billfold, where he put it. "Brad, I never went to school, not for a day. But I got a PhD in 'Street.'"

"These are different streets, Frank."

"Thanks for your concern. But I'll make out."

4. Past Due

The next afternoon, gray but not as cold as some recent days, Richie stood with his ex-wife Laurie in a Newark park, where their five-year-old son Michael could play in a grassy area with other youngsters, and not be party to their discussions about his welfare and future.

Already their talk wasn't going well, and when a jet screamed overhead and then faded away, the interruption was almost a relief; that Frank Lucas was on that jet, heading to the Far East, was a small irony Richie was not privy to.

"I'm sorry, babe," he said.

Laurie gave him a sideways glare that told him he'd long since lost the right to call her that. She was only one of a dozen moms in the park today, but probably the best-looking, with her curly dark hair brushing her shoulders, and a peasant blouse and slacks indicating what was still a nice body.

"You could have told me sooner," she said, watching their boy frolic with other kids, their laughter and screams tinged with the happy hysteria of childhood.

"I'm sorry." He sighed, shrugged. "I know. But it's the big exam. It's what all my work's been leading up to."

"I don't know, Richie."

"Can't be avoided." His hands were in his pockets and he was rocking on his heels; his eyes took routine stock of those other moms—one of whom rivaled Laurie at that, a hot young blonde. Got knocked up in high school maybe, and popped one out. "Next weekend I'm open. Be able to take Mike, no problem."

When he glanced back at his own wife, ex-wife, she was studying him the way a lab student eyes a slide with some squirmy thing on it, obviously aware he'd been sizing up the blonde competition.

Maybe that was why something else was in Laurie's expression, too: not disgust exactly, more . . . weariness.

Somehow that was worse than disgust to Richie; anger, disgust, were strong responses, emotional responses. Now, after all the loving and hating and cooing and yelling it had come down to this: she was tired of his cheating ass.

"Look . . . Rich." She shrugged, sent her eyes toward their son. "The thing is, I'm . . . I'm moving."

His forehead frowned, his mouth smiled. "What do you mean, moving?"

Her eyes came back to him, pointedly. "What do you think, moving? Pack your shit and get in the car and go, moving. Christ, Rich."

"Where to?"

She laughed bitterly. "To the St. Regis, maybe. What the hell do you care."

"I *care*."

"Right. My sister's."

"Your sister's. Your sister lives in Vegas."

Laurie grunted a tiny laugh. "Thanks for paying attention. I didn't know my family even made it on your radar."

He was shaking his head now, grinning, astounded. "Vegas? You want to take our kid to *Vegas*?"

The crunch and snap of breaking glass interrupted his words and his thoughts. He glanced over and a quartet of white kids were breaking pop bottles, hurling them onto the concrete path.

Richie picked up the thread, and tried to keep his tone civil. "Come on, Laurie. Be reasonable. You can't move to Vegas."

"Sure I can."

"Not with *Michael*, anyway."

Her eyebrows arched as she turned to him again. "Oh, there's another option? What else am I supposed to do with him? Leave him with you? There's a picture. You could turn the closet into his bedroom, long as you keep your box of weed on the top shelf where he can't get to it."

"That's not fair. . . ."

More glass shattering seemed to mirror the state of

his mind, and he yelled over to the smart asses, "*Hey!* You want to keep it down over there? Find a new hobby!"

The teenagers looked at him, started laughing and went on smashing the bottles.

Doing his best to ignore this shit, finding it hard to think much less reason with Laurie over the constant brittle background noise, Richie said evenly, "You know we have joint custody, Laurie. Court won't allow you to drag him out of state like that."

"Are you sure?"

His eyes tightened. "I'm sure *I* won't."

She smiled at him but it was mostly a sneer. "You? It's up to *you*, now?"

He slapped his chest. "You drag him out there, when am *I* supposed to see my goddamn *son*?"

Her eyes were wide and she was smiling, but it had nothing to do with the usual reasons for smiling; she was shaking her head, as if having witnessed something amazing.

She said, "How about *last* weekend? Or *this* weekend? Only you had to cancel. You had work. You had school. Maybe you had a bimbo or two, too."

Michael, playing with two other little boys, heard the edge in his mother's voice and turned to them with a pitiful little frozen smile.

Caught cold, both parents smiled and waved and nodded, and the boy—not entirely convinced, but placated, anyway—returned to his play.

Richie did his best to keep it low key. "Laurie,

please. You can't be serious about raising Michael in Las Vegas. What kind of place is that to—"

"Oh, and *this* is a good environment?" She looked at the sky for support. "What could I be thinking of? Mike would miss out on all your colorful friends, wise guys you grew up with, cop pals who're even sleazier." She gazed across the park toward the colorless Newark skyline. "Far as I'm concerned, there're less creeps per square inch in Vegas than in this godforsaken armpit."

Now Richie was shaking his head; it was his turn to feel amazed. "Vegas is the most mobbed-up town in America, Laurie! What's Mike gonna grow up to be in *that* cesspool? What the hell are you *thinking*?"

Her eyes bored into him and through him. "I'm thinking, Richie, of *him*. Not you. Not me. And not us. But *Michael*."

Another bottle breaking put an exclamation mark after Laurie's already pointed words; the noise was driving him fucking crazy. . . . *Little pricks*. . . .

"Goddamn it," he said. He raised a finger to Laurie, as if telling a dog to stay, and he strode over toward the teenagers, kids wearing letter jackets and smart-ass expressions.

Richie was a big guy, but there were four of them, who laughed as he approached, trading looks with one another before they all glared mockingly his way: *What are you gonna do about it, old man? Four against one!*

"I told you nice," Richie said evenly, "to shut the fuck up."

Their cocky expressions were curdling, but one of them managed, "Why don't *you* shut the fuck up, Gran'pa?"

Richie shook his head. "Okay. Have it your way. Now I'm gonna kill your punk asses."

And from under his jacket he snapped the revolver off his hip and aimed it at the one who'd just spoken.

One at a time Richie gave each formerly mocking face a look down the short but impressive barrel of the weapon. Instinct made them cover their heads, as if keeping the sound of a bullet from their ears would be enough to shield them.

One kid squeezed a few frightened words out: "What do you *want* from us, mister?"

"I want you," Richie said, smiling terribly, "to *pick up that fuckin' glass!*"

They almost dove to the pavement and the nearby grass, complying, finding every fragment, from jagged-edged chunk to splintery shard, and taking them to a nearby trash can, under Richie's casual but strict supervision, his gun still in hand.

Other people had noticed the confrontation, from the prettiest moms to the ones Richie's eyes hadn't bothered with, and the blonde whose inventory he'd earlier been taking asked nobody in particular, "Shouldn't somebody call the police?"

Laurie, having already collected Michael, passing by on the way out of the park toward her car, said, "He *is* the police. Hard to believe, I know."

Richie didn't see or hear any of this. He didn't even see his son's puzzled expression as the boy looked back at his father holding the gun on those bigger kids. The child felt a sensation that was far too complex for him to parse: shame intertwined with pride. But he would feel it again.

And by the time Richie had made the teenagers clean up after themselves, his wife and son were long gone, and so were most of the other moms and kids, leaving him alone on the grassy patch where, minutes before, his son had played under a blue-gray sky on a day that seemed suddenly colder.

Richie Roberts's apartment in Newark was nicer than a junkie's.

Barely.

Though the way he lived offered no proof, Richie was human and could hardly help but glance around his bleak little pad without thinking of the Manhattan town house or lovely suburban home he could be living in, if he weren't a stick-up-his-ass fool. He had no choice but to think about the great food—French cuisine maybe (though he'd never really had any, unless you counted fries)—that he could be eating right now, as opposed to standing at his gas stove pouring a can of Campbell's into a pot with his stitched-up black-and-blue hand.

But it wasn't just the nice digs he could be enjoying or the great food he might be chowing down on. It was denying those things to his family; that's what grated.

What kind of fucking idiot walks away from a cool million? Walks away, knowing he's alienated not just his own partner, but every goddamn cop in New Jersey and, when word got out (which it probably already had), New York to boot?

He could still feel the eyes on him when he'd walked out of that Newark police station, all by himself—even Javy Rivera hadn't been up to accompanying him—knowing this quiet, staring response was not out of awe or respect over Richie turning his back on all that crooked bread, no. These looks spoke of contempt, on the one hand, and fear on the other.

He would never be trusted again by his fellow cops.

The saving grace was that he wouldn't have to be a cop much longer.

He got himself a spoon and hauled his pot of soup over to the little cluttered desk, piled with law textbooks. Almost at random, he cracked open a text and started his night's studies for the upcoming New Jersey Bar exam. On the wall nearby, casting silent encouragement his way, was a framed photograph of one of his heroes: heavyweight champ Joe Louis, standing over the sprawled, vanquished Billy Conn.

When the soup was gone, the hunger sated but the tension gnawing, Richie went to the small wooden box that was his stash, where an ounce or so of grass waited along with rolling papers and clips.

He rolled a joint, smiling to himself at his hypocrisy, and soon was mellowed out and deep in his studies, smoke swirling to the ceiling like his conscience trying to find its way to freedom.

5. Ding Dong

A sprawling jumble of a city, Bangkok had all the humid heat, rank pollution, snarled traffic and diseased prostitutes its ragged reputation promised. Despite the colorful if grotesque palaces and temples, this was a world chiefly of weather-beaten cement with occasional splashes of tropical green poking through. Dirty, poor, crowded, its sidewalks clogged by stalls selling knock-off T-shirts and cheap jewelry, Bangkok made Harlem seem a paradise.

In the deceptive candy flush of neon at night, Frank Lucas—in a short-sleeved sportshirt and chinos, just another anonymous tourist—rode along in back of one of the three-wheeled motorized vehicles called a tuk-tuk. Bicycles darted around like flies (and flies were darting around everything and everyone else), but the tuk-tuk did its own share of weaving in and out of the impossible traffic.

Frank had checked into the Dusit Thani Hotel, where he'd skipped any tourist bullshit to catch the three-wheel taxi to his destination: the Soul Brothers Bar, which he'd been told back home was the top hangout for black GIs on R & R.

This was Frank's first trip to Southeast Asia, and—though he didn't impress easily—the sights and sounds and smells had overloaded his sensory system. What a shock it was to enter the Soul Brothers Bar and find the kind of black joint you might find in a funky corner of Atlanta or Chicago or Harlem itself.

The only way the joint could have been smokier was to be on fire. Otis Redding was singing "Dock of the Bay" courtesy of the Rockola jukebox, and at tables and booths and along the bar, black soldiers—Frank was the only man other than the two bartenders not in uniform—were putting the moves on slit-to-the-thigh-silk-dress Thai girls, who didn't look hard to seduce.

Frank ordered a Coke at the bar and found his way to a small table, where he sat and surveyed the scene. And some of what he saw would not have been allowed in the funkiest hole in Atlanta, Chicago or even Harlem. . . .

Not every GI had a hooker on his arm or in his lap; a few were zonked out, slumped in booths laughing lazily or flat-out sleeping, and a few others were drunk out of their minds. Dope was being rolled and smoked and even shot up. A staircase, up which went soldiers and their "dates," meant the second floor wasn't so restrained.

After a while a trio of ex-GIs started playing Southern blues tunes—"Gone Dead on You" by Blind Lemon Jefferson was their opener. *Authentic-sounding shit*, Frank had to admit.

Just as authentic were the smells that found their way through the smoke and general bar stench to tickle both his nostrils and his memory: ham hocks and collard greens served by waiters in stripeless army uniforms. Home away from home for Uncle Sugar's boys.

One uniformed figure stood out from all the others, perhaps because he wasn't wasted on dope or booze, and didn't have a hooker hanging on his arm, either: an army master sergeant. The tall, commanding figure, whose Apache cheekbones added an edge to affable, handsome features, threaded through the tables and patrolled the booths and bar as if on inspection.

At first the sarge seemed to be checking on the GI customers' well-being. Then at one booth, he shook hands with a patron and, through the smoke, Frank could barely see the pass-off of cash from the client for some packets of white from the sarge.

Frank must have been staring, because the sarge was suddenly squinting at him through the smoke, the guy's expression sinister at first, then shifting into a kind of loose-lipped shock.

The sarge called out, "*Frank?*"

Frank lifted his Coke in salute and smiled, just a little, and his old friend Nate Atkins beamed at him and made a beeline.

Nate sat and grinned and said, "You're too old to get drafted. What the fuck are you doing on this turf?"

"Thought maybe you could recommend a good Thai banker."

Nate blinked a couple times. "Got a major deposit to make?"

"Yeah. A major deposit. And maybe a sergeant major deposit, too."

Nate liked the sound of that. He gestured to the dingy, debauched surroundings. "What do you think of the place?"

"All the comforts of home. Soul food with dope on the side and a blow job for dessert. You're not still in the *service* . . . ?"

"No! Hell no." He gestured to the uniform. "This is just to make the fellas feel comfortable. So I heard about Bumpy. You taking over for him, or what?"

"What. Protection's out."

"But you're still moving powder."

"Yeah. And I want to move some more." He flicked half a smile at his old friend. "I hear the quality is high, your neck of the woods. Rumor or fact?"

Nate's brown eyes, always alert, took on a sharpness. He got up easily, saying, "You got a few minutes? Let me make a call."

Frank sat at the same table with Nate, but they had two guests, a couple of young Thai wise guys in sportshirts with big pointed collars and too much gold jewelry.

The conversation going on right now was in the Thai language, which Frank didn't understand; but he trusted Nate, a shirttail relation from North Carolina.

A skinny, dead-eyed Thai punk asked Nate, "He say how much stuff he wants?"

Nate, also speaking Thai, said, "He said 'a lot.' What that means I don't know. Four or five keys, maybe."

Both Thai hoods studied Frank like he was a modern art painting they were trying to comprehend.

Then the skinny Thai said, "And he's your cousin."

"My cousin-in-law," Nate said by way of full disclosure. "My ex-wife's cousin, actually. But he's family to me. I trust him."

The Thai kid thought about that. Then he said to Nate, "Ask your cousin-in-law how much he wants."

Nate asked Frank.

Frank said, "A hundred kilos."

Now it was Nate studying Frank like modern art.

"Are you fucking kidding me, Frank?" Nate asked.

"Am I known for my sense of humor, Nate?"

The next day, pushing through the paradise-for-pickpockets throng on the sidewalk along a row of steamy food stalls, Frank and Nate walked and talked.

"No one I know can get *that* much," Nate said.

"I heard you were connected."

"I am connected. I know every gook gangster in

town, and that's a lot of gook gangsters. I know every goddamn black soldier in the Army from the cooks to the colonels, and on up."

"Good to hear."

They stopped and bought mangos from a vendor, and munched as they went on.

"Well," Nate said reflectively, "I suppose I could piece together that many keys, from different suppliers. But ain't none of it gonna be one-hundred percent pure."

Frank shook his head. "Then I don't want it. Not what I want."

Nate grunted in exasperation. "I *know* that. I see where you're comin' from, my man. I just do not think it's possible, without risking floating facedown in one of these fuckin' canals."

"It's my risk."

"It's my risk, too!"

"If you want to get rich, it is."

Nate bit into the mango. "Means dealing with the Chiu-Chou syndicates in Cholon or Saigon . . . *if* they'll even deal with your stateside ass."

But Frank was shaking his head. "No. Not good enough."

Nate's jaw dropped, part in reaction, part for effect. "What the fuck . . . ?"

Frank was still shaking his head. "Too late. It's been chopped. I want to get it where *they* get it. From the *source*."

Nate slowed, and Frank didn't. Catching up, the big

man eyeballed his old friend and then started laughing. "Pullin' my chain, right?"

Frank's eyes said *Wrong*.

Astounded, Nate managed, "*You're* gonna get it. Your own self."

Frank shrugged with his face. "Why not? Good shit in life don't come around to hand itself to you. You got to go after it."

Nate tossed the mango pit in the gutter. "You mean *you're* gonna go into the fuckin' jungle like fuckin' Tarzan?"

Frank shrugged. "I lived in jungles all my life, Nate. Where I lived, fuckin' Tarzan wouldn'ta made it."

Nate put a hand on his friend's shoulder and stopped him, right there on the sidewalk, making a thousand people walk around the ex-soldier and the tourist. "No, you don't get it. This isn't *a* jungle. This shit is *the* jungle. Tigers. Vietcong. Fuckin' snakes *alone* will kill you!"

Frank raised an eyebrow. "And how is that different from Harlem?"

Khaki-clad Frank felt like he was leading the god-damn Dirty Dozen, so motley a bunch were these Thai thugs and black soldiers, riding mules with shoulder-slung automatic weapons through jungle dense as a pussy patch. Funny thing was, he was enjoying him-self, arrayed with pistol, rifle and ammo bandolier like a bronze Pancho Villa.

Days had passed since he'd sold Nate on the plan. They'd ridden in trucks and on boats and up and down every damn river in the Golden Triangle, as far as he could tell. And now they were about to arrive at the opium farm where Frank would do the deal that would change everything back home, that would make Bumpy Johnson a footnote in the Frank Lucas story.

If Frank didn't get himself killed, instead.

Right now they were under a pleasantly cooling canopy of foliage thick enough to blot out the sun. He could see the sunlight ahead, the light at the end of this tunnel, and when the canopy finally opened up, Frank Lucas found himself breathing in a syrupy sweet scent and staring down at a green-dotted-purple poppy field the size of Manhattan.

They stopped here and Nate had a confab with a Thai mercenary in the native gibberish. Frank waited for Nate to translate.

"He says," Nate said, "this whole area's controlled by the Kuomintang—Chiang Kai-Shek's army. *Defeated* army. . . ."

Frank nodded. "They're on guard down there." He'd already spotted the Chinese soldiers with their outdated weapons. "But what about those boys—*they* ain't Chinese."

He was indicating a handful of white sentries in camouflage jumpsuits, Americans probably, with weapons that were real up-to-date.

Nate said, "CIA, likely."

"Is that a problem?"

"I don't know. Let's see."

Nate dispatched the Thai he'd spoken to before, sending him down to talk to the Chinese guerrillas, having no idea how the American spooks would figure in.

But all went well. Before long Frank and Nate were in a natural cavern the size of an airplane hangar, which Frank gathered was a major processing center. In this rocky cathedral, Frank and Nate used their Thai point man to translate a negotiation with what turned out to be a vanquished Chinese general.

Not that this shit didn't get tense: Thais with CIA advisors guarded Frank and Nate and their boy, while the Chinese and *their* CIA advisors guarded the guards.

Pretty soon Frank found himself in a bamboo dwelling that was goddamn nice for a shack, sitting opposite the general at a desk where the mucky-muck sorted through Frank's papers—passport, visa, bank receipts and the really important paper: cash. Lots and lots of cash. . . .

The general had the kind of diamond-hard eyes that had seen everything (including lots of cash) before; and those eyes spent as much time examining Frank as they had the papers.

"How," the general asked, as if inquiring about the weather, "would you get it into the States?"

Frank's kept his face as unreadable as the general's. "What do you care?"

The general responded with a question of his own: "Who do you work for where you come from?"

"Again," Frank said, nonconfrontational but giving nothing, "why do you care?"

The general shifted his chair. His mouth tightened; his eyes, too. "Who are you . . . *really?*"

Frank nodded toward the passport and visa on the desk between them. "You read it. Says right there: Frank Lucas."

The general drew in a sharp breath. "I mean, who do you *represent?*"

"Frank Lucas."

The general studied Frank some more, seemed to understand that he wouldn't accomplish anything down this road, and let it go.

The general said, "You think you're going to take a hundred kilos of heroin into the United States, and you don't work for anyone? You expect me to believe that?"

"I don't care what you believe."

"Someone is going to *allow* you to do this?"

Frank shrugged.

The general glanced at one of his bodyguards, and said in Chinese, "I don't believe a word of this." Then he said to Frank, "After this first purchase, if you're not killed by Marseilles importers—or the Italians in the States—then what?"

Frank flipped a hand. "Then there'll be more—and on a regular basis . . . though I'd rather not have to drag my ass all the way up *here* every time."

The general thought about that. Then, after a glance at the various papers (including the cash), he said, "Of course not."

Frank did not smile, outwardly; but inwardly he was grinning.

The tough old general was ready to do business.

Two days later, at an army landing zone in Vietnam with monsoon rains pounding down, Frank climbed out of a UH-1 helicopter having traded his bandolier for the necklace of a press card. Nate, in uniform, climbed out of the Huey, too.

Nate alone was led by black enlisted men to an LZ tent where a black colonel was waiting. Frank cooled his heels under some dripping camouflage, hanging out with some other brothers in uniform. He could not hear the conversation that Nate and the colonel were having, but he knew what was going down.

The colonel said to Nate, "Jesus—that's a lot of powder. Where's it now?"

"Bangkok," Nate said. He shrugged. "I can bring it here. Or anywhere in between. Your call."

The colonel shook his head. "A hundred damn kilos. . . . I never seen that much dope in one place, have you?"

Nate grinned. "I just did. You ever see one of them Amana refrigerator-freezers?"

"Sure."

"Bigger than that."

". . . Let me talk to your partner."

Nate nodded out to Frank, who joined them in the tent and did some negotiating. Then they watched the colonel exiting the tent, rain still coming down like

God machine-gunning, to cross the torrent on duck-boards to another tent, where a white officer, a two-star general, waited.

This negotiation was brief: fifty grand in advance, covering the pilots and the guys on the other end, as well.

But Frank told Nate, "No."

Nate goggled at him. "*No?* Frank, we—"

"Give them one hundred."

"What? Give 'em *more* than we negotiated?"

Frank nodded. "A hundred. That's all I've got left, anyway. So if that dope doesn't arrive, for whatever reason, I won't need it, the extra. We'll buy a little good will."

"If you say so, cousin."

Then, suddenly, Frank embraced Nate and whispered in his ear, "Cousin or no cousin—don't let me down."

The words weren't overtly a threat, but as he handed the fat envelope of cash to Nate, Frank knew that Nate knew.

Knew that Frank would kill him, if things didn't go to plan.

Nate said, "Don't sweat this a second. I'm all over it. And I'll let you know when the shit's in the air. . . . Anybody ever tell you you're a kind of genius?"

"No. I been called a fool before."

Nate grinned. "Well, you're that, too. But aren't we all?"

6. Dick Down

Richie Roberts had never meant to hurt his wife. He had loved Laurie, and he still did love her, he supposed, in a mother-of-his-child kind of way. He'd never had an affair on her; he wouldn't do that to her, he wasn't some disloyal prick.

But he would knock off a piece here and there, strictly one-night-stand stuff, and yet the times she'd found out, Laurie reacted like he'd been seeing somebody behind her back.

He'd never bothered trying to explain it to her. That his job was high stress, max pressure, life or fucking death, and the only things that took the edge off, that took him out of his crowded head and into someplace free of thought, were the roll of a joint or a roll in the hay.

And that didn't count making love to your wife, with the kid in the next room and bills to pay and in-laws and PTA meetings and all the issues that made a bad habit of coming into the bedroom with you.

Yesterday was a (literal) textbook case of high stress and max pressure, and even in its way of life or death: he'd taken his law board exams. Maybe that anonymous chamber with its fifty or sixty student-type desks and as many asses dropped down in them, and the pinched-puss exam proctors prowling their beat, wasn't as literally dangerous as going down a dark alley or busting into some junkie shooting gallery.

But Richie's life did depend on it.

He felt he'd done okay, and anyway it was over. So he'd celebrated by calling up that sexy little brunette paramedic who'd stitched up his mitt last week. He took her out for steaks and a show (*M*A*S*H*) and they hung out in a bar a while, and his place was closer, so that was fine, and she hadn't even minded his overgrown closet of an apartment. They'd done it twice last night, once a fast frantic hump on the floor with their clothes half-hanging off, and then in bed, slow and sensual and romantic.

She'd stayed over and they rubbed against each other all through the night and at dawn he was balls deep in her again—*what was her name?*—and she was making so much noise, he was worried his neighbors might call the cops, and when the phone rang, it was almost a relief.

He reached for the receiver, but she slapped his hand, panting, looking up at him with big demanding eyes and orgasm-flushed cheeks; but the ringing wouldn't stop.

Neither would the paramedic, and he answered the phone in action and out of breath.

The voice on the other end was exploding words so fast, Richie wouldn't have had a chance to respond right away even if he could have.

Javy Rivera was saying, "Richie? Richie, man, I'm in trouble. This guy, this fuckin' *guy*, I don't know how, but he *made* me. And he went for his piece, Rich, Jesus Christ, he went for it like John Fuckin' Wayne and what choice did I have? I had to do it, swear to God. Now they're gonna kill *me*."

The paramedic was looking frustrated and annoyed, because she had lost Richie's full attention; and she didn't even protest, when he rolled off her and sat on the edge of the bed and got intense with the phone.

"*Who*, Jav? Who's gonna kill you?"

"Man, there's a hundred people out there, that heard the damn shots. I mean, if this goddamn fuckin' shit were any deeper I'd be gargling. Richie, man, you gotta help me. You gotta do *something*. Or my ass is grass, man."

Richie was getting it. "He's dead? Perp's dead?"

"*He's* dead, *I'm* dead. They're gonna *kill* me!"

Doing his best to calm his partner out of his hysteria, Richie said, "Cool it. Stay cool. Where are you? Javy? . . . Talk to me. Where are you, buddy?"

". . . That's the problem."

"What is?"

"Where I am is."

"Which is *where?*"

"Projects. Stephen Crane."

Oh shit, Richie thought, then said, "No problem. Stay cool. If it's not my voice, don't answer the door."

"Don't fuckin' worry."

And Javy gave him the building and apartment number.

Richie threw on a shirt, jeans, gun and his brown leather jacket, responding to his bedmate's question of "Should I wait?" with "Up to you."

Within minutes he was in his Plymouth Fury, moving quickly; this was Sunday, not long after dawn, traffic dead as Javy's perp.

The radio kept cutting in and out on him, but he didn't have any trouble hearing the male dispatcher's nasty news: "*There are no cars in that area, Detective Roberts.*"

"Bullshit," he spat into the mike. "I got a man in trouble and I need backup an hour ago."

"*. . . missed that . . . you . . . breaking up. . . .*"

"Put the call out again!"

"*. . . still can't . . . you're breaking . . .*"

"I said put the fucking call out *again*—"

"*I just did, Detective. Nobody responded. I'll try once more, but it won't do any—*"

"Fuck you very much," Richie said, and slammed the mike into its slot, thinking, *I'll bet he heard* that.

When Richie's car rounded the corner onto Central Avenue, the three dark thirty-floor towers of the Stephen Crane Projects loomed like massive tombstones from the war zone landscape. If a more forbidding place existed on the planet, Richie had no desire to see it. A torched and abandoned patrol car sat silent sentry just beyond the curb, dating back to one riot or another.

After he parked, Richie moved through the agitated all-black crowd swiftly and confidently, which was the only way to survive; the morning was unseasonably warm and, early as it was, the Crane residents and other neighborhood gawkers had come out to enjoy the fun and outrage. He spotted an ambulance pulled up on the sidewalk in front of one tower, and headed for that building.

Just inside the doors, a frightened female paramedic, pretty cute—*stop it*, Richie told himself— pointed the way for him: fifth floor. He went up the graffiti-adorned elevator and down a graffiti-adorned hall. Outside the apartment, two more scared shitless medics, male, were milling.

Richie displayed his badge in its wallet.

One medic, a white guy pale as his uniform, said desperately, "He won't let us in there, officer. There was a shooting and—"

Richie held up a hand and said, "I'm his partner. Give me a minute."

He knocked, said, "It's me!" and Javy, in jeans and a dark brown leather jacket, let him right in. Jav's shoulder-length dark hair, muttonchops and mustache overwhelmed his hangdog face.

"Thank God you come, Rich, thank God."

Then, without waiting for Richie to say anything, Javy made his zombie-like way over to the couch and sat, slumped, hands folded prayerfully, head bowed, though Richie was fairly confident nothing religious was going on here.

On the other hand, the skinny black guy on the floor in a blood-spattered yellow undershirt and jeans and no shoes was making like Jesus, in a crucifixion posture. Brains and lots of blood had drained out of him making a mostly scarlet Rorschach pattern on the cream-color shag throw rug. The dead dealer lay next to a low-slung white coffee table whose glass top was littered with drugs and drug paraphernalia, as well as a few empty beer bottles and soda cans.

Richie let the paramedics in; they wheeled in their gurney while the detective called in the shooting.

Before long he was saying into the phone, "Sergeant, does it sound like I'm asking? I'm fuckin' *telling* you: get some patrolmen over here, right now."

Richie hung up, hard, and the paramedics—their gurney not even unstrapped—were staring at him like his fly was open and his dick was hanging out. They'd been listening.

"You got no backup?" one of them asked.

The other added: "Why don't you? Have any back-up."

Richie pointed at the corpse and said, "Bandage that asshole's head."

"Detective," the pale paramedic said, "he's dead."

The other paramedic, a heavy-set guy, asked, "Should we even be moving him? Isn't this a crime scene?"

Richie walked over; the dead guy on the throw rug was between him and the paramedics. On the couch, hunkered over, despondent as hell, Javy sat staring at the shag rug, like a gypsy reading tea leaves.

"This *will* be a crime scene," Richie said, "if a couple hundred people start rioting and kill all our asses. As for our pal on the floor here? Yes, he's fucking dead, I *know* he's fucking dead. Now bandage his head, clean him up, put him on your gurney and . . . prop him up a little."

The pale paramedic squinted. "Prop him up . . . ?"

"Yeah, so he's sitting, kind of. Can you open his eyes? Use a little tape on his lids or something."

The paramedics were goggling at him, as if maybe they should be skipping the corpse's gurney and instead going down to get a straitjacket out of their ambulance for the detective.

Richie pointed to the stiff. "He needs to be less dead. Way less dead."

Pretty soon, Richie came out of the building fast— holding up his badge in its ID wallet Olympic torch-style—motioning and yelling at the crowd to get back, like it was a matter of life and death.

Which it was. Even more than his damn Bar exams. . . .

"We need a path here!" he called. "Step back— injured man coming through! Let these fellas do their job and he'll be all right. . . . Ma'am, excuse me. Step back. Sir! Please. . . ."

The paramedics were right behind Richie bearing a gurney whose rider had tubes in his nostrils, an IV in his arm and eyes open wide. If anybody had gotten a closer, longer look, the corpse would still have seemed a corpse; but nobody got much of any kind of look, and, wham, bam, the gurney was hauled up into the ambulance with one paramedic alongside, the rear doors shutting behind.

"Nothing to see here!" Richie called, motioning for Javy to come out of the building and join him. He was guiding his partner away in one direction, as the crowd began spreading out in the other, to trail after the siren-wailing ambulance as it pulled away from the ominous towers.

Richie and Javy walked.

Quickly. Not so quickly as to draw attention, but quickly enough, and in a nearby commercial area, Richie ducked into an alley, taking his partner with him, and they cut through almost to the next street. Near its mouth, they found a place between a bin and some garbage cans to stand and catch their breath and talk.

"Jesus, Rich," Javy said, shaking his head, sighing in relief, even grinning a little. "Thank you, man."

Richie shoved Javy against the brick wall. "You dumb bastard—you ripped him off, didn't you?"

"*What?*" Javy's eyes popped. "Are you *high*, Rich?"

"Look who's asking."

Javy held both palms up in "back off" fashion. "I don't know what the hell you're talkin' about, Rich."

Upper lip curled over his teeth, Richie leaned forward and stuck his hands into the deep pockets of Javy's leather jacket; he found the thickness of cash in both.

With a violent downward tug, he simultaneously ripped open both pockets—"*Rich! What the fuck!*"—and money spilled out, twenties, fifties, hundreds, onto the filthy alley floor.

"*This*," Richie said, indicating the fallen cash. "I'm talking about this, Jav. Where'd the bread come from, man?"

Javy's eyes were wild. "You *fucker!*" He got down on his hands and knees and recovered the money, stuffing it in his pants pockets and in his waistband, saying, "This is *my* money. Hard-earned! I never took dirty money in my life, you know that."

"What I know is," Richie said, watching his partner scramble after the literally dirty money, "you're a lying piece of shit."

Javy was on his feet again. "Jesus, Rich! Take the stick out of your ass. Every cop takes the *occasional* . . . you know, gratuity. You gonna tell me that's wrong?"

"It's wrong. Yeah."

"Hell it is!" Javy leaned in, not quite in Richie's face, and said, "It's part of our pay, guys like us. Above and beyond the salary, for little things, like getting the fuck *shot* at! You risk your fuckin' life to serve and protect, and in return? Certain courtesies are shown. In gratitude, like."

Disgusted, Richie grabbed his partner by the lapels of the leather jacket and tried to decide whether to shake him till he rattled or knock his damn head onto those bricks till it splashed or . . . shit.

He let loose.

Embarrassed, near tears, Javy said, "You'd begrudge me a little goddamn shitting consideration—a

discount on a TV, a Doughboy pool in the backyard . . . a new dress for my girl, maybe once a
fuckin' year."

"Wrong is wrong."

Javy's eyes flared. "Jesus fucking. . . . All I'm talking about is guys like you and me not living under the
fucking *poverty* level! You wanna call it wrong, go
ahead! Call it wrong."

"It's wrong."

Javy threw his hands in the air. "Fine! Then, god-
damnit, let the sons of bitches pay me fifty K a year,
like the manager of a goddamn supermarket. Pay me
something for putting my ass on the line, for getting
shot at. . . . You got a short fucking memory, man."

"Do I?"

His eyes were welling, his lips quivering. "Next
time . . . next time four guys come into your place,
with sawed-off shotguns? You take care of your *own*
ass."

Richie sighed. Held up a "stop" palm to indicate a
shift in conversation. "Okay. So you robbed him, and
then you shot him. And now I helped get you out of
there."

Javy said nothing.

Richie went on: "How many other pathetic low-end
dealers have you ripped off and shot over the years,
Jav? Two? Twenty?"

Suddenly Javy grew some spine, shoving Richie,
who stumbled back a step.

"Hey, you know what, Rich? Fuck you and the
white horse you rode in on. Guy accuses his partner

of something like that, accusing his own kind. You should be ashamed."

And Javy got his car keys out, and bumped by Richie, only Richie grabbed him, yanked his coat half-off to get at Javy's left sleeve, which he pushed up. The time had come to confirm a suspicion Richie had denied for too long.

There they were: *the puncture scabs and scars, the needle tracks of the junkie.*

Richie pushed his partner away. "You're the one should be ashamed. You're a fucking disgrace."

Now Javy did get in Richie's face. "I'll tell you what I am—I'm a fucking *leper*! And why? Because I listened to you, because I went along with Saint Richie of Roberts and turned in a million *fucking* dollars! God! Damn!"

Javy backed off and staggered around in a little half circle, saying, "And you know who wants to work with me after that? Same people wanna work with you, Rich—*no body!*"

Richie went to his partner, ex-partner, and grabbed the man's hand holding the car keys and squeezed and squeezed and finally the jagged teeth of the keys did their work and blood dripped from Javy's forced fist.

"Here's what I'll do for you," Richie said to the trembling Javy, "for that time at my place, when you saved my ass? I will write this up the way you say it happened. I will back you all the way."

"Richie. . . ."

"But that is it. That is it for us, Javy. Far as I'm concerned, that was you dead on the floor today."

Then Richie backed off, held his hands high as if in surrender and headed out of the dark alley into sunshine, not watching Javy slump against the brick and clutch his bleeding hand.

7. Payback

At a certain army base in New Jersey, in the cool blue dusk, a beat-up Chevy headed off a road, rumbled over the earth and stopped alongside a perimeter fence. The vehicle's driver, Frank Lucas, got out and waited, watching a military jeep with its lights off come gliding over the smooth ground of a firing range.

The jeep slowed.

Stopped.

Close enough, now, for Frank to make out the silhouettes of the driver and two passengers, and their M-16s at the ready. Frank took a few steps toward them and the silhouettes became three black servicemen, one of whom—the driver—was a captain.

Frank noted the peculiarity of a captain driving a couple of privates around, but said nothing.

The captain, accustomed to giving orders, gave one to Frank: "Open your trunk."

Frank nodded curtly and went around and opened his trunk, then stood to one side as the two privates—this is why the captain was driving, Frank decided—did the hauling, dragging four large taped-up duffel bags from in back of the jeep, tossing them in the junker Chevy's trunk, slamming it shut.

Then the privates rejoined the captain in the jeep and, without so much as a salute, took their leave, vehicle growling as it made a U-turn and headed back over the firing range.

Fitting, Frank thought. *We'll all be targets now. . . .*

In the relative safety and security of his apartment, Frank sat at his kitchen table with the four duffel bags—still taped and cinched up—slung there like big fat sausages, breakfast for a giant. Frank, nursing a glass of bourbon, kept staring at the bags, as if expecting them to speak.

He sat there a long time—going on an hour—putting off a moment of discovery that would mean one of two things: he would be a Harlem-based businessman (the word "gangster" did not cross his mind) at a level Bumpy Johnson had never dreamed of; or he had just squandered his life savings on four bags of nothing at all.

The German shepherd—which Frank had taken to calling "Bumpy" (in honor of a master who'd never bothered to name the animal)—was sitting nearby. The animal had finished his dishes of water and kibble and was staring at Frank with soulful eyes that meant he needed a walk.

Then the dog got interested in what Frank was doing—maybe thinking more food was in those duffel bags, the dog was always up for more food—as his new master tore the tape from one of the duffels, and loosened its cinching.

Frank let out a big breath that he hadn't realized he was holding in when he saw the multitude of brick-like packages within.

The other three duffels were similarly stuffed, brimming with oversized decks of No. 4 heroin wrapped in paper bearing Chinese characters and stamped with a label that was better than the Good Housekeeping Seal of Approval: two lions, up on their hind legs, paws pushing a globe.

And in English were the words DOUBLE UOGLOBE BRAND 100%.

By dawn Frank had found a better home for the enormous supply of dope than his own goddamn apartment, though that was where he was again sitting, and at the same table. The only evidence of any drugs on the premises was a small powder pile on a small slip of paper.

Sitting at the table with Frank was a slender, studious-looking young man with the wire-rimmed glasses and casual attire of a college student, who had just tested the powder and was about to tell Frank the good or bad (or in-between) news.

The young chemist said, "Typically what I see, before anybody on this end has stepped on it? Is twenty-five to forty-five percent pure."

Good news, then.

The kid's voice was businesslike but his eyes were glittering, like a woman studying a huge diamond some chump had given her. "No alkaloids, no adulterants, no dilutants. It's one hundred percent—holy grail of shit, Frank."

Frank nodded, flicked a smile, stood. "Thanks for coming around so early, such short notice."

The chemist flipped open a leather travel syringe kit, which the kid had set on the table along with his testing gear. The glittery eyes gazed up at him. "You mind, Frank?"

"Take it with you," Frank said. "Better cut it, some. Or your roomies'll be calling the coroner."

Nodding, the chemist quickly gathered his things, then on the way out offered one last piece of advice: "Store it in a cool, dark place, Frank."

"Sounds like you're talking about Harlem," he said, with another brief smile, and let the kid out.

Then Frank drew all the blinds and set himself down in his Eames chair, put his feet up and did his mulling, meditative thing. He needed a whole new way of doing things and probably a whole new crew and he had to think it through. . . .

8. OD

At the morgue, an assistant medical examiner pulled open a cadaver drawer for Richie Roberts to confirm an ID. The detective who'd called him down was an old friend of both Richie and his ex-partner Javy, who was the corpse in question.

Even knowing Javy had been using didn't prepare Richie for the wealth of scabs and tracks on not just his arms but the stomach, legs and toes of the longtime addict his ex-partner had become.

The detective, Jacobs, asked, "You know his girlfriend, Rich? Good-looker. Started out as one of his informants, and then he moved in with her."

Richie said, "Beth. Her name was Beth. Don't remember her last name."

The heavy-set figure in white that was the assistant medical examiner slid open another cadaver drawer, as matter of fact as an office worker at a file cabinet.

"That's her," Richie said, staring down at the skinny, once-attractive body with its own array of needle marks.

"Should've seen their pad," Detective Jacobs said. "Like a buncha animals lived there."

"I've seen it," Richie said. "Wasn't so bad, once."

"Well, trust me, you don't wanna drop by now." Then the detective said to the assistant ME, "Picked a good night for it, huh? Grand Central in here."

"It's been like this every night, lately," the ME said with a fatalistic shrug. "I'm lucky if I get home before midnight. Lot of careless people in the world."

"Less now," Jacobs pointed out.

Richie took a look at the small pile of personal effects on the chest of his ex-partner's cold corpse: a few crumpled dollars, car keys and a half-empty package of what appeared to be heroin in blue cellophane.

"This needs to go into evidence," Richie said, and took the bag.

The assistant ME filed Javy away, and on his way out with the detective, Richie held up the bag and asked, "This tell you anything? Blue cellophane?"

"That's the junkie's current brand of choice, my friend—Blue Magic. Stronger stuff than usual. May be why we're having such a carnival of ODs, lately."

Richie offered the bag to the detective. "You should take this. It's your evidence."

"Evidence of what? Javy Rivera being a first-class idiot?"

"He was a good cop, once upon a time."

The detective grunted. "That fairy tale is over."

* * *

In the lounge of the small police gym where Richie liked to work out, a television was going, though nobody was watching it right now. He found himself trying to listen, as he lifted weights in sweats and tennies, though the report wasn't telling him anything he didn't already know.

"Since 1965," a typically authoritative baritone intoned, *"law enforcement has watched the steady in crease of heroin addiction, no longer exclusive to big city neighborhoods, and along with it a rise in violent crime. Now unaccountably, it has exploded, reaching into cities as a whole—our suburbs and towns—our schools."*

Only a few other cops were working out, many of them overweight types who'd been sent here "or else," but whether fit or fat, the cops had one thing in common: none of them wanted a damn thing to do with Richie. Sometimes they'd even walk in, see him and walk out.

"Someone is finally saying enough is enough," the narrator was saying. *"Federal authorities have announced their intention to establish special narcotics bureaus in Washington, New York, Los Angeles, Chicago, Boston, Newark and other major metropolitan areas. . . . "*

Richie was jumping rope, now, and could see the sensational images on the fuzzy screen: quick shots of inner cities, junkies in shooting galleries, homicide victims in alleys and gutters, and, most shocking of all oddly enough, white suburbia.

And, of course, those who would fix all this: law-makers on Capitol Hill.

Richie heard somebody come in and saw it was his boss with the Prosecutor's Office, Lou Toback. To-back, his tie loose, stood with his hands on hips and listened to the last of the heroin story on the news.

Richie stopped jumping, said, "Dog and pony show."

Toback looked over his shoulder at Richie and half-smiled. "You think?"

In the locker room, Richie changed into his street clothes while tall, slender Toback paced and talked. Seemed Richie's boss had been selected to head up the Newark bureau in this federal drug inquiry.

"You heard the TV," Richie said, tying his shoes. "Like I said, dog and pony show."

"Not how I'm hearing it," Toback said, sitting on the bench nearby. "Not how it's being advertised, anyway."

"Well, where do I come in, in a federal deal? Who the hell would I answer to? FBI? I don't like the FBI."

"You answer to me," Toback said, "and the U.S. at-torney. Nobody else. No FBI. Hoover knows better than to mix his boys up with dope—too much tempta-tion for the feeble-minded."

Richie was dressed now. He sat on the bench and looked at his boss, who had always been straight with him, and said, "I know I'm not in any position to re-fuse this assignment, really. But I'm not convinced it's a good idea."

"Why, you'd rather stay where you are?"

"Well . . ."

Toback had a way of smiling that was at once mocking and friendly. "Rich, a detective who doesn't have the cooperation of his fellow detectives is by definition ineffective."

"What's that, French for 'fucked'? Anyway, you know why I don't have the 'cooperation' of my peers."

"*Why* you don't," Toback said flatly, "doesn't mean a damn."

"Doesn't it? Doesn't it mean anything that they're all on the take, and I'm not?" He shook his head. "Instead of giving you a medal or some shit, for turning in dirty money, they bury your damn ass."

"News flash," Toback said, "the world isn't fair. You're right, Richie. But what does being right get you?"

He frowned. "What does this assignment get me?"

Toback shrugged. "Maybe it's an opportunity to get away from all that. To go somewhere where you're not some kind of goddamn pariah."

The two men sat there and stared at each other.

"I'll do it," Richie said.

Toback grinned. "Good."

"*But* . . ." Richie held up a traffic-cop palm. ". . . only like this: I don't set foot in a police station again, not on either side of the river. I work out of a place of my own. And I pick my own guys. Guys I know wouldn't take an apple off a cart, a nickel off the sidewalk."

Toback thought about that. "Worked for Eliot Ness."

"My favorite show, as a kid, *Untouchables*."

His boss grunted a laugh. "That explains a lot."

"Well?"

Toback's eyes narrowed. "Done."

The two men shook hands.

Almost twenty-four hours to the minute from the time those GIs had stuffed four duffel bags of high-grade powder into Frank's trunk, a phone began to ring in a detached shed next to a decrepit clapboard house in North Carolina.

The house looked like Dorothy's tornado had picked it up and set it down hard; but this wasn't Kansas and it surely wasn't Oz. This was Greensboro, where crickets and bullfrogs were announcing the coming night, and a couple of black teens were playing catch.

Playing catch was understating it: one kid had a catcher's mitt, sixty yards away, and the other had a piston for an arm. The dark yew trees weren't impressed, throwing longer and longer shadows, making it hard for the kids to see; and the yard was an unlikely practice field, littered as it was with car parts and the scavenged, discarded vehicles that had given them up.

Within the shed, Melvin Lucas, in overalls and his early twenties, was reading *Players* magazine and paying no attention to the greasy, ringing phone on the workbench where he sat.

His brother Huey, working under a car nearby, yelled, "Will you please *answer* the bastard?"

Melvin took his eyes off Pam Grier's bosom and got the phone, saying into the receiver, "Yeah," unenthusiastically.

"Let me talk to Huey," a voice said.

Melvin didn't argue, merely said, "For you."

"Who is it?"

"I dunno." Melvin set the phone down on the work-bench and his ass on his stool and went back to Pam Grier.

In overalls he'd just gotten dirty today (as opposed to Melvin's, which had a month's buildup), Huey Lucas—bright-eyed, good-looking, a young thirty—came over, wiping his hands with a rag.

"Yeah," he said into the phone.

"Huey?"

He frowned. "Who's this?"

"Frank."

He gave Melvin a "what the fuck" look. "Frank who?"

"Frank your brother."

". . . Been a while since you called. Mom could use a damn phone call, time to— "

"You want to bust my ass over that, or come up north and get rich?"

Huey's smile was so big and pretty, it drew Melvin's attention away from the skin mag.

"Frank," Huey said, butter wouldn't melt. "What a damn treat hearing from you."

The brand-new two-story house in the housing de-velopment cost Frank fifty thousand dollars. Any mis-givings the Realtor might have had, selling to a man of Frank's complexion, were overcome by the sight of an open briefcase containing cash payment in full.

On a sunny spring afternoon, Frank was setting up Bumpy the German shepherd in the backyard with a doghouse and a fenced-in run when he heard the unruly caravan of cars arriving like the opening of *The Beverly Hillbillies*. All of his neighbors were white, and Frank had to grin to himself, thinking of the dozens of conversations his ragtag family's arrival would inspire around here this evening.

But his brothers and cousins would all learn to fit in. This wasn't Dogpatch, USA, it was Teaneck, New Jersey, and they would adapt. They would have to.

Still, their very lack of sophistication recommended these country boys to Frank. With what he had to accomplish, how could he turn to the usual sleazy Harlem suspects? But a country boy wasn't used to flashy cars and flashier women and diamond jewelry and expensive threads.

A city boy would take your last dime, then swear on his mother's grave he never touched it. A country boy wouldn't steal from you if his wife and kiddies were starving. City boys were selfish sons of bitches, but country boys were loyal as that German shepherd in Frank's backyard.

Assorted cars and pickup trucks soon lined the curb and jammed the driveway. Frank's five brothers, three cousins, their wives and kids and of course their gray-haired mother in cardigan and string-of-pearls climbed from the vehicles looking almost as excited as they did exhausted.

Just as Frank was coming out the front door with the

big dog trailing, Huey was arguing with Melvin about whether this was the right address or not: Huey thought it was. The new Lincoln Town Car parked just outside the garage may have given some of them doubts—how could that be their brother Frank's ride? One of the younger Lucas boys said he didn't want to get shot for trespassing or nothing.

And Frank's mother had said, "Shot for trespassing or *anything*, Cleon."

That was when Huey noticed Frank, and there were hollers and hoots as Frank went straight to Momma and took her in his arms and held her for the longest time.

Then he gave each of his brothers a quick hug, which may have surprised them, since he was normally not demonstrative. But he was happy as hell to see them, and could hardly contain himself.

Frank had spent two days picking out the furniture himself and the last of it had been delivered just this afternoon, so the place had not only a showroom look but smell. Momma had never seen a kitchen this big, even in the restaurants where she'd worked from time to time, and—Frank having anticipated her needs with his own trip to the supermarket—the new house was soon filled with the old smells of downhome cooking.

Within two hours of their arrival, the extended Lucas clan was sitting around a vast dining room table passing platters around. Even Nate's joint in Bangkok couldn't hold a candle to this soul food. And of course Frank, loving having everybody here, sat at the head of the table.

At the moment, brother Turner was bragging on his eighteen-year-old son, Stevie.

"Boy's got an arm on him, Frank," Turner was saying as he navigated a chunk of corn bread, "major league arm, I'm tellin' ya. Ain't that right?"

Nobody at the table argued, though Stevie himself just smiled shyly and shrugged.

Frank, spooning some black-eyed peas onto his plate, gave the kid a smile and asked gently, "Show me after supper?"

Stevie grinned and nodded.

But his proud papa wasn't finished: "You can't catch him, Frank. Why, he'll take your head clean off. Talkin' 95-mile-a-*hour*. Any idea how fast that is? Here's how fast: you see the ball leave his hand, and that's the last you see of it, 'fore it knocks you flat."

That made Frank laugh. "Is that right," he said.

At that moment, if pressed, Frank Lucas might well have admitted never feeling happier.

But before Frank went back outside, to try to catch a fastball in the dying light of day, he abducted his mother from the kitchen—the other girls could take care of clean-up patrol—and gave her the grand tour.

The downstairs remained alive with the noises of a big family, but was muffled and distant up here. Up here, it was just Frank and Momma.

Of his preparations over the last week, from buying this house to furnishing it and even doing the grocery shopping, Momma's room was Frank's proudest hour. He ushered her into a space larger than the shack he'd grown up in, and her eyes opened wide and her jaw dropped as she took in an array of Early American furnishings that would have staggered Betsy Ross.

"This," he said simply, "is your room."

Momma was clearly awestruck by the splendor of it. But of all the furnishings, an old vanity table, dotted with French perfume bottles, was what drew her eyes and herself.

She stood touching the table, as if testing its reality, asking her son, "How did you . . . ?"

"It's not magic," he said and found himself grinning like a fool. "It's something I put in motion months ago, to send you for your birthday. But now that you're up here with me? Well."

"I don't understand, Frank."

"I had it made. From memory."

She was shaking her head. "But you were *five* when they took it away. How could you remember it?"

"I remember."

"It's perfect," she said. She gazed around the bedroom, *her* bedroom. "It's all perfect."

He said nothing, but was glowing inside.

His gray-haired momma, eyes exaggerated behind the thick glasses, said, "I'm so proud of you, son."

He took her in his arms, and he kissed her forehead, and he swelled with the pride she'd bestowed upon him.

He *had* done good, hadn't he?

The building Toback found for him was an old deconsecrated Episcopal church, long since abandoned. The city maintenance worker who let Richie in did not enter deep himself, merely stood near the door and watched the fool wading in through the debris-strewn former church.

Richie immediately liked the idea of this place, standing in the colored light filtering through stained-glass windows. God's house, where cheating and lying and stealing wouldn't be allowed. But he'd make it an Old Testament house of God, where judgment wasn't forgiving.

Getting the feel of the place, acknowledging to himself that the clean-up work wouldn't be pretty, he almost stumbled on something among the rubble: a framed photograph, the glass already broken, the wood cracked.

He bent and picked it up, and a faded photograph of a priest smiled at the Jewish cop in benediction.

Well, what the hell, Richie thought. *We've already been blessed.*

"This is the only floor we'll be using," Richie told the maintenance man.

9. Can't Get Enough of That Funky Stuff

Across the river, in Newark, at a groovy little neighborhood dive with a black-dominated clientele, Richie Roberts—in a funky brown leather jacket and jeans—sat in a booth with Freddie Spearman, a scrawny-looking mustached guy with stringy brown hair whose pseudo-junkie style made him an ideal undercover cop.

"Freddie," Richie was saying, talking louder than he'd have liked because of the jukebox blasting "Signed, Sealed, Delivered," "this task force has got to be squeaky clean."

"These *are* cops you're looking for, right?" Spearman asked dryly, and sucked on his cigarette. He was so skinny he seemed to swim in his paisley shirt.

Richie grinned. "Yes. Cops who value a good bust more than a free season ticket to the Knicks."

" 'Good bust,' " Spearman said, "in the strip joint sense?"

"All right, all right," Richie said with a laugh, and he sipped his beer. "I don't wanna come off as some damn Boy Scout. And these guys gotta be hard-asses to begin with. At some point on this gig, more than likely, the guns are comin' out."

Spearman blew a smoke ring. "Does sound like a good time."

Richie leaned forward. "But, Freddie, you gotta understand—I'm reluctant to bring anyone in I don't know, personally."

"You know *me*, don't you?" Spearman flicked cigarette ash onto the floor. "Well, I vouch for both Jones and Abruzzo. Stand-up guys all the way."

"Yeah, yeah, I know but—"

Spearman held up a "stop" palm. "No 'buts,' Richie. We work together, Jones and Abruzzo and me. You want Ringo, you got to take Paul and George, too."

Richie shook his head. "What about John?"

"Hell, *you're* John."

Richie laughed again. "Gimme a break. . . . So where are they, these two stand-up guys?"

Spearman pointed over to the smoky joint's crowded dance floor. "That's Moses Jones. With the skinny-legs-and-all chickie."

On the jukebox, Stevie Wonder had given over to Eric Burden and War doing "Spill the Wine." A lanky black dude was dancing with a skinny white girl, so wild and uninhibited they might be leaving their best game in the practice gym. The dude had a serious Afro, a Fu Manchu mustache and a dark untucked shirt with collars pointed enough to put an eye out, and looked about as much like a cop as Spearman.

Which was to say, not like a cop at all.

"And that," Spearman was saying, "is Al Abruzzo. With the big black mama."

Abruzzo was a criminally good-looking young Italian in an untucked light blue shirt with its own eye-hazard collars; his sleeves were rolled up and some tattoos were showing, dating to his days in the military, most likely. The heavy-set gal seemed giddy having the attention of this cut-rate Marcello Mastroianni; and he was lost in the sight of her big bobbling bosoms.

Both Spearman's buddies looked more like crooks than cops, so that was a good start. What Richie had in mind didn't involve deep undercover, but his squad members would have to work the streets without getting made.

"Both are good with wires," Spearman was saying. "Hooked up with good informants. They're honest, far as it goes. And they're fearless, farther than that. They'll do whatever it takes to get the job done."

Richie raised an eyebrow. "Good to hear. Anything else to recommend them?"

Spearman grinned. "Well, they're insane. Like *you*, Richie. What more could you ask?"

He couldn't think of a thing.

Spearman's trio made the last of Richie's fifteen Untouchables, the rest of them handpicked by the detective, not from going through endless files, but out of his own knowledge of which other cops he'd encountered over the years worth recruiting—cops who seemed motivated by putting away bad guys and not money in a safe deposit box.

So it was time to go to church—that ground floor of the former Episcopalian house of worship had been cleared of refuse but otherwise little renovated, with a loose bullpen of desks moved in, some files and lockers on the fringes and at the front of the room a folding banquet table behind which two bulletin boards loomed like big blank slates, waiting for the work of the sixteen men in this room, in the days and nights ahead, to fill them.

Morning sunlight filtered in, turned shades of burnished yellow and brown thanks to the tall stained-glass windows along one wall, filling the gutted room with amber-tinged light, and reminding everybody that God was watching.

Richie perched on the table with the bulletin boards at his back and said, "Our mandate is to make major arrests. No street guys—small potatoes are of no interest. Main course meals only, guys—suppliers, distributors."

His latest recruits, Spearman, Jones and Abruzzo, had taken the desks in the back, like delinquent students hoping to evade the teacher's notice. Of the entire group, these three amigos were the most disreputable-looking, which made them ideal for what would soon come.

Richie got up and pinned to the bulletin board its first exhibit: a single, half-empty packet of heroin, bequeathed to him by his late partner, Javy Rivera. The blue of the distinctive cellophane bag popped against the brown of the tackboard.

He pointed to the little blue bag. "Heroin," he said. "We'll also target cocaine and amphetamines—we can skip the grass, unless we have a major haul on our hands."

Spearman's voice echoed up from the back. "Define major haul."

Richie shrugged. "Thousand pounds? Less than that, let somebody not as important as us waste their damn time."

A few grins blossomed at that remark.

In the back of the room, where they sat on one of their desks, side by side, Jones nudged the sleepy-looking Abruzzo, and Abruzzo nudged him back. Richie gave them the kind of hard look he'd received himself, over the years, countless times from countless schoolteachers.

And they gave him their attention, if grudgingly.

"We'll be handling big shipments," Richie said, "big money . . . and big temptation."

Jones raised his hand.

"Yeah," Richie said with a nod of acknowledgment.

"What's with this story going around about you?" Everybody's eyes were on Jones. "About you turning in a shitload of cash. That true?"

Everybody's eyes were on Richie now.

"You're half right," Richie said.

Those eyes all widened.

"It's a load of shit," he said.

And everybody grinned in relief, their "teacher" going on with his briefing, in charge but one of the guys.

They began the next afternoon, on the streets of Newark.

Abruzzo needed to look like a junkie, and it hadn't been a stretch: dirty jeans and wool cap were all it took to sell the story. He shuffled up to a dealer on the corner as Richie, Spearman and Jones watched from an unmarked vehicle, Jones discreetly snapping photos.

The exchange they saw take place was a simple one: ten bucks for a blue cellophane packet of H.

When they tested the powder back at the church, Jones taking the honors, the results were impressive.

"Stuff's ten percent pure," Jones said. "Strong enough to smoke, for all those suburban white kids who don't like sticking needles in their pasty little arms. And the ghetto junkies? They'll get high just on the *thought* of stuff this strong. . . ."

The whole squad was gathered around the impromptu lab test taking place on Jones's desktop. These were seasoned cops, but they all wore incredulity on their faces—none of them, Richie included, had ever heard of anything this pure on the street before.

Richie, his voice hushed enough for the church in its former glory, said, "Ten bucks. That's all you paid for it."

Abruzzo nodded. "Who says you don't get bang for your buck these days?"

Jones was frowning. "Crazy thing is, this blue packet stuff's about all that's out there right now. Somebody's cornered the market."

"How's it possible?" Richie asked. "Who can afford to sell shit twice as good for half as much?"

"I dunno," Jones admitted, "but I'll lay you odds that's *how* they cornered it."

Richie turned toward the bulletin boards.

One of them represented a project that had taken him all of yesterday afternoon: arranging surveillance photos that Toback had given him to display the hierarchies of crime families in New Jersey and New York, the known dope kingpins, almost all of them Italian.

"But who?" Richie asked. "*Who?*"

Jones shrugged. "New player, maybe?"

Richie and his squad had no way of knowing they were up against not only a new player, but a whole new ballgame, that in fact somebody from the minors had just moved up to the big leagues.

The process started overseas, in a cave in the Golden Triangle, where the poppies were processed, each bulb pierced, its white liquid oozing, changing into filthy liquids in wooden bowls, finally forming a gray paste.

It continued back home, in the Bronx, at the Chemical Bank where Frank Lucas would sit with a respectable Caucasian vice president who wire-transferred a sizable amount overseas to a Bangkok bank, where Frank's friend, former Master Sergeant

Nate Atkins, sat with a respectable Thai banker, who proceeded to convert the transfer to cash.

Nate would carry the ball for a while, sliding cash across a table at his Soul Brothers Bar to a pair of Chinese Triad gangsters.

Then in a tent at a jungle army base in Vietnam, Nate would hand still more cash to the two-star general he and Frank had met on his first East Asian business trip—the military brass had to get their cut, after all.

Nate's next stop was Vietnam, at a landing strip where the air was chopped by propellers as wounded soldiers on stretchers were lifted onto a transport plane. Nearby, four large crates of Japanese TVs waited under cargo netting. And the pilot of the transport was stuffing more cash in a pouch, after he saluted Nate, as if the master sergeant's uniform still meant something.

Nate's role in the process had now played out.

Before long, at dusk at an army base in North Carolina, that transport plane had come and was about to be gone, taxiing for takeoff, leaving behind a pile of discarded TV boxes outside a supply warehouse.

At the perimeter of the base, several black servicemen transferred heavy, taped-up duffel bags from an army jeep into a station wagon, hoisting those that wouldn't fit inside a roof rack. Two civilians—brothers of Frank Lucas—supervised, helping tie down the duffels with twine.

The Lucas boys headed north in their station wagon, down a rain-slicked highway, canvas tarp atop their vehicle flapping like the tongue of a happy hound. Before long, in the distance, the glow of the Washington Monument beckoned like the American dream coming true.

The process finally got to Harlem, as a black mom exited a discount drugstore into a parking lot, pushing a shopping car loaded down with her baby, bundles of Pampers and several cases of milk sugar.

That milk sugar found its way to Red Top's apartment, where the ruby-haired woman in charge tended not just to the cutting of the powder, but to the cleanup. Her five table workers, in street clothes now, surgical masks dangling, wiped down surfaces, scales and other apparatus. Tens of thousands of blue cellophane packets of heroin were neatly arranged on two folding tables.

The process was complete.

The product was ready to hit the street.

Richie and his squad were hitting the street, too. But the squad leader's bulletin board of dope kingpins did not include a shot of Frank Lucas, nor would that name have meant anything to Richie Roberts.

10. Kill Kill Kill

Frank Lucas marched the small army of his brothers down 116th Street in Harlem. In his Armani suit, Frank looked like the Pied Piper, leading these country boys in their plaid and checked shirts and jeans and clodhoppers. The Lincoln Town Car was gliding along just behind them, keeping the same pace as they walked and talked and toured the street they would soon own.

He'd been telling them about Bumpy Johnson. How Bumpy ran one of the biggest companies in New York City for almost fifty years. That he'd been with Mr. Johnson every day for the last fifteen of those years, looking after him, taking care of things, protecting him and, most of all, learning from him.

His words seemed to impress these country boys, though they may have been even more impressed by the storekeepers who waved and smiled at their big brother, and the grown men who stepped out of his path like a red carpet was rolling out from under his well-polished shoes.

"Bumpy was rich," Frank was saying, "but never white-man rich. Why? Because he didn't own his own company. Oh, he *thought* he did. But really, he only managed it; somebody else *owned* the thing. So they owned *him*."

This lecture continued as Frank led his brothers up the stairs of Red Top's apartment building.

"Nobody owns me," Frank told them. "Why? Because I own my own company."

Soon they were heading down a hallway.

"And my company," Frank continued, "sells a product that's better than my competitor's . . . at a lower price."

Frank stopped outside Red Top's apartment door.

Huey, bright-eyed and as naive as a kid at his first county fair, asked, "What are we sellin', Frank?"

"See for yourself."

Frank unlocked the door onto a world his brothers had never seen before, outside of maybe a blaxploitation picture at a drive-in movie.

Five naked women—all in their twenties, with the kind of nice bodies that could make any boy's mouth hang open, country or city—sat at worktables with their faces veiled by surgical masks. Four of the top-less quintet were cutting heroin with lactose and quinine in a precise Frank Lucas–dictated mixture of controlled purity. Another of the women was stamping small packets of blue cellophane with the words "Blue Magic."

Frank shut the door behind his slack-jawed brethren as Red Top—in a halter top and leather miniskirt—came over and smiled in that way of hers, both friendly and businesslike.

"Hi, Frank," she said. "What turnip truck did these boys fall off of?"

"A truck out of Greensboro, honey," he said good-naturedly. "These are my brothers."

She grinned at them and started shaking hands, saying, "Any brother of yours, Frank. Any brother of yours."

Huey was watching the women work, not just taking in their titties like the other boys. He asked Red Top, "Why are you putting 'Blue Magic' on the packets?"

She said, "There's lots of brands of dope in Harlem—Tru Blue, Mean Machine, Could Be Fatal, Dick Down, more than you could count even with your shoes off."

Frank picked it up: "Blue Magic's a new brand name, *our* brand name, for this new, stronger shit."

Red Top put in: "Ten percent purity, when other brands are five percent or less."

Huey was paying close attention, even if Frank's other brothers were still ogling the help.

Next stop on Frank's nickel tour was just across the way, his favorite diner, where they pushed a couple of tables together and ordered lunch. As they waited for Charlene to bring their blue plate specials, Frank continued to hold court.

"What matters in business," Frank was saying, "is honesty, integrity, hard work and loyalty."

Out the window Frank spotted Tango Black, wearing his Shaft-like black leather jacket, bald head gleaming in the sunlight, standing at a fruit stand and helping himself. A fine-looking long-legged gal hung on his arm, and that bodyguard as big as Tango stood watch.

"Most important," Frank said, reaching for the glass sugar dispenser, screwing off the lid, "is never forget where you come from."

His brothers watched with eyes wide as Frank dumped the contents of the dispenser onto his plate, as if he was preparing to chow down on a hill of sugar.

"You are what you are," Frank said, "and that's one of two things: you're nothing, or you're something. You following this?"

His brothers managed to nod, though they remained fascinated by the empty sugar dispenser, its abandoned lid and the pile of sugar on his plate.

"Excuse me, fellas," he said, and stood. "I'll be right back."

His brothers watched, bewildered, as Frank exited the diner and, weaving between this car and that one, headed across the street, where a big bald guy with a good-looking girl on his arm was filling a brown-paper grocery sack with fruit.

Empty sugar dispenser in his left hand, Frank approached Tango cheerfully, saying, "Hey, man, what's up? I was just thinking about you."

Tango turned and frowned, more confused than irritated.

Frank was saying, "You know, I was looking at the jar

you told me about?" He held up the empty sugar dispenser. "And you know what? I didn't see nothing in it."

Tango sneered and snarled, "What the fuck you want, Frank?"

But Frank's answer wasn't words.

Frank's answer was to pull his revolver from its shoulder holster and shove the gun's snout into Tango's forehead.

Right out on the sidewalk, on the street, in front of the fruit stand, in front of his brothers and Tango's girl and bodyguard and God and everybody.

The ranks of "everybody," however, were thinning, as people faded away in the deadly silence, including the bodyguard, who backed way the fuck off. Even the young long-legged gal wasn't on Tango's arm anymore—she was heading down the sidewalk, her high heels clicking on cement, like she had a doctor's appointment she just remembered.

If Tango was worried, though, he didn't show it. He just stared at Frank, eyes cold under the gun barrel whose nose was dimpling his forehead, and the would-be king of 116th Street sneered some more as he said, "What're you gonna do now, boy? Shoot me in broad daylight? Front of *everyone*?"

The world froze.

Life on the street stopped, like an atom bomb had just dropped, nobody moving, everybody looking at Frank and his captive audience.

"Big show," Tango said derisively. "Everybody looking at the big man. But what next? You really gonna shoot me, motherfucker?"

"Yeah," Frank said, "I am."

Frank squeezed the trigger and Tango was dead so fast it didn't have time to register in the insolent eyes, and the big man fell back and hit the pavement, hard, but feeling no pain. Blood and brains drained out under the bald head like somebody had dropped a melon off the stand.

Tango was history but Frank still had a point to make.

He emptied the revolver into the corpse's chest and the shots made little cracks yet echoed like thunder down the canyon of buildings.

When the gun was empty, and the echo had died away, silence again shrouding the street, Frank just stood there and, one by one, looked into the face of each spectator, including the bodyguard and the fruit vendor, daring them to remember him.

Then, calmly as a meter maid giving a parking ticket, he knelt and reached inside Tango's jacket and found a money clip fat with cash. He set the empty sugar dispenser down and jammed the money in.

To nobody in particular, Frank said, "For the cops. Should be plenty."

Then he got to his feet, crossed the street—no cars at the moment, for some reason—and went back into the diner and sat back down with his brothers. He ignored their astonished stares and tucked his napkin back into his shirt collar, like any good country boy. The blue plate specials had arrived, steam rising off meat loaf.

"That's basically the whole picture," Frank said. He smiled from face to face, then asked, "Any questions?"

11. Nice to Be Nice

At the same time Richie Roberts was settling in with his squad at an abandoned church in New Jersey, Frank Lucas was being shown around an Upper East Side penthouse in New York. Just as a city maintenance worker had watched Richie deciding, so did a real estate broker—an attractive white woman—stand patiently on the sidelines while Frank considered the high-ceilinged spaciousness of a grand, unfurnished apartment.

Frank liked the modern look of the place, which probably dated to the 1950s when things got sleeker and all atomic and shit. The light streaming in from the garden terrace was right out of an old painting in a museum, and the curtains were themselves twelve feet high; this wasn't an apartment, it was a damn cathedral.

Without looking at the real estate agent, Frank said, "No loan, no contingencies."

"That's fine. How—"

"Cash sale."

"Fine! I know you'll just love it here. . . ."

And he did know he would love it there. The penthouse would be his refuge, his sanctuary, from the streets and business, and even from Teaneck and his family. Country boys made good help and were great family, but Frank had goals and tastes that were not at all country.

His home away from home, however, was a nightclub called Small's Paradise at the southwest corner of 135th Street. Harlem had lots of choices in the nightlife department, Mr. B's, the Shalimar, the Gold Lounge. But Small's had history; it was the kind of place where a guy like Frank Lucas, even back when he was a glorified bodyguard for Bumpy Johnson, could rub shoulders with the likes of Wilt Chamberlain or even Howard Hughes.

Rain had turned the streets as slick and glistening as black patent leather, and off that sheen reflected the neons of the night, including the Apollo sign itself, the famous theater just across the way and down—James Brown appearing. Outside Small's, a welldressed lineup of blacks and whites waited behind a velvet rope for the doorman's decision on whether they were cool enough for the room. In a beautifully tailored Brooks Brothers, Frank, of course, brushed right on by and in; he was a silent partner, after all.

Frank didn't take a ringside table—he preferred not to be in the spotlight—and sat talking and drinking and laughing a little with two business associates, Charlie Williams and Cattano's man, Rossi. Like

Frank, the two men favored expensive threads, nothing flashy, but sharp. Even their women, two pretty black call girls, were tastefully attired, not so heavy on the makeup or jewelry, some cleavage but no *Playboy* Bunny spillage.

Up on the stage Joe Williams was tearing it up, doing his signature tune, "Every Day I Have the Blues." The acts at Small's were always big-time—last week King Curtis, next week Jimmy Smith and his Hammond.

When applause for his signature tune died down, the singer said, "We have a special guest here at Small's Paradise tonight, ladies and gentlemen—Mr. Joe Louis!"

The legendary champ, still a powerful-looking man despite his age, stood and bowed, smiling shyly, and waved to the crowd, which was going wild with applause and whistles and cheers.

After one more tune, the singer went on break but the band started up again, "Green Onions" inspiring couples to flood out to claim their tiny pieces of real estate on the postage-stamp dance floor.

Frank looked past the dancers toward the table where the former champ sat with his dignified wife, Marva, and their guest, a stunningly beautiful young woman in her mid-twenties, her slender shape poured into a gold lamé gown, shoulder-length dark hair cascading to bare shoulders.

Rossi, noticing Frank's eyes were on the Louis table, said, "Twelve years. No champ'll ever pull that off again."

"Who's the beauty queen?"

Charlie chortled and said, "You called it, Frank: a beauty queen."

Frank gave Charlie a sideways look.

"A *real* one, Frank," Charlie said with a grin. "Miss Puerto fuckin' Rico. No kiddin'."

He found himself staring at her—her smile so real, so natural, her eyes dark and bright and taking everything in . . .

. . . including Frank, when her gaze momentarily caught and held his. He didn't look away. He didn't mind her knowing he was admiring her; he wasn't some gaping pervert, but a man respectfully taking in a vision of beauty.

Anyway, their eyes didn't lock long enough for her to get uneasy or him to be embarrassed, because both had their eyes drawn to a noisy group entering the club, some young dudes and their women striding in, loud as a gospel choir but not near as righteous, with a big ridiculous Superfly figure out front.

Christ, Frank thought, *what idiots*, and then he *was* embarrassed: it was his brothers, with Huey (who should the fuck *know* better!) in the lead, wearing a damn parrot-green suit with floppy wide-brimmed fedora and slung with a showcase worth of gold chains, acting like he owned the place.

When, after all, it was his *brother* who owned the place. . . .

Frank didn't even let the boys and their wives and girlfriends find their way to a table before he got up, went over and took Huey by the arm and hauled his ass unceremoniously in back to a small dressing room used by singers like Williams and comics like Nipsey Russell, empty at the moment and perfect for Frank's purpose.

"What is this nonsense?" Frank demanded, turning Huey toward the mirror.

"What?" Huey said, mildly indignant, as if he had no idea what the hell his big brother was talking about. "These are my *clothes*. This is a very nice expensive—"

"Piece of crap," Frank said, holding onto his brother's green-clad arm. With his free hand, he gestured to his own sharp but not ostentatious apparel. "*These* are clothes. *You're* wearing a costume. Fuckin' Halloween, Huey."

"That's bullshit, man!"

"Is it? Why don't you just hang a sign around your neck says, 'Arrest My Ass'? You look like Nicky fuckin' Barnes."

Huey blinked, looking more hurt than mad. "And what's wrong with that? What's wrong with Nicky Barnes? I like Nicky. He's cool."

"Cool? You wanna be like Mr. Cool? You wanna be Superfly, when you don't grow up? Then go work for him, Huey. End up in a cell with him, why don't you?"

"Maybe I will." Huey pulled himself free from his brother's grasp. Trying to regain some pride, he smoothed his ruffled shirt and adjusted his outlandish hat.

Frank sighed. He took the edge out of his voice, stayed calm and even soothing. "Listen for a second, bro. Gotta understand, man—guy making all the noise in the room, he's the weak one. That's not who we are. That's not who you want to be."

Lightly, as if changing the subject would make all this go away, Huey said, "Nicky wants to talk to you, by the way. Told him I'd tell you."

Frank's found his primping brother's eyes in the mirror. "You talked to Nicky about *me*?"

"Not *about* you," Huey sputtered defensively. "We was just talking. Shooting the shit, y'know? And it come up in passing, like, that he had something he wanted to rap with you about."

"Do I look like I want to have anything to do with that fool Nicky Barnes?"

"I'm just passing it along is all."

Frank said nothing. He looked at his brother in the mirror, took in the gaudy threads and shook his head. "I am definitely taking you shopping tomorrow."

"Why? I went shopping today."

Frank's eyebrows went up. "Yeah, I can see you did. Seems like you go shopping every day, Huey, like a goddamn girl."

"That's no way to talk."

"That's no way to dress. I'm introducing you to my tailor. God help us if he sees you in that getup."

Frank waved his brother away, and the vision in green went out to find the other country boys and their womenfolk.

Half an hour or so after the Lucas brothers ended their conversation about Nicky Barnes and his influence on fashion, a cream-color Bentley rolled up at the curb outside Small's Paradise and Barnes himself—and his entourage—piled out.

When Frank's chief rival in the powder business swept in, Barnes—in a sable coat and brown leather suit and feathered fedora—had his arms full of copies of the recently released *New York Times Sunday Magazine* that depicted him on a cover emblazoned "Gangster Chic." The flamboyant druglord was passing them out like a newsboy peddling an "extra," often stopping to sign them.

At the same time, Barnes's chief rival was occupied in a conversation with Joe Louis, the champ having table-hopped his way to Frank's, where he now sat and spoke respectfully to the man responsible for filling Harlem's streets with a product called Blue Magic.

"It's a tax thing," Louis said with an embarrassed shrug of his massive shoulders. "It's a mistake my lawyers'll straighten out, you know? But for the time being, Frank, it's a real headache."

"How much you owe?" Frank asked.

"Nothing, nothing. Something like—fifty grand?"

Frank studied the battered, puffy and yet still handsome, iconic face of America's greatest heavyweight champ, black or white. Was it an honor to have a celebrity of this stature asking to borrow money? Or a curse?

Either way, Frank could only smile and nod, a king granting a request from a down-on-his-luck knight.

Louis beamed in a shy country boy way that Frank could relate to. "Thank you, Frank. You're tops. I'll pay ya back soon as—"

"No. Joe. It's a gift. Not a loan. You don't owe me nothing. Just keep comin' around the club here. You honor us with your presence."

Meanwhile, Nicky Barnes was gliding around the club with his magazines and his crew, a long-legged good-looking gal on his sleeve. As Louis chatted with Charlie and Rossi, Frank watched the flashy fool make his rounds, lingering at Louis's table where Mrs. Louis was introducing him to Miss Puerto Rico, Barnes holding onto the beautiful creature's slender hand longer than a man with a girl on his arm should.

Frank had had enough. He glanced and nodded at Huey at a nearby table, by way of announcing he was splitting. Frank's big bodyguard/driver, Doc, didn't require a glance or a nod, knowing Frank's moods well enough to read that he was ready to go. Doc got up even a beat before Frank.

At the hatcheck stand, Doc had Frank's topcoat ready and he was slipping into it when Miss Puerto Rico—stepping from the ladies' room into their path—came through.

She gave him that open, no b.s. smile, making no bones about them earlier having shared a look across the crowded club.

"I'm Eva," she said.

"I'm Frank," he said, and smiled just a little. Just enough.

That made her smile grow, and she said, "You're Frank, and . . ." She gestured around the hopping club. ". . . this is your place."

He kept the just-enough-of-a-smile going but otherwise didn't reply.

She took that for "yes," and said, "Then why is it called Small's?"

"Fellow named Small opened it. Back in the days of the Harlem renaissance. Cotton Club and all."

"That was a long time ago." There was something impish, and nicely teasing, in her voice, which was lilting and musical, the Puerto Rican accent adding faint percussion. "Why don't you call it 'Frank's' now?"

"Because," he said, "I don't have to."

And now he let the smile all the way, full-wattage. Normally he could make a girl forget her own name with that smile. Only right now, with her smiling back at him, he wasn't sure he could remember his own. . . .

12. The Judge

In the middle pew of a crowded courtroom, Richie Roberts, in a somber suit and tie, sat with his attorney, Sheila Allison, also in a severe (if stylish) suit, waiting their turn. Everyone in the courtroom was half of a divorced couple sitting with his or her attorney. Laurie Roberts and the male attorney representing her were on the other side, in more ways than one.

Richie had noticed the odd sight of attorneys bearing papers clipped with five-dollar bills or tens and sometimes even twenties, heading down the aisle toward the bench.

Sheila, a dark-haired woman, her professional demeanor taking not a whit off her blonde prettiness, was saying, "You should be prepared for your wife's counsel to hit below the belt."

"Who I had relations with," he said, mildly defensive, "since we broke up, isn't any of her business."

He was specifically thinking of the fact that he and Sheila were sleeping together, and was wondering if having sex with your divorce attorney could be a black mark against you in a custody case.

"I wasn't talking about your *proclivities*, Richie," she said, patient but having to work at it. "Those I know only too well. This isn't about you having a wandering eye."

"What is it about then?"

Her expression was regretful, like a mother feeding a spoon of castor oil to her kid. "I'm talking about you being a cop."

He made a face, waved that off. "You kidding? What, about me taking *money*? I don't do that." He laughed once, harshly. "You've seen where I live. Does it look like I care about money?"

But Sheila, like everybody else in this part of the world, couldn't seem to get it through her lovely head that maybe not every cop was in it for the graft. "If you *have* taken money, Richie, I promise you, it will come out."

"Fine. Swell. I haven't."

An eyebrow arched in the oval face. "You're going to have to sit down with shrinks and social workers."

"Big deal."

"*And* your wife's lawyers, *and* the judge, and there will be a lot of questions."

"I'll have answers." He nodded toward the bench, in front of which a man in a gray suit was arranging the folders the lawyers had been bringing up to him. "What's that about?"

She smiled tightly. "Scheduling."

"I mean, the money."

"The money is about scheduling. That's the judge's assistant. He's rearranging the pre-trial cases in order of . . . rearranging them."

"In order of the amount of gratuity, you mean?"

She didn't answer his question. Instead she asked her own: "What about your old friends from the neighborhood? You still hang out with them?"

He shrugged. "Summer softball on Sundays with some guys."

"With some *wise* guys, you mean. That's going to look good, Richie. Just great."

He felt red rising up his collar. "I grew up with those guys. Went to school with them. Big deal. I never did any business with them."

Too casually, she asked, "What about Joseph Sadano?"

"What about Joseph Sadano?"

She paused. Took a deep breath. Let it out. "Richie, I'm just trying to understand certain things your wife has said. If they're not true, just tell me. But if they *are*, well . . . what I don't know can definitely hurt you."

"Yeah, Joey's a guy I hang with sometimes. Basketball. Poker."

"You bet on basketball with him?"

"No. We play it. Badly."

"What kind of poker games? High stakes?"

"Yeah, all the way up to a quarter a raise. Are you kidding me, Sheila?"

"Joey Sadano . . . he's also your son's godfather?"

He nodded, rolled his eyes. "Not that kind of godfather. Jesus."

Sheila's mouth tightened—it was not exactly a smile, and was almost a frown. She nodded toward the side of the courtroom where Laurie and her counsel sat. "Do you really care about this, Rich? Or do you just not want your ex to win—even when maybe she should."

"What's that supposed to mean?"

Sheila's gaze wasn't any more cutting than a laser beam. "How often do you see your son as it is?"

"Not enough as I should," he admitted. "And it's my fault, kind of work I do. But Laurie, Christ, she wants to make it *never*."

Sheila studied him. She laughed, once, a tiny thing that didn't make it out of her throat. "You want this bad enough to invest another twenty?"

They'd been keeping their voices low, but now Richie whispered: "What, pay some prick judge off?"

She sighed. "Well, *I'm* not to going to sit on a hard bench all day."

And Sheila got a twenty dollar bill from her purse, and took it up to the judge's assistant with it clipped to Richie's paperwork.

When the bailiff said, "All rise," Richie rose, but he wasn't in a hurry about it.

Finally Frank Lucas got the nerve up to make an important call. He got the number from Joe Louis, who after all owed him a favor; this one might be well worth the fifty grand.

"I want you to know who I am," Frank said to her.

Even over the phone her voice retained its music, its magic. "That you're an important man in Harlem?"

"No. Who I *am*. Where I come from. Are you free Saturday afternoon?"

And at one o'clock Saturday, Eva was waiting on a corner in Riverside, right where they'd arranged, just as much a vision in a dark sweater and skirt and hand-bag as in the gold-lamé gown.

Doc pulled the Lincoln Town Car up to the curb, and Frank told him, "I got this," and opened the rear door and stepped out and stood before her as awkward as any downhome suitor.

"I hope you weren't waiting long," Frank said.

"No. No, you're right on time."

"A woman as beautiful as you shouldn't have to wait for anything."

She smiled at that, almost laughed, and then she saw he meant every word.

The perfect gentleman, Frank held the door for her, then slid in after her.

"And where are we going?" she asked.

"Teaneck," he said.

"What's in Teaneck?"

"My mother."

Before long the lovely young Hispanic woman was studying family photos on the mantel of the living room's fireplace, with Frank at her side.

"Is that your father?" she asked, indicating a photo-graph of a well-dressed, respectable-looking Bumpy Johnson.

"No."

"Who is it?"

"Martin Luther King."

"It's not! You're a big tease."

"You're right." Frank smiled at Bumpy's visage. "To me, he was just as important as Dr. King. More so."

"What his name?"

"Johnson."

"What did he do?"

"Lot of things. And he had a lot of friends. He served New York and it served him back."

Eva wasn't looking at the photo now; it was Frank she was studying. "What was he to you?"

"Well, let me think about it. . . . More than an employer. *Teacher.*"

"What did he teach you?"

Frank's head moved to one side; his eyes narrowed. "How to take my time."

"Is that important?"

"Yes. It is if you're going to do something, do it right, with care . . . with love."

He hadn't meant to make the words sound seductive, but she clearly was warming to him, standing closer, her voice softer now as she asked, "What else did he teach you?"

The images flew unbidden into his brain: *men beaten to a pulp, guys shot to death, Bumpy watching as gasoline was poured onto a competitor and a match was lit. . . .*

"How to be a gentleman," Frank said.

Bumpy's calm, benign face in the photograph seemed to agree with this assessment.

"Is that what you are?" She slipped her arm in his. "A gentleman?"

Her smile said she doubted this; but it also said she didn't mind. She was clearly marking the time before he tried to take her upstairs. His mother's house— *right. Sure.* . . .

But Frank said smoothly, "I got five different apartments in the city I could've taken you to. I have a penthouse that would steal your breath away. But I brought you *here*, instead. . . ."

A voice from the nearby staircase said: "Oh, is this *her?*"

Eva turned toward the voice and so, smilingly, did Frank.

His gray-haired mother was making her way down the stairs, beaming at them.

"I brought you here," he whispered, "to meet my mother."

Who was crossing the room with her arms wide open, saying, "Oh, she's *beautiful*, Frank. Just look at her—an angel come down from heaven."

Then Momma was embracing Eva, who looked at Frank questioningly, wondering if she'd been had.

Not yet, he thought. *Not yet.*

13. Mean Machine

Every street cop gets used to the spike of fear that certain sights send through you. But that sick feeling usually didn't come in the middle of sitting at your desk and going through the morning mail, which was what Richie Roberts was doing when he came across the deceptively mundane-looking envelope from the New Jersey Bar Association.

He sat staring at the thing, holding the letter in both hands, trying to get up the goddamn nerve to open it, the only color in his face provided by the amber light of the sun's rays slanting in through the looming stained-glass windows.

Over at the bulletin boards, the trio who had become his squad within the squad—skinny Spearman, Afro-sporting Jones and matinee-idol Abruzzo—were revising the organized-crime food-chain chart, pinning up new surveillance photos of various Italian wise guys.

Jones was saying, "Ice-Pick Paul goes here—"

"Naw," Abruzzo insisted, "he's under Benny Two-Socks."

Jones shook his head. "No, man, you're thinkin' of the *other* Benny, Benny the Bishop. Benny *Two-Socks* is Cattano's deadbeat son-in-law."

Spearman was nodding. "Jonesy's right. You put the wrong asshole up there. . . ."

Richie rose from his desk, came over, and the others looked over their shoulders at him while he studied the table of organization for several long moments. Then, as he began untacking photos, from the top down, the three detectives exchanged wide-eyed glances and shrugs.

Finally Jones asked, "What're you doin', Rich? We just put them up there—"

"For a cop," Richie said, not lecturing, just stating facts, "the uppermost thing is the arrest. For a prosecutor, the arrest is nothing without the evidence to convict."

Spearman said, "I'm in favor of evidence. Evidence is cool."

Richie went on: "But we don't have any real evidence on anybody on this board, so . . . down they come."

"Gonna look awful blank," Abruzzo said.

"We'll fill it with new pictures."

"New pictures?" Jones asked.

Richie nodded. "We're starting over. From the street up."

Abruzzo's handsome mug twisted sarcastically. "What are you, all of sudden, a fuckin' prosecutor?"

Richie just smiled at the guy, then tacked up his exam results on the bulletin board.

"Son of a bitch *passed*," Spearman said, eyeballing it.

With a self-satisfied little smile, Richie went back to his desk and got back to work.

That afternoon, on a street in Newark, the four detectives sat in an unmarked car watching blue cellophane packets change hands. This particular dealer, a nondescript moke who might have worked in a drugstore or supermarket, seemed to specialize in white kids, college-looking types, who were making expeditions to the "bad" part of town for their fun powder; but the dealer was democratic: he sold to street junkies, too.

The buyers Richie and his team ignored; it was the seller who had their attention—though they did snap pictures of him, he was hardly their chief concern. Where he might lead them was.

When he'd sold his last packet, the dealer got in his own wheels and drove half a dozen blocks to a gas station/car wash, where he ducked into the service garage and was glimpsed by the detectives as he spoke with a burly black automobile mechanic. They got a blurry pic of what seemed to be money handed over to the mechanic; and then the dealer walked off.

At that moment, Richie's interest in the dealer died, and they watched the garage for what seemed like hours and was minutes. A mechanic stepped out for a breath of fresh air, rubbing his hands with a rag—yes, this was the same brawny guy the dealer had handed money off to, meaning Richie now had his camera lens trained on a supplier.

He snapped a picture; it too came out a little blurry, but would suffice to go up on the new, almost bare bulletin board where a new table of organization was being built, each surveillance photo another brick in the wall.

The next day, Spearman—looking every bit the telephone lineman in his hard hat—was up top of a telephone pole outside that gas station. He was working hard, all right, but not improving the quality of phone service in the neighborhood. . . .

And the day after that, an empty apartment above a storefront across from the gas station made the perfect place for Richie, Jones and Spearman to enjoy their take-out Chinese as a reel-to-reel tape recorder picked up various interesting conversations.

These seemed innocent enough, but sometimes the codes these mental giants used was just plain pitiful: *"Those, uh, snow tires you give me last time come in yet? I'm gonna want some more of them . . . gimme one and a half more of them."*

Spearman almost choked on his Chinese, laughing.

"Wish I wasn't just some poor dumb honest cop," Jones said, grinning. "Then maybe *I* could afford one-and-a-half snow tires. . . ."

A week later, Richie was getting a mini-tape recorder, no bigger than a pack of ciggies, taped to his bare chest, which he'd shaved for the occasion.

Spearman wondered aloud if Rich had shaved his legs, too, but Richie was too preoccupied to toss a smart remark back at him.

On the table next to the bulletin boards rested a gym bag, nothing much to look at, but inside you wouldn't find a jock strap, swim suit and socks: twenty grand in neat banded packets was stacked in there.

At the prosecutor's office earlier today, Toback had sat in shirtsleeves and loosened tie, looking like a low-end disgruntled accountant, counting out the $20,000 in cash onto his desk.

"This is more than a year's salary, Richie," his boss said grimly. "If it disappears, I won't be able to get you this kind of cash for a case again."

"It'll never be out of my sight," Richie said.

"And here's two bills out of petty cash," Toback said, getting a much smaller packet from a small metal box in his desk drawer. "So you can look the part."

The cashmere sweater and sharp slacks that gave Richie the correct mid-level wise guy appearance had taken the full two C's and a little more out of his own pocket. But it was worth it: the mechanic at the gas station/car wash accepted Richie at face value, though maybe it was the gym bag of money that dazzled the guy, not Richie's clothes sense.

The mechanic wiped his hands off on a rag and then again on his greasy jumpsuit before starting to count the ten thousand Richie had handed over. The bills were on a cleaned-off area of a workbench; the other half of the twenty grand was still in the gym bag, in Richie's grasp.

"It's got to be Blue Magic," Richie said.

"Yeah, yeah, it's the 'Blue,' all right. You can pick it up here, tomorrow." The grease jockey completed counting the money, which he'd done by thumbing through, keeping the bands on the packets. "Where's the rest? This is only ten K."

"Ten K is half. You'll get the other half tomorrow, on delivery."

"No, no, no," he said, lifting a hand that didn't really have all the grease off after all. "We don't play that, we ain't fuckin' Sears Roebuck."

"I don't think it's unreasonable," Richie said gently, "half down, half on delivery."

"Well, go fuck yourself, then. That reasonable enough for you?"

Richie sighed and lifted the gym bag onto the workbench and gave the bastard the rest of Toback's money.

Soon Richie was back in their unmarked car, with Spearman behind the wheel as they headed toward the George Washington Bridge, changing lanes to keep up with a pickup truck driven by the mechanic. They had seen the guy get in the truck with a grocery bag filled with their money (or at least it had *better* be filled with their money).

Richie, wrestling his way out of the cashmere sweater, was in the process of exchanging it for a T-shirt.

"I guess you see where he's heading," Spearman said dryly.

"I see."

"New York. Is that where *we're* going?"

"Yeah. Why not?"

"Not exactly our turf."

"What are they gonna do, arrest us?"

Behind five-buck Aviator sunglasses, Spearman arched an eyebrow. "We're talking New York cops, Richie. They can do worse."

Richie shook his head. "We're not losing that fuckin' money. We're out of business, we lose that fuckin' money. Go."

Spearman went.

Followed the truck over the George Washington Bridge, with Manhattan right in their faces, looming in the windshield like the world's biggest cemetery.

Before long they were in East Harlem; neither Spearman nor Richie was thrilled about that, but neither were they surprised. The pickup pulled up to a curb outside a Pleasant Avenue grocery store—Italians did dope business in this part of Harlem.

As the mechanic—no longer in his coveralls, but anonymous street clothes—entered the grocery, Spearman stopped just for a second, for Richie to get out, and went on. Richie crossed the street, just another honky getting honked at, and from the sidewalk did his best to glance inconspicuously through the grocery window, to see who the mechanic was contacting.

Only all the guy was doing was buying a cup of to-go coffee.

In the meantime, Spearman had taken the corner, going around the block. Richie was wishing he'd caught his partner, before that trip began, and almost missed the mechanic and his coffee exiting the grocery—in fact, almost got bumped into, and had to double back quickly so as not to be made.

As the mechanic got in the pickup, Richie looked around desperately for Spearman. This was the kind of street where trucks routinely double-parked for un-loading crates and fuck you, if we're blocking you. Horns were honking, and one of them could be Spearman, caught on a side street.

The mechanic started the pickup, and began to pull out.

Richie could not afford to lose that guy—and he sure as hell could not afford to lose that twenty grand. He hurried over to a taxi stopped at the light, and flashed his badge.

"Get out," Richie said.

The taxi driver, a black kid alarmed by seeing this wild-eyed cop, just sat there; he managed to blurt, "What?" But that was all he did.

"Get the fuck out of the car!" Richie yelled, leaning in the cab like a demented car hop. "I'm commandeer-ing your vehicle!"

The taxi driver had no idea what "commandeering" meant, but he knew this guy, cop or not, was a lunatic, and began hurriedly rolling up his window.

Richie reached in, got his arm stuck as the window came up, but managed to send his fingers down to pull up on the lock; then he yanked the door open and dragged the driver out, hurling him to the pavement, hard enough to make the guy yowl in pain.

Richie hadn't meant to hurt the guy, but first aid was not his top priority right now; he jumped behind the wheel, swung the cab into opposing lanes to maneuver traffic, and then the vehicle was screeching around the corner.

Far ahead he spotted the pickup truck. That wasn't great, but any closer and the guy might have seen or heard the commotion Richie had just made. Anyway, Richie had lost time to make up for: he gunned the engine, flew through a red light and glanced nervously at his rearview mirror where cars that had just missed him were almost colliding themselves.

The truck took a right turn, still way up ahead, and Richie barreled through another red light, took the corner and kept the truck in his sight—a couple car lengths ahead, now.

Several blocks later, Richie pulled the cab up to a yellow-painted curb as the mechanic, already parked, got out and went into a pizza parlor with windows as greasy as the pizza probably was. The detective got out, crossed the street, walked past the restaurant, trying to get a good look inside without breaking stride.

Then, from around the nearest corner, coming right at him, strode a quartet in dark leather coats, like a modernized pack of gestapo thugs, big guys with dark sleek slicked-back hair. He could also make out, beneath the heavy, expensive coats, the silk ties and dark, tailored suits and Italian loafers; Rolexes gleamed on their wrists. They might have been top Mafiosi, only they were cops. The so-called Princes of the City.

Special Investigations Unit guys—he had heard of them, and seen them around, or anyway one of them: the big guy in front with the Zapata mustache, that was

Detective Trupo, though Trupo wouldn't know him from Adam. These guys—much feared and often admired by other cops, both sides of the river—were known for two things: unlimited authority and outrageous corruption.

Richie ducked into the nearest alley, just as the Four Horsemen of the Apocalypse were riding into the restaurant. In the alley he found a grimy basement window down into the kitchen that gave him a view on a tableau that made his guts tighten. . . .

Trupo and the other SIU detectives burst in, guns in hand. The mechanic and a white guy in chef's attire were in the midst of doing business, a metal food-prep table home to a meal of stacked money packets and a pile of blue cellophane baggies. Trupo supervised while one of his men slapped the mechanic and chef around, and then another detective gathered the money, stuffing it into a black bag, and the final detective slid the dope packets into another bag. The mechanic, who was a bruiser himself, started to protest, and Trupo slapped him with his automatic, a nine millimeter that opened a red gash on the black cheek.

No arrests were made. They just strode out of the kitchen, as abruptly as they'd appeared, the four lawmen departing with no suspects, just two black bags, one filled with dope, and the other with money courtesy of the taxpayers of the state of New Jersey. And Richie.

They came back up through the front door, same way they'd come in, and Richie was waiting.

They paused on the sidewalk, just outside the restaurant, frozen with casual contempt as this slovenly figure in a T-shirt had the balls to get in their way.

Richie, pointed at one of the black bags, said, "That's my money."

"*What* money?" one SIU cop asked.

Another said, "Who the fuck are you? The janitor?"

Richie discreetly passed around his Bureau of Narcotics ID in its little wallet. Trupo hung onto it.

Quietly Richie said, "Those bills are sequenced and registered with the Essex County Prosecutors Office. All begin with CF3500. Appreciate it if you'd check it out."

A frowning SIU dick got in the black bag and thumbed through a few.

"I'll be damned," he said. He grinned good-naturedly, a rapist offering his victim a post-coital smoke. "Here I thought we had a score. Figured I had a fuckin' Chris-Craft sitting in my driveway, for sure."

"Honest mistake," Richie said. "Just hand it on back."

Another of the detectives wasn't smiling. "*This* time we will."

Then this dick smiled, too; and all of the cops, except top dog Trupo, laughed, one even patting Richie on the back. An affable lot of thieves.

But Trupo still had Richie's ID, and was studying it like a clue at a crime scene. "When's the last time I was in New Jersey," he said. He had a pleasant baritone. "Let me think . . . a week ago never."

His guys smiled.

Trupo smiled, too, but it was nothing to write home about. "What're you doin', Detective Roberts, coming over here without letting anybody know? Don't you know you can get hurt doing that, overlooking the niceties?"

Richie returned Trupo's smile. "Sorry. We followed that mechanic over here from a stakeout in Newark. We were kinda doing things on the fly."

"That's the way cases get kicked out of court," Trupo advised, "doin' things on the fly. . . . Now you got your money. And we're cool with that. Aren't we guys, cool with that?"

Nods all around.

Trupo kept smiling; Richie would have preferred a frown. "Now never, Detective Roberts, *ever* come in our city again, unannounced. You come in to catch a fuckin' Broadway show, you call ahead first and clear it with me."

Then Trupo gave Richie a pat on the back, and the lead SIU detective and his fellow servants of the people went off, still hauling their bag of confiscated heroin.

Which somehow Richie doubted would ever find its way to an evidence locker. . . .

At night the narcotics squad HQ still felt like a church; but the unholy quartet Richie had encountered that afternoon didn't do much for encouraging him that God was in His Heaven and all was right with the world.

Toback, who was sitting with Richie at the banquet table by the bulletin boards, was waxing philosophical.

"What do we hate most?" his boss asked. "Isn't it the transgressions of others that we fear we're capable of ourselves?"

Richie said nothing.

"Thing is," Toback said with an easy shrug, "cops are just people. They're like—"

"Everybody else," Richie finished, "yeah, I know. And some of 'em will steal no matter what. There can be a camera on 'em and they'll still do it. And some'll never do it."

"Right," Toback said. "But a lot of 'em are in between, Richie."

Richie nodded. "Capable of doing either, depending on which way the wind blows, and how their department leans. Only these SIU guys—their department isn't leaning, it's falling down. Patrol cars don't even *stop* in Harlem—just slow up and roll down the window so the dealers can toss the money in. Man, I've seen drops go down on precinct *steps*. . . ."

"I know, I know." Toback sighed, his eyes searching his new prosecutor. "What the hell were you doing on their side of the world?"

Richie shrugged elaborately. "That's where the dope is coming from—Blue Magic. Out of New York. What am I supposed to do, ignore it? You think a narcotics squad can make it, busting two-bit dealers?"

"No. But can a narcotics squad *leader* make it, when a cab driver files aggravated assault and grand theft charges?"

Richie scowled. "Prick wouldn't give up his ride!

Motherfucker rolled his window up on me, would've dragged me from here to Kingdom Come."

"Well, that'll be handy, because Kingdom Come is where he's suing the State of New Jersey to, unless he reconsiders when a settlement amount is offered."

"I told him I was a cop. I showed him ID."

"You stole his cab and broke his arm."

"That was an accident."

"Stealing his cab?"

"Breaking his arm! Hey, I was chasing *your* twenty thousand bucks!"

Toback's face was unreadable, utterly bland, as he said, "I don't want to hear about you going into New York anymore."

Richie shook his head glumly. "Then this investigation is over. Might as well dismantle the team and go home."

Toback smiled and something almost evil was in it. "You're not *listening,* Richie—I said, I don't want to *hear* about it."

"Oh."

Toback folded his arms, leaned back in his cheap swivel chair and rocked a little. "You do whatever you have to do, go wherever you have to go, to find out who's bringing this nasty shit into our country. . . . *Just don't tell me.*"

". . . Thanks, boss."

Toback got up, stretched and yawned, and said, "I think I'll get some sleep. Why don't you do the same?"

And that was just what Richie did.

14. Cooley High

The domination of Blue Magic on inner city streets, both sides of the river, was complete within months. On this typical August afternoon, hot enough to fry eggs on the sidewalk, kids were wrenching open a fire hydrant to cool off, inadvertently splashing the beat-up Chevy parked down the street and across from the 23rd Precinct in Harlem.

Frank Lucas was in casual clothes, sitting in the junker he called Nellybelle. He owned one hundred custom-made suits, and his automobiles included a Mercedes, a Corvette Sting Ray, a 427 muscle job for kicks, and of course his Lincoln Town Car. But for keeping an eye on things, looking like just another homeboy, loafing in a T-shirt and slacks in a three-hundred-buck piece-of-shit car, was just the thing.

He was like a ghost haunting the domain he owned—116th Street, between Seventh and Eighth

Avenues—a shadow, what back home they called a "haint." He would sit there in Nellybelle, invisible, and just watch the money roll in.

Right now, inside that dingy gray stone precinct house, a clock in the locker room would be reading 3:58 . . . two minutes till shift change. Cops, in the synthetic breeze of fans sending humid air around, would be getting a jump on quitting time, exchanging uniforms for street clothes. Other guys were reversing the process, as outside blue-and-white squad cars came and went.

A minute later, a bus moving down 116th Street would turn down an almost empty Eighth Avenue. Nothing shaking. A haunted house of a street.

And the haint haunting that house sat in his clunker with its windows up and its top-dollar air conditioner blowing full blast, listening to the wicked Wilson Pickett wrapping up "Mustang Sally" so an announcer could mark the arrival of 4 P.M.

With quiet, even smug pleasure, Frank watched out a window smeared with hydrant juice as 116th Street transformed into Times fucking Square. From alleys, storefronts, tenements and around corners came junkies and dealers, flooding the sidewalks and the street with black faces.

"'Nuff niggers to make a Tarzan movie," his brother Huey had said on first seeing this phenomenon, prompting Frank to scold him for his negative language—he would not suffer that kind of self-denigrating talk from his family and employees.

Taking his product out for sale at cop shift change was another of Frank's innovations. He knew it would take a couple of hours for those lazy bastards to get their uniforms on and their asses in gear and out of the break room and onto the pavement.

And his buyers, man, you could set your watch by them. Word was the Transit Authority was planning to reroute the Eighth Avenue bus, 'cause of all the congestion, cars and delivery trucks getting snarled up by the stream of customers and sellers.

Small blue cellophane packets changed hands for the ten-buck-per-bag fee Frank insisted upon. Within minutes, in alleyways and dank, grim rooms, the contents of those packets would be cooked up and sucked into syringes, and plunged into eager veins.

Within the hour, decks of rubber-banded tens and twenties would be stuffed in envelopes and runners would deliver them to the Lucas brothers: Melvin at his metal shop; Dexter at the dry cleaners; Turner at a tire service shop; Terrence at an electrical shop; Huey at his body shop—hardworking souls, the Lucas boys.

Later, at Red Top's apartment, the brothers would converge with their envelopes of cash, which became piles of cash, which initially had been a problem. Those boys, with their backwoods math skills, could simply not deal with all that paper money. First time they tried, Huey shook his head and said, "We're gonna be here all night, if we count every bill."

So Frank had bought them a money-counting machine, a mechanical marvel that would flip through the bills with its counter rolling up impressive numbers, while the brothers rubber-banded it all into new decks of $100,000. Huey jotted down the numbers, and his brothers stuffed the money into cardboard file-type boxes, which were then taped shut.

From these boxes, the 100G stacks would be transferred by Frank into safety-deposit boxes at the - Chemical Bank in the Bronx. He was alone in the safety-deposit vault, of course, but the vice president who'd been so helpful was now a friend, who even got invited to parties at Frank's penthouse.

The banker and Frank were sipping drinks in the middle of a shindig that Hugh Hefner couldn't have topped, which was fitting since the penthouse was now beautifully furnished in a modern *Playboy* pad kind of way.

This was an office party of sorts, celebrating Blue Magic's success, with Frank's brothers, cousins, wives and girlfriends partying alongside certain business associates, including distributors like mob-guy Rossi, trusted old-timer Charlie Williams and assorted East Harlemites, plus a scattering of plainclothes cops on the payroll.

The stereo hi-fi system was pounding out soul tunes, and right now Marvin Gaye's "I Heard It Through the Grapevine" had guests dancing in Frank's living room—which had more space for the activity than Small's Paradise's dance floor, anyway.

The banker was asking, "You got a stockbroker, Frank?"

Why did these white people insist on doing business at parties?

But Frank, the perfect host, merely said, "I deal with enough crooks as it is."

Juggling his drink, the banker managed to get a business card out and jot down a name and phone number on the back.

Working to be heard over Marvin Gaye, the banker said, "This broker is as honest as he is discreet. Just ask around. He's got a list of clients in your field."

"Yeah, well, thanks, but—"

The banker shook a finger. "No 'buts,' Frank—you can't go around leaving all of your money in safety deposit boxes. Promise me you'll give him a call."

Frank took the card and nodded and the banker went off to look for food or maybe a spare female—Frank always pumped a few high-class working girls into a bash like this.

Sipping his drink, Frank was happy to see his family, friends and business associates having a good time; but the truth was, this level of noise and this degree of rowdiness made him uncomfortable. He would rather be spending the evening alone with Eva, listening to jazz or watching TV.

Eva was playing hostess, charming everybody with her smile and bright eyes and lilting accent; and the way she filled an evening gown didn't hurt, either.

Charlie, the veteran affable dope dealer, came ambling over with his arm around a balding, mustached white guy in a black suit and white shirt and no tie, who looked like he might've been an athlete half a lifetime ago or so.

With a wink and a grin, Charlie said, "Frank, this is Mike Sibota."

Frank recognized the name: this was a former Yankee

player who was now scouting for the team. Right now Sibota seemed to be working hard not to look nervous.

"Mr. Sibota, a pleasure," Frank said, and extended a hand. They shook, and Frank asked, "What can I get you?"

"From what Charlie tells me," Sibota said, "a left-hander. Your nephew?"

"My nephew," Frank confirmed. He tilted his head and risked a grin. "Got an arm on him."

"Any experience?"

"Just sandlot. Didn't graduate junior high. But I bet you're not in the market for a scholar."

Sibota, relaxing, said, "I'm in the market for a *left-hander*."

Frank gave him his patented easy smile. "Well, it's been Stevie's dream, all his life, to play for the Yankees."

Sibota laughed. "A Southern boy likes the Yankees?"

"He has good taste, Mr. Sibota. Plus, he's good enough to start tomorrow."

"So I hear." The scout handed Frank a business card. "You have your nephew come see me. And we'll give him a tryout."

"Just a chance. All he asks."

The conversation continued, about baseball and how the Yankees were doing (not that great—playing .500 ball), but Frank was only listening with one ear. He was picking up on a noisy conversation ten or so feet away, and glancing over there as well.

His brother Huey, in tinted goggle glasses and a polyester pantsuit, was holding court with his wild-ass driver Jimmy Zee, and their fine-looking if coked-up girlfriends, as well as a white cop, a detective whose name Frank couldn't recall.

The little group was gathered around a glass-top coffee table with a pile of coke on it that hadn't been among the appetizers Frank's caterers set out. The brazenness of it irritated Frank, and the grab-ass game Jimmy and the dick were playing made the back of his neck tingle.

The dick was play-acting, flashing his gold shield and patting Jimmy down for a frisk.

"What's this?" The cop yanked a .45 automatic from under Zee's jacket. "Oh, that's *it*, man, I am takin' you down for this, I'm takin' your black ass in."

Jimmy laughed and batted the air. "You can't take me in for that shit, motherfucker—I got a *license* for that."

"Okay," the dick said, handing back the gun, which Jimmy slipped back in its shoulder-rig. "Then what about *this* shit?" The dick gestured to the pile of coke on the coffee table.

"They don't sell no licenses for *this*," the dick said. "In fact, I best confiscate this shit. . . ."

And the cop bent down, and sucked up a line.

The females were laughing like Flip Wilson was performing, and not some thickheaded, bent cop, who was about as funny as a fall down the stairs. Frank, still talking to the baseball scout, was wondering if he ought to get over there and put an end to this foolishness. . . .

Powder on his nostrils, the dick took out his handcuffs

and said, "All right, Zee, all right—*now* I'm busting your ass!"

The women howled with laughter, and Huey and Jimmy were laughing, too.

Huey dug in his pocket and got out a fat money clip and peeled off a C-note. "Let me bail him out, officer—I need the man to drive for me."

"What is that, a *bribe*?" the dick demanded in mock indignation. "Now *all* your asses are under arrest."

So the dick made a big show of pretend-arresting the group. Frank, with one ear and half his attention, took this in, thinking he ought to shut this high school nonsense down; but Frank was busy with Sibota, and Sibota was Stevie's ticket to the big leagues, and if the scout wanted to chat, Frank would chat.

So Frank didn't see what turned the fun into something ugly. He didn't see the dick pretend-frisking Jimmy Zee's woman Darlynn and putting his hand all over her right breast.

But Jimmy saw it, all right, and said, "What's *this* shit?"

Huey's opinion (which he later told Frank) was that what really riled Jimmy was that his girlfriend didn't complain about the grope; but Jimmy considered himself a gentleman, and wouldn't slap the bitch in public.

Right now the dick was fooling with his handcuffs and playing at taking Huey away, saying, "I gotta take *all* you evil lawbreakers in!"

But Zee wasn't having any.

Huey's skinny mean driver/bodyguard glared at the

handsy dick and demanded, "I said, what the *fuck* was *that*?"

The dick blinked. Huey stepped away. The dick, innocently, asked, "What was what?"

"Fuck you," Jimmy said, and then the .45 was in his hand and the report of the weapon in the high-ceilinged space was like thunder.

And the dick was on the floor, right now, clutching at his leg, blooding running through his fingers onto the shag carpet.

"Are you fuckin' *crazy*?" the dick gasped.

"Man touches my woman's *titty*," Jimmy said, "is crazy. And next time, he's dead."

Frank didn't have to excuse himself, as he moved away from the baseball scout and through his guests, because they were all so stunned and scared. . . .

Jimmy saw Frank coming and held up the gun like it was a party favor and smiled, unconvincingly, as he said, "Aw, he's all right. I just shot him in the leg, is all." Jimmy bent over the fallen, bleeding, whimpering cop. "What are you complaining about? You got a health plan, ain't you?"

Frank approached. "Jimmy—a word?"

Jimmy said, "Aw, Frank, come on, he's fine. Here. . . ." Jimmy got in his pocket and brought out a wad of bills and dealt C-notes off like a poker hand.

The bills floated down onto the shaking cop, who looked like he might pass out any second.

Jimmy said, "Five hundred, all right, bro? Six?" He dealt another C-note and it fluttered to the floor into a pool of blood. The cop snatched it out before the bill got ruined.

Then Jimmy grinned at Frank, and around at the other guests, saying, "See? He's feeling better already."

Frank took Jimmy gently by the arm, and this time he did excuse himself, as the host moved with the man through the partygoers and brought him over to a wall and, finding a nice space between framed modern-art paintings, slammed his misbehaving guest into the wall.

Jimmy was shaking.

Frank got in his face. "You want to take your gun out again? No. Didn't think so."

"Frank . . . honest . . . I. . . ."

"Shut up, Jimmy."

Frank hauled the idiot, who seemed on the verge of tears, by the arm and across the room and tossed him at the door. Jimmy thumped into it, then opened it, and scrambled out without closing it.

Frank did.

As Smoky Robinson sang "Tears of a Clown" courtesy of the hi-fi, Frank strolled out among his guests and smiled with every ounce of charm he could summon, and lifted his arms as if in welcome. "No cover charge, folks! Please—enjoy yourselves."

But Zee had put a damper on the festivities. Frank had Doc take the wounded cop home, where a real doc on the Lucas payroll would make a house call. Within an hour, the penthouse was empty but for Eva—who, still in her gown, was doing her best to clean the blood stain off the rug with salt and soda water—and Frank's five brothers.

And Frank.

They sat, mostly on a sofa. He paced. Slowly. Like a cat. A big, pissed-off cat.

"This kind of stupidity," he said, and shook his head, the cold rage obvious in his voice, "I can't have."

Looking like the Lone fucking Ranger in those tinted goggles, Huey said, "It was an accident."

"Accident. You don't shoot a man by accident, Huey."

"I . . . I know, Frank. But Jimmy feels terrible about it."

"*Feels* terrible?" Frank planted himself before Huey, stared down at him. "Jimmy don't feel shit, coked up all the time, way he is. *This* is who you have drive for you? *This* is who protects your ass? Get rid of him."

Huey's eyes widened behind the big tinted lenses, his expression half-shocked, half-sorrowful. "Frank, you can't mean that. . . . He's your *cousin*! What's he gonna do?"

"I don't care what he does. Just so he doesn't do it in my world."

"He can't go back home. We brought him *up* here! There's nothing left back there. . . ."

"Does any of this sound like my problem?"

Huey risked a smile and patted the air. "Listen, give him a chance, give *me* a chance, to go and talk to him. I'll straighten his ass out."

Frank just stood there looking at his brother behind

the ridiculous glasses; what was Huey trying to be, a goddamn spaceman? It was like talking to a cartoon character.

"Give those here," Frank said, and held out his hand, palm up.

"What?"

"Glasses." Frank's fingers made the "come here" gesture.

"What? Why?"

Frank grabbed the things off his brother's face and threw them to the carpeting and cracked and crushed them under his shoe.

Then he backed off and, one at a time, he caught their eyes and held on until each brother had to look away.

Finally Frank said, "Jimmy Zee goes back to North Carolina, or to hell, for all I care. Cousin, brother, doesn't cut shit with me. I'm giving you the chance of a lifetime. Blow it, and you're gone."

There were gulps and nods and mumbled apologies.

"Now get the fuck out," he told them.

And they went, as the Jackson 5—the hi-fi not so loud now, but still distinct—sang "Never Can Say Goodbye."

15. Boody

On a beautiful, lazy Sunday afternoon in the New Jersey suburbs, Richie Roberts whiled away a few hours with mob kingpin Dominic Cattano's nephew, Joey Sadano.

Richie had gone to high school with Joey, and when the weather allowed, he and Joey and other mutual friends would play softball in a park, then head over to the Sadano ranch-style digs—very nice, with swimming pool and all the modern conveniences, if not a castle like Uncle Dominic's.

As on many a Sunday afternoon, Richie and Joey and other pals—wise guys like Joey, if truth be told—transformed into a bunch of eternal teenage boys in their brown-and-orange *Weequahie* jerseys, talking sports, drinking beer, cooking burgers and hot dogs on the backyard grill.

As things began winding down, Richie nodded to

Joey that he wanted a word. Joey—mustached, pock-marked, hair receding, but attractive and affable—ushered Richie into the den-like poolhouse and they sat at a table where the guys sometimes played poker.

"You're getting that constipated look again," Joey said.

"Other day," Richie said, lifting his eyebrows, "I coulda got killed, chasing bad guys in heavy traffic. Makes you think."

Joey's eyebrows also went up. "Yeah. And I know *what* you're thinking—you're off playin' Lone Ranger, and here you are with a kid to worry about. Well, don't. When you asked me to be your son's godfather, I took it very serious."

Richie flicked a smile. "I know."

Joey gestured expansively. "I said, yes, I'll take on this responsibility, take care of your son, God forbid something should happen to your crazy, sorry ass. . . ."

Richie felt like a boulder had settled on his shoulders. He'd known Joey forever. He loved Joey like a brother. But Joey was a problem.

"Joey, the thing is, Laurie's telling Child Social Services stuff that makes me look bad, real bad. Tells 'em I'm out all night. . . ."

"Aren't you?"

Joey didn't know the half of it. Just yesterday morning, Richie had gone to the door in his robe and underwear and found an attractive, professional-looking black woman with a briefcase standing there, looking at him like he was the Ghost of Christmas Past. Was she a one-night stand he'd filed away and forgotten?

Speaking of which, the stewardess he'd spent the night with had taken just that moment to hip-sway out of the bedroom, one hand buttoning her blouse, the other hauling her little wheeled travel thingie into a living room that somehow managed to be both minuscule and a huge mess.

"Mr. Roberts," the woman in the doorway had said, "I'm here for our appointment. . . . Child Social Services?"

Now here he was sitting in his friend's poolhouse, needing to sever a tie that stretched back decades.

"The women are bad enough," Richie said. "I take full blame on that one. I take full blame on *all* of it— all-night stakeouts, chump change for pay, lowlife informants hanging around."

"Not to mention," Joey said softly, starting to get it, "certain old friends. Like me?"

Richie sighed. He sat in silence cut only by the muffled laughter of their friends out in the yard and kids shrieking around the pool. He felt like a total shit. Then Joey's hand settled on his shoulder.

"Buddy," Joey said, "it's all right. Really. I understand. It's the waters we swim in. Look, these social workers come sniffing around, I'll tell them whatever you want me to. I'll lie my ass off for you, man."

"Thank you. I don't deserve a friend like you."

"You got that right. . . . What *else* is it? There's something else."

Richie drew in a breath. Let it out. "You don't have to talk about it, Joey, if you don't want. But have you heard anything about this Blue Magic shit? Anything at all?"

Joey's mouth tightened and his eyelids lowered to half-mast. "Not much *magical* about it. Lot of sorrow and misery from guys gettin' put out of business, is all."

Richie leaned forward. "Nothing about who's bringing it in?"

"Guys down South, is all I heard."

"Down South, where? Florida? Cuba?"

Joey held up a palm. "All I can tell you is, whoever it is? They're upsetting the natural order of things."

Neither Richie nor Joey had the slightest notion that Joey's uncle would soon meet with Frank Lucas in accordance with the natural order of things—specifically, the law of supply and demand . . . he who controls the supply can demand whatever the fuck he wants.

But of course Frank Lucas was not yet even a blip on Richie Roberts's radar.

On a perfect sunny morning in quietly suburban Livingston, New Jersey, Frank Lucas and his fiancee Eva were guests in a palatial residence where the old expression "king of his castle" made perfect sense.

Outside the literally castle-like residence, on grounds so perfectly manicured a country club might well be greenly envious, a series of statues rose above an elaborate European fountain: a Napoleonic representation of Mafia capo Dominic Cattano on horseback, and next to him a woman and two children (Mrs. Cattano and their offspring) astride marble horses of their own.

Cattano was a cruelly handsome middle-aged man

whose baronial bearing made this tribute to himself seem less ridiculous than it should—centuries ago, Frank thought, Cattano would have been the kind of Italian who paid painters and sculptors to do works of art that would last forever, in between said patron poisoning relatives and rivals.

Somehow, though, Frank didn't think the Cattano family on horseback would go down through the ages.

A shotgun in his hands, Cattano, in tailored hunter's attire, was (as usual) giving an order: "*Pull!*"

A clay pigeon sailed out across a vast backyard bordered by stunningly colorful gardens—the target obliterated by Cattano's well-aimed blast.

His turn over, Frank's elegant host indicated another shotgun resting nearby and Frank—in *GQ*-worthy sportcoat and slacks—took it, getting poised to shoot.

Within the opulent residence, Eva was being entertained by Mrs. Cattano, a handsome dark-eyed, dark-haired woman getting the better of middle age. Mrs. Cattano was explaining that their "house" had been imported, brick by brick, from Gloucestershire. Eva had assured Mrs. Cattano that the Cattano home was "very nice." But mostly the two women sat in polite strained silence thicker than the hanging tapestries.

Eva's unease was only heightened by the occasional muffled yet distinct reports of shotguns booming just outside.

Frank, who'd never before seen a clay target much less aimed at one, had held his own shooting with Cattano. So far this afternoon, the two men had been all smiles and friendly remarks—guarded respectful behavior from longtime business associates who'd lately become rivals.

That Frank had been a glorified bodyguard to Bumpy Johnson, with whom Cattano had collaborated for decades, made the atmosphere a little stiff and awkward, but that was to be expected.

Lunch (Mrs. Cattano called it "luncheon") in the formal dining room had been pleasant enough, with both Cattanos expressing interest in hearing about Eva's experiences as Miss Puerto Rico; and the two men had chatted a little about the upcoming Ali/Frazier match. Afterward, Mrs. Cattano—prompted by a look from her husband—led Eva away for a tour of the house.

Shouldn't take any more than four hours, Frank thought dryly.

Flashing his disarming smile, Cattano escorted Frank by the arm down a hallway. The two men had taken their drinks from the table with them, a goblet of red wine for Cattano, a glass of ice water for Frank.

"A lovely girl, Frank," Cattano said as they walked. "You really should marry her."

"We've talked about it. She seems willing."

"Good!"

"But we won't rush into it. Too many things to look after, right now, to think about that."

Cattano squeezed his guest's arm a little. "Frank, if I may—take it from a man who's gone down this road. Waiting is a mistake—don't take her for granted, a girl like this. A man needs a strong, smart woman for a partner. To bring smart, strong children into your family."

They were going down a corridor lined with framed

family photographs. If those were Cattano's kids, they looked more goofy than smart and strong, to Frank; but he kept that opinion to himself.

Frank nodded. "I appreciate the advice."

"Good. I'm glad you don't think I overstepped. I wouldn't ever want to overstep, Frank, but I know you and Bumpy were like father and son. He'd say much the same to you, I think."

"Bumpy had a dog not a wife. And I have the dog now."

With a polite laugh, Cattano led Frank into a richly wood-paneled study lined with leather-bound volumes, the kind more for decorative purposes than reading. Soon they were seated in comfortable, leather-upholstered chairs in subdued lighting with a golden tinge, as if Frank's host's Midas touch extended even to illumination.

Cattano settled back, sipped his wine, then gestured to the library around them. "It's good to have a sense of history, Frank—the events that have brought us to where we are today."

Frank thought, *I'd rather make history*, but said nothing.

"You know, Frank," Cattano was saying, "Bumpy Johnson had a real interest in history."

"Bumpy had a lot of interests."

With his eyes gliding down the rows of books, Cattano said, "I always wonder if people *know* when history's being made . . . that they're part of it, that they're *in* it."

"Hard to say."

"They're living their lives, doing any number of in-consequential things—for instance, this could be a historic moment, right now, this second . . . and you're just sitting there sipping a glass of ice water."

As droplets trailed down his glass like rain along a window, Frank thought, *Finally you're getting to it. . . .*

Cattano held the wine goblet in both hands; he looked down in it as if reading tea leaves, then up at Frank and said, almost casually, "Bumpy and I did a lot of business together, of course."

"I know."

"Whatever he needed, he'd come to me. And I would do my best to provide whatever it was. *He* came to *me* . . . I did not go to him. Is the point I'm trying to make. And d'you know why that was?"

Frank shrugged. "Bumpy didn't have what you needed. You had what *he* needed. I believe it's called supply and demand."

"That's right."

"Which is why," Frank said, "we've always come to you."

"Yes." A tiny bit of edge came into Cattano's voice. "Until lately, that is."

Frank sipped his ice water. His glass was sweating but he wasn't. He had the best poker face in Harlem and knew it. Cattano could search Frank's features forever and not come up with anything.

Maintaining his vaguely professorial tone amid all these books, Cattano said, "Monopolies are illegal in this country, Frank . . . because nobody can compete with a monopoly."

"A lot of things are illegal in this country, Mr. Cattano."

"Call me Dominic, please! . . . Imagine the dairy farmers, if the powerful ones threw together and formed a monopoly, that is. Why, half the dairy farmers in America would go belly up!"

"That's a shame," Frank said, "but I'm just trying to make a living."

"Which is your right. Because this is a free country." The don's head tilted and a patronizing smile formed. "But not at the expense of *others*, Frank. That's un-American."

"Sounds like capitalism to me, Dominic. And that's as American as apple pie."

Cattano's smile began to curdle like some of that dairy-farmer milk gone bad. "You know the price you pay for any commodity doesn't represent its true cost of production. It's controlled. Set. So that a fair profit can be made."

Frank shrugged. "I think my price is very fair. I haven't had any complaints."

Cattano's nostrils flared. "Your customers are happy, but what about your fellow dairy farmers? It's very unfair to them. You're not thinking of them at all."

"I would say," Frank said calmly, "that I'm thinking of them as much as they ever thought about me."

"All right," Cattano said dismissively. "I can see you're getting excited. No need to get excited, Frank. That's not why I invited you to my home, to get all excited."

But Frank was not excited at all. Cattano seemed mildly worked up, though.

Then, with a suspiciously benign smile, Cattano rose and indicated Frank should do the same. "I have something for you. Something nice."

In a small, pungent, climate-controlled, tobacco-laden room just off the study, Cattano opened a humidor and extracted two fat Cuban cigars.

Casual again, Cattano said, "Now what if . . . and I'm just thinking out loud, here . . . you sold some of your inventory wholesale, and I helped you expand your avenues of distribution."

Frank shook his head, gently. "I appreciate the offer, Dominic. But I don't need it."

"Oh?"

"I already got everything from 110th Street to Yankee Stadium, river to river."

Cattano waved that off. "Which is a little mom-and-pop operation, compared to what I'm talking about. I could make you bigger than Kmart or McDonald's. I can take you nationwide—Chicago, Detroit, Vegas. And I could guarantee you peace of mind. And I think you know what I mean by that."

Just in case Frank didn't, Cattano used a little gold guillotine to clip a Cuban.

"Frank," Cattano said, soothingly. "You see how I live. You've seen my wife, you know the kind of family I have. I fancy I'm a kind of Renaissance man."

"I got that."

Cattano shook his head regretfully. "Unfortunately,

not all my associates are as . . . enlightened. You ask them, what is civil rights? They don't know. To them, black power is a couple of boxers hammering each other bloody. They're not open to change from the way things've been done in the past, and who's done it, and who is doing it now."

"Do you anticipate a problem, Dominic?"

Cattano held up a palm. "No, not if I talk to them, so there won't be any misunderstanding. That, Frank, is what I mean by peace of mind."

Frank realized that he was not really being given a choice here. Funny—he'd dismissed the old protection racket as antiquated, and yet this Italian don, Renaissance man or not, was squeezing Frank's balls in a time-tested fashion.

Still, maybe this really was an opportunity. Frank operated internationally, procuring his product; but for merchandizing, he was limited to Jersey and New York, turf he knew and was familiar with. Cattano and his Cosa Nostra pals could open the world up. . . .

All business, Frank said, "You pay what, now? Seventy-five, eighty a kilo? I'd consider taking fifty. And I can get you as much as you want. And better than anything your other sources have ever come up with."

Now it was Cattano's turn to put on his best poker face; but Frank saw right through it: the capo's eyes had dollar signs in them. Fifty thousand a kilo, for the highest-quality shit on the planet, would be a hell of a coup for the Mafioso on the marble horse.

"You see," Cattano said, and put a hand on Frank's

shoulder, "I was right. This is one of those historic moments we were talkin' about. Frank, you're going to be bigger than Bumpy Johnson himself."

And Cattano handed Frank a Cuban cigar, expertly prepared for his guest.

"Can't smoke it here, unfortunately," Cattano said, with a funny little grin and shrug. "Grace doesn't like it. Take it with you."

Half an hour later, Frank and Eva walked across a driveway smaller than Rhode Island to the Lincoln, where the massive driver Doc waited. Frank slipped the cigar into his top shirt pocket and they climbed in back. From the front step of the reconstructed castle, their host and hostess smiled and waved.

In back of the Lincoln, Eva gave Frank a raised-eyebrow glance. "Why would you trust these people, the way they look at you?"

"What do you mean?" he said, and grinned and laughed. "Why, baby, they look at me like it's Christmas and I'm Santa Claus."

"Please," she said and shivered. "They look at us like we're the hired help."

Frank leaned over and kissed her cheek. "That's impossible."

"Why?"

"They work for me now."

In the bedroom of the penthouse, the dusk outside giving way to evening, Frank—in shirt-and-tie and trousers—stood gazing into his closet where his extensive color-coordinated racks of Phil Cromfeld suits and sports jackets awaited his whim.

On the TV on the dresser opposite the bed, Howard Cosell—already ringside at the Garden—was (in his trademark nasal bleat) expounding on tonight's fight . . . or anyway, talking about Muhammad Ali's antiwar stand. The battle ahead with Joe Frazier seemed almost an afterthought.

Eva, in her lacy underthings, was sitting at her makeup table, getting herself even prettier than God had managed, and God had done a hell of a job. Frank selected a linen jacket, laid it carefully out on the bed, then strolled over to the lovely young woman, catching her eyes in her mirror.

"What?" she asked. She had just a tiny bit of attitude left from this afternoon's tea party at the Cattano castle.

He set a little jewelry box down on the vanity.

She gazed at the small square object and reached for it, but her hands couldn't quite manage to touch it. So Frank opened it for her, showed her the four-karat diamond engagement ring, which he then slipped on her finger.

Her lips trembled. A tear formed and trickled down a perfect cheek and messed up her makeup, just a bit.

Then she was on her feet, hugging him.

Kissing him, long and lovingly.

"Yes, I'll marry you," she said. "Yes."

After that, still in his arms, she held her hand out in the way all newly engaged women do, appraising their own worth via the size of the diamond their men had provided.

"Funny thing," she said with an impish grin, "I bought you a surprise, too."

She eased from his arms and moved past the TV and opened her own closet; she made her selection—a man's garment bag—and rested it on the bed next to the linen jacket. She touched her fingers to the zipper, but then stalled, giving him a girlish, teasing look.

"What?" he asked. "What is it?"

She giggled.

As if unveiling a great work of art—one that would at least rival the Cattanos on horseback—she unzipped the bag and revealed the full-length chinchilla coat.

Frank, his anticipation turning to embarrassment, said, "I don't know, baby. . . . I don't think that's exactly my style."

"You don't *have* a style, Frank," she said firmly. Probably in the same kind of voice Grace Cattano used to tell Dominic not to smoke his Cuban cigars in the house. "And it's time you *got* one. . . ."

16. Capone

Saturday afternoon, at the narcotics squad's church HQ, the guys had given up paperwork and sorting through surveillance photos to gather around the portable TV, watching a press conference where Muhammad Ali was telling the world that he was the black man's black man, whereas Joe Frazier was the white man's black man.

"Frazier is gonna kill that conceited clown," Spearman said.

"What odds you give me?" Jones asked.

Richie Roberts wasn't paying any attention to the TV. He was studying the bulletin boards, specifically the work-in-progress that was the table of organization of drug suppliers and their higher ups. Only the lowest level included black faces—one of them Charlie Williams—but Frank Lucas (whose name Richie had never heard) was not among them.

The other faces were white, mostly Italian, and stopped midway up—the top slots remaining empty. The squad had hit a wall, and Richie didn't know where the hell he was going to find a ladder.

He was still preoccupied with the problem that evening, attending the Ali/Frazier match via a press pass as he and his camera blended in with the media crowding the rear entrance of Madison Square Garden.

Celebrities were arriving in their limousines, including showbiz figures like Sammy Davis, Jr., and his wife, Altovise, and sports figures like Joe Louis and his wife, Marva. Some celebrity gangsters attended, too, like Nicky Barnes and Joey Gallo, all with flashy jewelry and flashier girls hanging off of them.

But one VIP couple—also likely belonging to the gangster category—Richie did not recognize. The beautiful Hispanic gal in a showy white dress—according to buzz among the press photographers around him—was a recent former Miss Puerto Rico. She stepped out first and basked in the flashbulbs, but then seemed to have to coax her escort from the backseat of the Lincoln Town Car.

"You want to miss the fight?" she was saying. "Come on, baby. You look *great*. . . ."

A black patent leather shoe poked out of the vehicle, followed by a tall, handsome black guy in a floppy wide-brimmed pimp fedora and full-length chinchilla coat so ostentatious, Nicky Barnes would've thought twice about being seen in public like that. Miss Puerto Rico, casting a dazzling smile on the media boys, hooked onto an arm of the chinchilla-coat character like she thought her squire might make a break for it.

To Richie, the coat's owner seemed ill at ease, and yet there was something commanding about this presence, an undeniable charisma that had no trouble competing with the likes of Sammy Davis and Joe Louis.

In the arena itself, Richie was seated with the press photographers, so taking pictures of organized crime celebs with his long-lens Leica was no more suspicious than eating a bag of popcorn. He was intrigued to note that the striking, lanky dude in the chinchilla coat and ridiculous fedora had snagged second-row ringside for himself and Miss Puerto Rico, just behind the sportswriters.

Not just anybody got seats like that.

The odd thing was how uneasy the decked-out Nicky Barnes imitator seemed, like he'd rather be anywhere but next to a stunning woman in the best seat at the hottest ticket in town.

Filing that away, Richie and his camera roamed the faces of other prime ticketholders ringside, assorted celebrities, politicians, and organized crime figures . . . and of course stacked trophy dolls with platinum hair and plunging necklines.

To get a better shot of the mob figures, Richie got out in the aisle and, almost immediately, a massive figure brushed by, saying, "Excuse me."

Joe Louis.

Stunned, Richie felt like a ten-year-old and managed to blurt, "Mr. Louis!"

The Brown Bomber in his black tux glanced at Richie as the eager figure moved alongside him.

Grinning like a fool but unable to do anything else, Richie let the words tumble out: "I'm sorry, sir, but I just have to tell you, you were my hero growing up, my absolute hero. To this day I still push elevator buttons *eight times* for the rounds you beat Billy Conn in. You know, for luck!"

Louis met Richie's face but not his eyes and something that might have been a nod—maybe an eighth of an inch worth—was all Richie got for his trouble before the great champ moved on to catch back up with his friends moving down the aisle.

Richie's smile froze on his face, his eyes glazing, his expression a death mask of disappointment, as a very old dream withered and passed away in the aftermath of his hero's disregard.

And so he got back to work, taking pictures of various Italian wise guys, including Dominic Cattano himself (and his bodyguard), edging into the third-row ringside, behind Miss Puerto Rico and her chinchilla-coat escort. Cattano and the handsome black dude spoke to each other, friendly—the mob capo even seemed to be kidding the guy.

Richie's surveillance-bred lip-reading skills confirmed as much, Cattano saying: "*Hey, Frank, you keep that hat on, I'm gonna miss the fight!*"

Somebody next to Richie leaned in to get his voice above the din of the arena: "Only in America, huh?"

Richie turned and Detective Trupo was grinning at him, the Zapata-mustached, devilishly handsome SIU cop resplendent in a black leather sportcoat.

Taking the bait, Richie asked him, "What is?"

Trupo nodded toward where the celebrities were seated. "That spade-in-chinchilla's seat is better than the guineas. Makes you wonder."

And Trupo was gone, heading down the aisle, taking the identity of Miss Puerto Rico's date with him, if indeed the crooked piece of shit knew it.

But Trupo had a point. As Richie watched through the telephoto lens, he saw top Italian OC guys came over to the stranger in chinchilla and pay homage. So did various showbiz types and sports world figures, from Sammy Davis to Don King.

Then fate turned its knife blade in Richie's belly: Joe Louis himself came up to pay his respects to the man in the chinchilla coat, punching at him playfully, smiling warmly. Richie's hero, who hadn't had the time of fucking day for him, kissing up to some . . . some *what*?

As much as he'd studied the guy through his telephoto, Richie hadn't yet snapped any shots of Miss Puerto Rico's dream date, and he was about to correct that when a roar came up from the crowd and the lights went down but for a spotlight on the ring. An announcer's voice echoed throughout the massive arena unintelligibly. Then other lights found Ali and Frazier coming down the steps through the crush of fans and reporters, preceded by an honor guard of soldiers bearing American flags.

Between the lack of lighting and all those flags, Richie lost sight of that chinchilla-coat dude; but then, would you believe it? Ali himself stopped to shake the bastard's hand!

Flashbulbs popped throughout the arena as Robert Goulet sang the national anthem, while Ali in his corner pointedly did not sing along.

And dim lighting or not, Richie caught the chinchilla-coat dude in his camera sights and, focusing as sharp as possible under these conditions, snapped the shutter; and snapped it again, and again. . . .

On Monday morning, the best photo Richie had snapped of this new player got tacked to the table of organization—low and off to the side with other puzzle pieces that didn't fit in just yet, other new faces needing names.

Richie handed a slip of paper to Spearman, seated on top of a desk, not his own.

"What's this?" Spearman asked. "A number you're hoping to hit?"

"Kind of. It's the plate on the limo Mr. Chinchilla climbed out of. Check with the company, see who rented it."

Spearman smirked humorlessly, unimpressed. "What, you think there's a new Capone in town, a *black* one?"

Richie shrugged, smiled.

Spearman made a farting sound with his lips. "Just a small-fry with a big head. Supplier, at most, or just another fuckin' pimp. Otherwise we'da heard of his ass."

Richie had started shaking his head halfway through Spearman's spiel. "No, Freddie, he's bigger than that.

His seats were phenomenal—better than Dominic goddamn Cattano's. I saw Joe Louis and Ali *both* shake his fuckin' hand."

And Spearman, taking this more seriously, nodded over at the bulletin board and pointed at Cattano, up top, and the new face whose name, Frank Lucas, they did not as yet know, low, to one side.

"How do you get from down there," the skinny, scruffy cop said, "to up there?"

Richie said, "I don't know. But we better find out. 'Cause Cattano was sitting behind that dude, and the dude did *not* take off his hat. . . ."

17. Swear to God

Frank Lucas took Dominic Cattano's advice and did not let the "girl" get away—barely two months passed between Frank's presentation to Eva of the engagement diamond and a wedding day that, for a while at least, was so perfect his North Carolina momma might have conjured it in a dream.

In the biggest Baptist church in Harlem, his brother Huey at his side as best man, Frank—in a beautifully tailored sky-blue tuxedo—stood on the altar looking out at a sea of ladies' hats, all coral and pink. Eva's family and friends were on one side of the aisle, and the extended Lucas family on the other, Frank's mother gazing up at her eldest son with teary-eyed pride.

As expected, Eva was a vision in radiant white as her father escorted her down the aisle; then, in a blur, Frank was slipping the simple gold band on next to the honking diamond, and Eva was putting a gold band on his finger. The minister pronounced them man and wife, Eva lifted her veil, and their first married kiss was to applause so resounding you'd have thought Jesus Christ himself had made his long-promised return visit.

Charlie Williams, Bumpy's old friend and a current associate, was at Frank's side when Eva threw her bouquet.

"Most beautiful bride I ever saw, Frank," Charlie said.

"Only wish Bumpy could've met her," Frank said. "And I wish she could've met him."

Eva's father had given the bride away; but Bumpy, the man Frank thought of as *his* father, was in the ground. Maybe the great man had been there in spirit. . . .

A photographer took the official photographs of the wedding party on the church steps, and Frank would have been surprised to know an unmarked car shadowing the festivities held another photographer, snapping a different breed of official photographs.

On this happy day, Frank was blissfully unaware that he had finally registered on Richie Roberts's radar.

While members of Richie's squad were attending the wedding that glorious fall afternoon, the narcotics squad leader himself was concerned with other photographs, surveillance shots dating back over the last two months.

Right now Richie was catching up his boss, Lou

Toback, on their progress. Stacked on the banquet table in front of the bulletin boards were documents Richie and his guys had gathered, including the car agency records where the Lincoln Town Car had been purchased (*not* rented); Frank Lucas's scant arrest record, including mug shots of a years-younger version of the suspected Harlem drug kingpin; and photographs of Lucas in his chinchilla coat and pimp fedora while holding court at the Ali/Frazier bout.

Toback said, "I've never even heard of this guy. And you say he's a *player*?"

"Originally from Greensboro, North Carolina," Richie said with a curt nod. He was on his feet in front of the bulletin boards. "Couple arrests, years ago. Gambling, robbery, unlicensed firearm."

"Small time."

Richie shook his head. "Not really—Lucas was Bumpy Johnson's right-hand man."

That perked Toback up, his eyes glittering now.

Richie allowed himself a smile. "Fifteen years, guy was Bumpy's chief collector, bodyguard and driver."

"No shit. . . ."

"None. Fact, he was at Bumpy's side when the old boy fell down and died there on the street."

Toback—in shirtsleeves and loosened tie, leaning back on a metal chair—said nothing, but he was clearly keenly interested now.

For the first time in all these months, Richie felt a surge of excitement and a sense of accomplishment.

He went on: "Five brothers—Frank's the oldest, and there's lots of cousins, all living up here now, spread out around the boroughs and Jersey. On the street, they're called the Country Boys."

"We got *names* on these Country Boys?"

"More than just names," Richie said, and he began pinning up pictures as he introduced Frank's brothers to Toback, one at a time: "Dexter Lucas, in Brooklyn, operates a dry-cleaning establishment, where lately our guy Spearman has been doing business."

"Spearman gets his clothes cleaned? Now that *is* a surprise. . . ."

Richie tacked another photo to the board. "Terrence Lucas in Newark—owns an electrical shop. Jonesy got a lamp fixed there, recently. . . . Melvin Lucas has a metal shop in Queens—Abruzzo bought a door there, last week. . . . I had my tires rotated a couple weeks ago in the Bronx, at a garage operated by Turner Louis. . . . Then later I got a nasty dent in my fender—funny what can happen when you kick a Dodge—but a body shop, out in Bergen County, fixed it up fine. Run by Huey Lucas, second oldest. When Huey isn't in grease-monkey workclothes, he's a Mack Daddy type in the threads department."

"More than Frank?" Toback asked, with an arched-eyebrow nod toward the photo of the dude in his chinchilla coat and floppy hat.

"Except for the getup he wore to the fight," Richie said, "Frank seems to keep it low key. Suit-and-tie-type, sharp but not exactly zoot. Leads an orderly and, outwardly, legitimate life . . . gets up early—five A.M. Has breakfast at the same midtown diner, usually alone. Then he goes to work."

"Define work," Toback said.

"Meets with his accountant, or one of his various lawyers. Drops in on several office buildings he owns."

"What about nightlife?"

Richie shrugged. "Usually stays at home—who wouldn't, with that beauty he's marrying today . . . and turns out she *is* last year's Miss Puerto Rico."

"And this year's Mrs. Frank Lucas," Toback said dryly.

"When he does go out, it's with her—to a club or dinner. He likes Small's Paradise. Likes to hobnob with celebs and sports figures—Joe Louis, Wilt Chamberlain. Never with organized-crime guys."

"You mean, never with *white* OC guys."

"Right. He pals with the other Country Boys, of course. But I did see with my own eyes Dom Cattano and other top wise guys bowing down to him at the Garden."

"Sit, would you?" Toback asked. "You're making me nervous."

Richie hadn't realized he was pacing excitedly up and down in front of his newly revised table of organization.

Richie sat across from his boss. "That's about it—other than his Sundays."

"What about his Sundays?"

"You'll love this," Richie said with a chuckle. "He takes his little gray-haired momma to church."

"Fuck he does."

"Every Sunday, rain or shine. Then he drives out to a certain cemetery and changes the flowers on a grave."

Toback frowned. "*What* grave?"

"Bumpy Johnson's."

"I may bust out crying."

"Every Sunday. No matter what."

Toback's eyes went to the pinned-up surveillance photos. "Not your typical day in the life of a dope kingpin."

Richie flipped a hand. "What was a typical day in *Bumpy Johnson's* life like? And that motherfucker *owned* Harlem."

"Bumpy had class," Toback said reflectively, "for a lowlife shakedown racketeer."

"And Frank Lucas learned from Bumpy. Was like a son to him, by all reports."

Toback's eyes tightened, skeptically. "You think Lucas took over for Bumpy? His damn *driver*? That's a little far-fetched."

Richie just smiled. "Is it? Everything Lucas does, he does like Bumpy."

"Not everything." Toback gestured to the Ali/Frazier photos again. "Bumpy never wore a goddamn chinchilla coat in his life."

"We haven't seen that again—hat and coat from the Garden seem to've been retired to a closet."

"Okay. So what do we have on him we can use in court?" Toback gestured to the stack of documents. "Because interesting as all of this is, Richie? You don't have anything that'll stick. You try this, without informants and confiscated powder? No one's going to jail, except maybe you, for contempt of court."

Richie was shaking his head. "We won't get any

informants. Not inside Country Boy circles. It's like a Sicilian family—structured that way, to protect the Godfather."

This annoyed Toback. "Where the hell'd Lucas learn that?"

"Where else? From Bumpy. Bumpy did big business with the Cosa Nostra crowd, remember. And Frank was always at Bumpy's side—enough so to learn how the guineas got things done."

Toback threw a hand in the vague direction of the table of organization. "You're talking like Lucas oughta be up at the top of that chart. . . ."

Firmly, Richie shook his head. "He's not even the man I want. I want to know who *he's* working for— which Italians he's wired up with, which white faces are bringing in all this high-grade heroin."

Toback leaned back, his eyes traveling over the new pictures, the array of black faces that had invaded the white chart they'd been assembling.

"Okay," Toback said. "You're doing good."

"Not sorry you put me in charge of this?"

His boss stood, the lanky man seeming to unfold himself, as he gave Richie a wry, rumpled grin.

"Not yet," Toback said, and ambled out, leaving Richie to his work.

The reception at the church was loud and fun and sentimental, with Frank and Eva dancing before the assembled guests and receiving another resounding round of applause, plus the requisite *ooohs* and *aaahs*.

When the bride and groom finally left the church, God played a trick and sent rain machine-gunning down on them, as they raced to the back of the Town Car. Then Doc was behind the wheel and the vehicle was pulling slowly out through the crush of happy faces below umbrellas, guests waving wildly and throwing kisses.

The downpour stopped as suddenly as it had come. A gentle blue twilight had fallen as the Town Car made its way along the rain-slicked streets, flanked fore and aft by security vehicles. In the backseat Frank and Eva held hands and cuddled and smiled goofily at each other, a couple of giddy kids. Neither of them saw the Shelby Mustang roll up alongside.

Doc instinctively reached for his rod, but then he saw the badge in the hand of the smiling, handsome, devil-bearded SIU cop: Trupo his own self, shaking his head gently, *no, boy, you wouldn't want to do that.* . . .

Pulled over in Central Park, the Town Car, security vehicles and Mustang sat and idled, making clouds of gray poison.

"Stay in the car," Frank told Eva, giving her the slightest reassuring glance when he saw her fear; then he was walking toward the man in the black leather topcoat. Doc got out, too, but Frank said, "I'll handle this," and Doc passed the word to the other bodyguards, who were getting out of their vehicles, as well.

Trupo walked loose and confident across the damp grass, not far from the parked cars, and Frank met him halfway.

"Hello, Frank," Trupo said, though they'd never met. The two men stood facing each other.

"Detective," Frank said with a professionally courteous nod.

Trupo glanced toward the Town Car. Eva's worried face was in the backseat window. The detective smiled at her, gave her a little salute, and she glared at him and turned her head away.

The cop sucked in his breath and hiked his eyebrows. "Hope you've done the right thing, Frank. Beautiful girl, no question, but seems to got an attitude on her."

"Listen to me," Frank said. His tone was even, the threat strictly in the words themselves. "Before you say another word about her ... or about me ... remember that you're saying it on the most important precious fucking day of my life."

Trupo said, "Respect is a two-way street, Frank."

"Meaning?"

The cop shrugged good-naturedly. "Meaning, guy walks around in a fifty-grand coat, and he never even buys me a cup of coffee? Something wrong there. Something out of balance."

"I don't know what you're talking about."

Trupo's smile would have been charming, in other circumstances. "You pay your bills, Frank?"

"You want to keep talking," Frank said, an edge coming in, "talk to my lawyer—here's his card." Frank gave it to the cop. "You call him, 'cause we're done here."

And Frank started to go, but Trupo's gaze stopped him. "Do you pay your *bills*, I asked you."

Frank stared coldly at the son of a bitch. "If you're not getting your share, it's not my fault. Go talk to your chief."

Trupo's eyelids went up and something vaguely maniacal was in his expression now. "My share? What *is* my share, Frank? I don't think you even know me. How do you know I'm not a special case?"

"You guys all look alike to me."

Trupo still had his shield in his hand and showed it to Frank. "See what that says? I know you can read. I know you're smart."

Frank said nothing and did not look at the badge.

Trupo went on: "Special . . . Investigations . . . Unit. See, it's right in there, the word we're discussing: *special*." With care, the detective took a business card from his breast pocket, under the leather coat. "I have a restaurant; little investment. Drop by anytime, and it's on me. . . . But first of the month? It's on you. Ten grand. Delivered to this address."

Frank did not take the card. He regarded Trupo with open contempt. "Detective," he said, "there are some things you don't do, unless you're a damn fool. This is one of them—you don't do this kind of business on a man's wedding day."

Trupo's confidence buckled, just a little, his rhythm thrown by Frank's resolve. "Yeah, well, later then. . . . Have a nice honeymoon."

And the detective saluted again and ambled off.

* * *

Truth be told, the honeymoon got off to a rocky start. They weren't flying to Nassau till tomorrow, and this first night of their marriage would be at the penthouse, where—instead of carrying Eva over the threshold—Frank left her standing in the doorway, while he strode to the gas fireplace.

He lighted it with a match, then made a beeline to the bedroom without his bride and returned with the fifty-grand chinchilla coat, and threw it onto the flames. The floppy hat, too. The garments smoked and stank like hell, but they burned just fine.

Then he walked over to her and smiled and took her into his arms. She was a little afraid, but he kissed her, making it better, and they never spoke about it, the coat and hat and everything they represented now history.

But Eva Lucas would never again attempt to dictate her husband's wardrobe.

18. Praise Praise Praise

Huey Lucas's driver, Jimmy Zee, had been given a rare reprieve by his cousin Frank, after Huey vouched for him, and after that Jimmy had really tried to straighten up and fly right.

And what happened to screw it all up, in Jimmy's view, wasn't his fault at all. It was that damn Darlynn. A man should never get involved with a goddamn junkie. A goddamn junkie will use up a man's dope her own self.

The TV was on, *Kung Fu* interrupted 'cause them damn hippies was protesting in Washington again or some shit, and Jimmy could not care the fuck less, all he wanted was his goddamn dope, and Darlynn wouldn't give it to him.

"Where *is* it, I said!" He was following her past the TV into the kitchen. They were both walking around with their shoes off.

"Fuck you," she said, waving her hands like she was praising Jesus. "I ain't tellin' you."

The kitchen table had all kinds of dope paraphernalia spread out on it, like a junkie's banquet except for there being no junk.

He got up in her face. "Where is my fuckin' dope, woman? You and your girlfriends take it again? You and your girlfriends *take* it again, I'm gon' fuckin' *kill* your skanky ass!"

Darlynn got a kitchen drawer open and found a big old knife and slashed it in his general direction, so he went off after his gun, and when she saw the .38 in his hand, she started to scream and ran for the door and went out down the stairs, still waving the knife.

Jimmy did what any reasonable man would do in that situation, which was chase her junkie ass out into the street, yelling questions at her, which she declined to answer.

But she could run faster than him, and the cement was cold on his damn feet, so he planted himself and raised his gun and popped a cap in her ass.

Right in her ass: she went down on the pavement, clutching her left butt cheek, moaning.

Moaning was the order of the evening in Richie Roberts's apartment, too, though nothing between him and his current girl friend had led to running out into the street or knives or gunplay.

Richie was in bed with his lawyer, Sheila, her

briefs filed who knew where, and he must have been distracted by the weight of work, because she was under him, urging him on: "Come on, Richie, fuck me like a *cop!*"

As opposed to a lawyer, which he was himself now, technically at least. Because he was still cop enough to answer the ringing phone on the nightstand even while Sheila was still pumping under him, moaning, *"Yes, Richie, yes. . . . "*

This of course turned into "No, Richie, no!" when he reached for the receiver, still inside her, doing his walk-and-chew-gum-at-the-same-time best when Spearman's less than seductive voice whispered in his ear: "Richie, sorry to bother you, man, but the Newark fuzz just picked up one of our celebrities."

"Celebrities?" Richie asked, still at it.

Sheila was saying, "No . . . no . . . no . . ." But her protests had nothing to do with the phone conversation Richie was managing, and in fact weren't protests at all.

Spearman said, "A face climbed right down off our Wall of Shame, Rich—Huey Lucas's driver, Jimmy Zee."

"What *kinda* bust?"

"Attempted murder."

". . . Call our friends over there. Get him shaken loose into our custody."

"Can we do that?"

"Get Toback on it, if we can't. I'll meet you over at the church in half an hour. . . ."

Which was all he needed to complete his attorney's case, and get his clothes and gun and go.

* * *

The narcotics squad HQ may have been in an old church, but the basement was closer to hell than heaven, a dank, dark dungeon where Jimmy Zee had been sat down in a hard wooden chair. A naked bulb above threw Jimmy's angular features into stark relief, as Richie paced in front of their captive, whose handcuffed hands were in his lap.

Spearman, Abruzzo and Jones were on the periphery, outside the pool of light, shapes that lurked and watched. Jimmy was obviously unsettled, even scared, and that was fine with Richie.

Frank Lucas's cousin was in a bad place, and this church basement wasn't it: Jimmy was coming down off a high that hadn't been high enough to make him forget he'd recently attempted his girlfriend's murder.

"Things aren't as bad as they seem, Jimmy," Richie assured him.

"They ain't?"

"Attempted homicide, that's Grand Jury. Now a Grand Jury, a bunch of average citizens like yourself, Jimmy? They might come in very favorably."

"They might?"

"They might. Attempted manslaughter, maybe. Self-defense even."

Jimmy was looking all around. "What the fuck *is* this place? Why'd they take me out of lockup?"

"Darlynn had a knife," Richie said, still pacing the small patch of concrete in the pool of light. "You were trying to protect yourself. Fact she was shot in the ass, well, that's mitigated by circumstances."

"It is?"

"The knife. You know, this could turn out okay for you, Jimmy."

"It could?"

"Depends on how I decide to deal with you. . . . You see where this is going, Jimmy? Get the picture yet?"

Jimmy didn't—he was too busy trying to make out the shapes that were Spearman and his guys. "You guys Homicide or what?"

Richie stood in front of the seated suspect. "So let's say you *do* beat it, somehow. What do you think your cousin Frank'll think of that? He knows you had to sit down and have somebody like me tell you something like this."

Jimmy blinked repeatedly. ". . . What?"

"You beat attempted murder, and *walk*?" Richie laughed, once. "Is Frank stupid? He'll think you talked. He'll *know* you talked."

Jimmy thought that through. "You mean you'd . . . help me to *hurt* me? To make me look bad?"

Richie shrugged. "Maybe I'd just be really trying to help. Is it my fault if your cousin Frank thinks you rolled over?"

Jimmy slumped in the chair. He began to shake his head as he stared past Richie into the darkness and the shadowy figures.

"You fucked up, Jimmy," Richie said. "Still, you got one thing going for you—nobody knows."

Jimmy looked up at Richie. "What?"

"Nobody knows—I got the arrest report folded up in my back pocket. So even Frank doesn't know—*yet*. Of course, if I send you and this arrest report back over to the Newark PD, Frank could read about your bust in the papers tomorrow, and the whole chain of events I outlined would begin."

Jimmy's eyes narrowed. "Or?"

Richie gestured with open palms. "Or you just walk out of here—no bail, no trial. Just walk out now. Insufficient evidence—your girl already says she doesn't know who shot her."

"Yeah?"

"Yeah." Richie began to pace the little area again. "Of course, I could always find a witness that saw you shoot her, if I tried. And any time I change my mind about letting you walk, I know who I'll pull in for questioning first; I even know what he'll look like—just like you, Jimmy. Just like you."

"That's cold."

"And it won't be discreet, like your visit here tonight. Be real public, Jimmy." Richie smiled and leaned in, putting a hand on the suspect's shoulder. "And Jimmy? If I decide I don't like the quality of your work? This case'll get reopened."

"Quality of *what* work?" Jimmy asked.

Richie smiled. "Like some coffee, Jimmy? Let's go upstairs and talk in more comfortable surroundings. . . ."

Jimmy hadn't left the old church till dawn, slipping out the back way into the chilly morning air. That cop, Roberts, when he raised his voice, it had echoed down in that basement; and his threats, his promises, went on echoing in Jimmy's mind.

Over the coming days, Jimmy did something he never dreamed he'd do: he wore a wire.

He wore a wire, and he'd learned to live with twenty-four-hour fear. Driving for Huey, Jimmy would spend half his time looking in the rearview mirror at what seemed to him to be the evident cop tail, wondering how fuckin' obvious those pigs could be.

But Huey never spotted the tail, and even Frank, when he was in the backseat with his brother, didn't notice.

On this day in late November, in the meat-packing district, Jimmy was unaware that Richie Roberts, following him, was checking his own rearview mirror, keeping tabs on a small procession of cars behind him—the full narcotics squad. Talk on Jimmy's wire about "picking up the big delivery" had sent them into action, for what could be their first major drug bust.

Soon the detectives' cars were parked behind a warehouse near another warehouse whose loading dock was where Jimmy had parked Huey's car. Through binoculars, Richie could see Frank and Huey getting out, chatting casually; then some black guys in bloody white smocks exited the warehouse and approached Frank—words and gestures, but Richie couldn't make anything of it.

Richie snapped pictures as Frank Lucas returned to his brother's car, opened the trunk and removed a briefcase. Using the telephoto, Richie saw—and recorded—the moment when Frank clicked open the briefcase and revealed stacks of cash. Frank took out a number of banded packets of green and carried them over to the men in bloody smocks.

Then Frank strolled to a nearby semi-truck, and— *damn!*—seemed to have spotted Richie, or anyway was looking right in his direction, and, hell, *waving!*

But then Richie realized Lucas was merely waving to the semi driver to pull out.

And in half an hour, on a Harlem street corner, Richie Roberts was watching—not bothering to snap any pictures—as Frank Lucas stood in the back of the semi and handed out hundreds of freshly butchered turkeys— continuing Bumpy Johnson's tradition.

The next day, Thanksgiving, Richie spent alone in his tiny apartment, eating a cold sliced turkey sand- wich at his kitchen table and half-watching the Macy's parade playing on the little portable TV.

But Richie wasn't taking in the big balloons or the happy crowd or Santa Claus on his fucking float. Richie was picturing, in his mind but as clear as if he were there, the Norman Rockwell painting come to life that would be Frank Lucas's Thanksgiving dinner at his fifty-thousand-dollar suburban home, his family around him, lovely wife, brothers, cousins, other womenfolk, including his momma. The man of the house probably wearing a nice white apron for carving the turkey.

And what had made the feast possible? Richie could picture that, too: addicts spending their holiday shoot- ing up and nodding out in alleys and dingy hovels.

Thanksgiving with all the trimmings, all the fixings: needles, spoons, veins, filth. . . .

In another suburb, Detective Trupo of the Special Investigations Unit, with his wife and kids, had enjoyed a Thanksgiving as idyllic as the Lucas family's. And just like the homeless in Harlem, Trupo received a free turkey from Frank Lucas, though it arrived late, well after the cop and his loved ones had partaken of their holiday feast.

The pumpkin pie with whipped cream was already a memory, and a football game was in full sway on the tube, when the bell summoned Trupo to the front door. There, on his welcome mat, he found a live turkey, squawking its ass off, flapping its wings.

The detective was still trying to process that when his precious Shelby Mustang, parked out front, seemed to speak to him: he glanced up at where the *whoosh* had emanated, and saw flames engulfing the interior of the car; soon the windows had blown apart and flames were licking.

He stood and stared, bathing in the seasonal reflection of orange-and-blue flames. Then the vehicle, as if this were July Fourth and not Thanksgiving, exploded like a big fat firecracker.

Even the turkey seemed impressed.

Jimmy Zee had seen, firsthand, the lavish Lucas family Thanksgiving. Right now he was in the bathroom, his shirt off, changing batteries on the little tape recorder stuck to his chest.

Most of the brothers and cousins, Frank included, were out in the backyard sitting on patio chairs, watching nephew Stevie, the baseball whiz, knock pop flies for the younger kids to catch.

Jimmy took a chair not too far from Frank. The afternoon was just starting to turn into dusk, and the crispness of the day had become almost cold. The big German shepherd, in the run by its fancy doghouse, was lounging after too much leftover turkey, sleepily watching the ball as it went back and forth between older boy and younger ones.

Frank called out to Stevie: "Come over here!"

Stevie, in a short-sleeve shirt and Sunday slacks, came over, tossing the ball up and down in his palm.

"Stevie, heard you didn't show up the other day."

Funny, Jimmy thought, *how much disapproval Frank could put into his voice without half-trying.*

The lithe, athletic kid said, "Yeah. I missed it. Sorry."

Frank's eyes flashed. "You're too busy to meet with Billy Martin himself? After I set it up?"

Stevie was shifting foot to foot, not exactly afraid of Frank but in any case not wanting to make him mad.

Finally the teenager said, "I don't wanna play pro ball, I decided."

Frank leaned forward in the metal chair. "What are you talkin' about? It's your dream since you was *their* age. . . ." He gestured to the younger kids. ". . . Look. Maybe I can set it up again. . . ."

Stevie sighed. Shifted foot to foot.

"What?" Frank asked, impatient.

"It's not what I want, Uncle Frank. I wanna do what *you* do—I wanna *be* you some day."

Jimmy was surprised by Frank's stricken expression, on hearing that; didn't remember ever seeing his cousin look more unhappy.

Huey came from inside the house and ambled over to Frank. Jimmy sat forward: he could tell from Huey's gait, his manner, that they'd be going somewhere soon, and Jimmy *was* the driver. . . .

"Bro," Huey, leaning in, said to Frank. "We got a problem."

Jimmy could only hope that problem wasn't him.

19. Harlem Hijack

In the back of his brother Huey's Cadillac, Frank—in a tan cashmere topcoat as anonymous as the chinchilla had been flamboyant, yet almost as expensive—sat and listened, trying not to be irritated that business was taking him away from his family on this day of thanks.

Huey was saying, "I keep hearing our shit is weak. Man, our shit is *strong*, you *know* our shit is strong. . . ."

"Nicky's been stepping on it?"

"Stepping on it! He's been jumping the fuck up and down on it! Been cuttin' it so much, it's down to two, three percent pure."

Frank frowned. "And you tested it? You're *sure*?"

Huey said, "Does the pope shit in the woods? Is a bear Catholic?"

Frank noticed driver Jimmy's eyes on them, in the

rearview mirror, and scowled at his stupid cousin, saying, "The fuck *you* lookin' at?"

And Jimmy's eyes went back to the road.

Frank breathed out and, half under his breath, said to his brother, "Shoulda never let you talk me into hanging onto that chump."

Dusk had fallen when the Cadillac drew up in front of a nondescript building in the clothing district. Frank instructed Jimmy to stay with the car, and he and Huey went on inside.

The interior was chrome and mirrors and Naugahyde and looked like a nightclub out of *Cotton Comes to Harlem.* This was Nicky Barnes's "members only" club, and today had been open only to family and staff—turkey carcasses and empty pie tins on the bar indicated those partying here today had, to some degree, enjoyed a traditional Thanksgiving.

But things got less traditional quickly, as a bodyguard led Frank and Huey into an area resembling the VIP section of a strip club, right down to the naked girls who were cavorting with Nicky and a couple of his pals.

"Frank!" Nicky said, a long-legged wench on his lap. Nicky was in purple velour and lots of gold chain work. He gestured around the naked woman, a magnanimous host. "Welcome. Make yourself to home."

Frank just stood there. "We need to talk."

"Great!" Nicky moved the naked girl off his lap, like a guy moving a potted plant to one side. "Girls, get the fuck out."

The girls, giggling, a little high, gathered their scanty things and disappeared into the adjacent bar. At

Nicky's nod, his two bodyguards exited, too, so Frank gave Huey a look, to wait in the other room.

Across from Nicky, with a little black table between them, was a modernistic black-leather chair, the seat of which Frank cleaned off with a handkerchief, which he then discarded.

Nicky leaned forward and laid out several lines of coke, then offered his guest first sniff, handing a rolled-up C-note as a straw toward Frank.

"No thanks," Frank said.

"You must've been talking to Charlie," Nicky said good-naturedly.

Frank hadn't been, but said nothing.

"You must wanna hear about this big idea of mine, this Black Coalition. It's great you're here. I'll explain it to you. . . ."

That is, Nicky would explain as soon as he'd bent over to suck up a line of that coke.

Frank sat back, folded his arms. Despite the numerous bodyguards in the next room, Frank felt safe enough; he had a nine millimeter in his waistband and, anyway, he was the golden goose of dope suppliers. Even Nicky Barnes wasn't dumb enough to kill the golden goose.

"This Black Coalition," Nicky was saying, as high on this idea as on the coke, "it'll change *everything*—"

"Not why I'm here," Frank said flatly. "Glad to talk about that another time, Nicky. But not today."

Nicky looked up quizzically before doing the second line. "Why you *here*, then, my brother? We ate all the fuckin' turkey."

And Nicky grinned, teeth as white as the coke.

Frank did not grin. "You look happy, Nicky."

"I *am* happy."

Nicky did another line.

"No," Frank said. "You're not. Everybody's happy—Charlie, Baz, cops, Italians . . . everybody. Everybody but you."

"I'm fuckin' *happy*! All right?"

Frank grunted. "Then I don't understand. If you're happy, why take something that's perfectly good the way it is, and ruin it?"

Nicky shook his head, not getting it; or, anyway, pretending not.

Frank rolled out the charming smile. "This is America, Nicky. We're capitalists. In wholesale business, working through retailers. And in a capitalistic country, brand names *mean* something. Consumers rely on brand names, to know what they're getting."

Nicky was staring at Frank like maybe this was a hallucination.

Frank continued evenly: "Consumers know a company they've relied upon, done business with, isn't gonna try to fool them with an inferior product. They buy a Ford, they know they're gonna get a Ford—not a fuckin' Datsun."

Nicky was shaking his head. "What the fuck are you talkin' about, Frank?"

"Blue Magic, Nicky. Blue Magic is what I'm talkin' about. It's a brand name, like Pepsi or Coke, and I don't mean that snow you're sniffing. I own the Blue Magic brand name, Nicky. I stand behind it. Guarantee it, and people know that, even if they don't know me personally any more than they know the chairman of General fucking Mills. They *know* Blue Magic and what they get from it and what it stands for."

Nicky waved his hands. "You're over my fuckin' head, Frank! I have no idea what the fuck—"

"What you're doing," Frank said, still superficially pleasant, "far as I'm concerned, when you chop my dope down to five percent or three or two? Is trademark infringement."

Finally Nicky got it.

The gaudy dealer sighed, nodded, then said, in a reasonable tone (for Nicky), "All due respect, Frank, if I buy something, I can do whatever the hell I wanna do with it."

Frank shook his head. "Not true. That's where you're wrong."

But Nicky was insistent: "I buy a car, I can paint the fucker, can't I?"

"For your personal use. You can't pass it off as a showroom model, anymore."

Nicky frowned; if the creases on his forehead had been any deeper, you could hide dimes in there. "You can't tell me how to do my business, Frank."

"No, but I can tell you how to do mine." Frank sat forward. "Nicky, you don't need to dilute my stuff. You don't need to make more money than you already can with Blue Magic, just the way it is. Nobody does. Christ, at a certain point it's just plain greed."

Nicky's eyes flared. "That's easy for you to say, on your high horse. I got my own expenses, and needs, and I got customers for this shit, even *stepped* on—hell, stepped on it's still good shit."

"Better than what some sell, yes. But that's not the point."

Nicky was clearly working to control himself. "What can I do about this, Frank? You want me to call it something else?"

"Yes," Frank said simply. "I have to insist—you cut my shit, and then call it Blue Magic, that's misrepresentation."

Nicky shrugged, and some defiance was in there, despite the capitulation. "Fine. I'll call it Red Magic. Don't sound as good, but it'll do just fine out on the street."

Frank shrugged back at him, gestured with open palms. "That's all I'm saying. Wrap it in red cellophane, and—"

"Pink magic," Nicky was saying, thinking out loud. "Black magic, maybe."

"I don't give two shits," Frank said. "Whack it down to nothing, tie a bow around it and call it Blue Scumbag, if you want, just don't let me catch you doing this again."

Nicky's eyes grew cold, and their coldness settled on Frank, who felt the chill but did not show it.

" 'Catch' me?" Nicky said, a lilting threat in his voice. " 'Insist?' 'In-fuckin'-*fringe*-ment?' I don't like words like that. Better to hear 'please,' 'thank you,' 'sorry to bother you, Nicky.' These are better words for business associates to use, especially when they come into my fuckin' place without a goddamn invitation."

Frank just looked at him. Nicky seemed to be waiting for a response, a diplomatic word or two, but Frank wouldn't dignify the fool's rant with any.

Then Frank lifted an eyebrow as if to say, *We cool?*

Nicky sighed, shook his head; but then he nodded. "Okay, fine," he said, but it sounded more like a warning than an acceptance.

On his way out, Frank found Huey off to one side in a chair with one of the naked broads grinding on his lap and Huey grinning goofily into space. Frank pulled her off his brother and she said, "Hey," but Huey didn't argue, just followed Frank dutifully out into the twilight.

Frank went to the Caddy, where Jimmy was leaned against the car, smoking as he waited. Holding out his hand, Frank said to the driver, "Keys. Take a cab home."

Jimmy nodded, handed over the keys and disappeared down the street.

Huey drove. Both brothers were in the front seat. Neither said anything for a while.

Then Frank said, "Don't go around there any more."

"What?"

"I don't want you hanging with Nicky. Problem?"

"No."

They rode in more silence, then Frank noticed that Huey's eyes were staying on the rearview mirror, his expression turning sick. The reflection of blazing white light caught Frank's attention, too, and he glanced back to see a car behind them, flashing its brights.

Cops in an unmarked.

Frank touched Huey's arm. "It's okay—pull over. What are they gonna do? Give us a ticket? We'll live."

Huey pulled over, but Frank's words hadn't calmed him much.

Behind them, Detective Trupo and another SIU dick, both in their black-leather dusters, were climbing out of the unmarked, heading for the Caddy. The garment district was deserted on this holiday, and if this were a hit, nobody would see it but those involved, living and dead.

Huey whispered, "Frank, Jesus, Frank, I'm sorry . . . but there's some stuff in the trunk."

Frank glared at Huey, who reacted to the look as if his brother had slapped him.

Then Trupo was standing outside Frank's rider's window. Frank powered the window down and Trupo leaned in, like a satanic car hop.

"Why, hello, Frank," Trupo said and grinned his terrible handsome grin.

"Detective. How's it going? You have to work Thanksgiving? That's too bad."

"Yeah," Trupo said slowly, "it's been a fucked-up Thanksgiving at that, matter of fact. . . . Get out of the car, fellas."

The Lucas brothers got out and convened on the sidewalk with the two SIU dicks.

The unmarked was a Chevy Caprice, nothing special.

"Didn't recognize you in that car, Detective," Frank said easily. "Save the Shelby for off-duty these days?"

"The Shelby's gone, Frank."

"Too bad. It was a beauty. You trade it?"

Trupo said nothing, but his upper lip curled in a sneer as he walked around to the driver's side, reached in and snatched the Caddy keys from the ignition.

The detective went back to the trunk and opened it up, and Frank and Huey swapped glances.

Silence, but for distant bridge traffic, accompanied Trupo standing there, looking down into the trunk for what seemed the longest time, and was maybe ten seconds.

"Wanna come over here a minute, Frank?" Trupo asked politely.

Frank came over.

Six kilos of heroin basked in the meager illumination of the trunk light.

"Now what are we gonna do about this?" Trupo asked. "This is illegal contraband, you know."

"We're gonna shut the trunk," Frank said, "and say good night, and forget you even pulled us over."

"No." Trupo raised a forefinger. "You know, I think I have a better idea."

Then the SIU dick leaned in, plucked two heroin bricks from the group, and tucked them under his arm. "Okay with you, Frank? 'Cause we got other options."

"Do we."

"I mean, if you rather I took it all and threw you and your brother in the fuckin' river, is another option."

Frank, expressionless, said, "Here's a third: next time it's your whole fuckin' house blows up and not just your candyass car."

The two men stared at each other. Neither face held any expression; neither man blinked, either.

Not until Trupo, genuine sadness crawling into his expression, said, "I loved that car."

"A pity."

"You wouldn't know where I could get a turkey butchered, would you? Do they keep overnight, once they been shot in the head?"

"Couldn't help you with that."

Trupo sucked in breath, then slammed the trunk closed, yelled to his partner, "Let's go," and walked away with his cut of the heroin tucked under his arm like a couple loaves of bread.

Frank got in on the rider's side of the Caddy, Huey on the driver's, and Huey was about to start the car when Frank slammed his brother's head into the window so hard, the safety glass cracked.

Huey groaned, and choked off sobs.

Frank leaned in and his upper lip peeled back over his teeth as he said, "Don't you *ever* put me in a car with dope in it again. Or you'll be the one thrown in the fuckin' river."

In another unmarked car, Richie Roberts—pleased with himself for abandoning his bleak Thanksgiving for staking out Nicky Barnes's club—sat and watched through binoculars. He couldn't see exactly what happened in the parked Caddy, but he'd seen the SIU detectives, helping themselves to a small fortune in heroin.

Someday, Richie thought. *Someday. . . .*

20. Insured for Life

Last night Joey Sadano had called, and asked Richie to stop over this afternoon, Saturday. And Richie Roberts was nothing if not loyal to his friends, so his best intentions to curtail (if not cut off) any contact with his high school buddies, due to their Organized Crime ties and such, well, those seemed to be going the way of most best intentions. . . .

The two old friends were in Joey's spacious white modern kitchen, the windows over the sink looking out on the backyard and the pool, where Marie Sadano and the kiddies were splishing and splashing.

Joey, in Bermuda shorts and a paint-factory explosion of an Hawaiian shirt, was showing off something called a microwave oven. Richie, in a T-shirt and white jeans and a cap with a "W" for Weequahie, was wondering if his friend's pride over this big boxy kitchen-counter doohickey could really be the reason for Joey calling to insist Richie come over.

Right now, through the TV-screen-like glass door of the box, popcorn was bouncing off the inner walls and the sound was like every firecracker in China going off.

"What the fuck is a 'micro' wave, anyway?" Richie asked, working his voice above the racket. "Micro like in Mr. Microphone? Cooks so loud you can wait out in the other room and know it's done?"

"You are *so* fuckin' out of it," Joey said, laughing. He gestured to the squat fat gizmo. "It's a scientific force like atomic energy. It rearranges molecules and shit."

"Molecules of what?"

Joey shrugged. "You name it. Of popcorn, for starters. But you don't wanna put your head in there. Or you'll get *your* molecules rearranged like Hiroshima."

"Sounds delicious."

It smelled like scorched shit, when Joey opened the door and raked the popped kernels out into a bowl, most of them burnt. Joey insisted Richie try some. It tasted like scorched shit, too.

"I can get you one of these," Joey said, nodding at the microwave. "Just like this, brand-new. Have it delivered and everything."

"Thanks, but no thanks." This fad would never catch on.

Richie moved away from the smell, noticing a snapshot stuck with magnets on the refrigerator: Joey and his wife and kids outside a snowy cabin under a perfect blue sky. "Looks nice. Where is this, anyway?"

"Aspen," Joey said, coming over. He plucked a

packet of snapshots off the counter. "Here's some more. Man, it's paradise."

Richie thumbed through the photos—skiing, snowball fights, kids making a snowman, Marie looking pretty with a glass of wine by a rustic fireplace.

"Yeah," Joey said, "we just got back. Had a great time. That's where we were, case you was trying to get a hold of me."

Richie hadn't been. "I'd like to go there some time, Aspen. Always wanted to go skiing those slopes."

"Oh, yeah, man it's wild. You know who we met? Burt Reynolds. Saw Robert Redford, from a distance. Johnny Carson, too. I ain't kiddin'—all kinds of Hollywood people go up there. Hell, they're buying everything's not nailed down."

Richie held onto the photos, then jerked a thumb at the shot on the fridge, of the family grouped outside the cabin. "That your place?"

"Are you kidding?" Joey said, grinning, waving the suggestion off. "You think *I* could afford a log-cabin palace like that?"

"I don't know. Can you?"

"You know what it's worth? Ski-in-ski-out, five bedrooms, sauna, everything. Naw, we were guests. . . . No, that's not my place. Richie . . . it's yours."

"What?"

"If you want it. That's *your* place, Richie."

Silence hung in the kitchen along with the scorched smell. The only thing Richie could hear was the distant splashing of the girls outside the window, only that sounded a world away, somehow.

Richie was trying to find a way to say what he needed to say, when Joey jumped in.

"Rich, isn't there some way we can accommodate this situation? Something we can do about you . . . leaving the big guy alone? You know who I mean."

The elephant in the kitchen, the elephant that was always in any room with Joey and Richie: Joey's uncle Dominic Cattano.

Richie said, "You know, don't you, that if I don't report what you just said to me, I could be in a lot of trouble. And if I *do* report it, *your* ass'll be in a sling."

Joey's shrug was an effort to be casual but the tightness in his voice belied the gesture: "I'm hoping you won't do that. A lot of cops make certain accommodations, Richie, a lot of good, underpaid cops who understand that certain things in this world ain't gonna ever change, so why buck it?"

Richie, for the first time, began looking around the kitchen with an eye on where microphones could be hidden: Joey's deck wear wouldn't allow a wire.

Mr. Microphone is right, Richie thought.

But Joey held up his hands as if in surrender. "I'm not taping anything, Rich."

Richie just looked at him.

Joey answered the unspoken question: "Because we're friends, Richie, that's how you know I ain't bullshitting you. We're friends and I'm telling you. Nobody's listening but you and me and God, if He's got nothing the hell better to do. This is a real, legit offer."

"Legit isn't the word I'd use. Who's this from, your

uncle? Or some wise guy insulation?" Richie shook his head, sick to his stomach and it wasn't the awful popcorn smell. "How can you *do* this, Joey? Why would you risk our friendship?"

Joey's gaze was steady. "Because I care what happens to you. I'm hearing things I don't like about what could happen to you."

Richie let out a single, harsh laugh. "What, a *threat* now?"

Joey raised a peaceful palm. "No. That's a friend telling a friend to watch his back. Officially, I'm just conveying an offer. Which I think you should seriously consider."

Richie shook his head. "You shouldn't've done it."

"I had to, Rich."

"You had to."

"No choice." Something desperate came into Joey's eyes. "Neither do you, Richie. Not a threat, not from me, not between us. But just between us? You have *got* to leave Frank Lucas alone."

Richie blinked. "Frank Lucas?"

"You heard me, Rich."

"What the fuck, Joey . . . he's not *important* enough for you to make a move on me like this."

Joey's eyes locked onto Richie's. "Yes he is."

So the elephant in the room, for once, had not *been Uncle Dominic! When Joey had said, "You know who I mean," he meant Frank Fucking Lucas. . . .*

Richie pressed the packet of photos into Joey's hand.

"Tell Marie I'm sorry I had to leave," he said. "Up to you, whether you tell her *why. . . .*"

* * *

That afternoon, Richie went over to HQ and sat
with the sun's dying light streaming through the amber
stained glass and he studied the table of organization
they'd been building on the bulletin boards.

He stared for a long time and he considered what
Joey had said, and the things that had been between the
lines of what Joey said. The Organized Crime chart
currently had Italians up top, the uppermost figure
Joey's Uncle Dominic. The black faces, among them
Charlie Williams and the Lucas brothers, were way
down on the board, in a position reserved for lower-
echelon Harlem crooks.

Finally Richie got up, untacked Frank Lucas's photograph and moved it from its lowly position to a place
of rare honor (or perhaps dishonor) as the first
African-American to reach the top of the pyramid.

Above the Mafia.

When Toback came in the next morning—at
Richie's request, before the rest of the team—the boss
sat, leaned back in a metal chair, staring up at the chart
and the new, black face atop it. At first Toback thought
Richie was either kidding or insane.

But they talked a long time and, finally, Toback
came around to Richie's thinking.

The squad was trailing in as Richie wrapped up,
saying to Toback, "INS, FBI, IRS—I can't get anything out of them on Lucas. Nothing on his travel, his
bank accounts, property holdings—nada."

Toback chuckled dryly. "That's because they all think you're on the take."

"Fuck them! *They're* on the take!"

Toback raised an eyebrow. "How do you know your assumptions about them aren't as unfounded as theirs are about you?"

Richie leaned forward, putting both palms on the banquet table. "Because these bent bastards don't *want* this to stop. This drug traffic, it employs too many people—cops, lawyers, judges, probation officers, prison guards. The day dope stops coming into this country, what? A hundred thousand people are out of work?"

But Toback was shaking his head. "Richie, I thought *I* was cynical. . . ."

Spearman threaded over through the desks and came up to Richie. "Excuse me—couple of suits want to see you."

Richie frowned. "Feds?"

"Yeah. J. Edgar flavor."

Richie went over near the entrance and conferred with two FBI agents as interchangeable as their dark suits and short haircuts and stony expressions. One might have been ten years older than the other, but otherwise they were strictly Frick and Frack.

"We understand that you're doing a good job, Mr. Roberts," the older of the two said. "And we want you to know we'll do everything we can to cooperate with your efforts."

"Good. Fine. *And . . .* ?"

The two men exchanged glances.

"We have it from a very reliable source," the older agent said, "that a contract's been taken out on your life."

Richie, not wanting to show the feds anything, said blandly, "Yeah? Who took it out?"

"It emanates from Organized Crime circles."

"No kidding. *Where* in OC circles does it 'emanate' from, guys?"

The feds again traded looks.

The lead agent said, "We can't say without compromising our source. You understand about not compromising sources."

"No," Richie said, shaking his head, "I don't. Not when it's *my* life, I don't."

The younger agent chimed in: "If you like, we can assign someone to protect you."

"What?" Richie laughed. "The FBI is going to protect *me*? Guys, I been working on the street for fifteen years. I appreciate your concern, and your offer, but . . . I'll take a pass."

Richie would say this much for the feds: they took no apparent offense. The lead agent gave Richie his card, and they went out.

"Hilarious," Richie said, walking back over to Toback.

But his boss's expression was grave. "None of this is funny, Richie," he said, sitting up in the metal chair. "And you *know* it. . . ."

Spearman, Abruzzo and Jones had taken all of this in—with or without electronic aid, they were born eavesdroppers—and even they had no wise-ass remarks to offer.

* * *

So maybe it was natural that Richie did start to feel a little spooked.

That night he was walking down a dark side street, on his way back to his apartment with a bag of groceries in his arms, when he started thinking a guy was following him.

This character was medium build and wearing nondescript working-class clothes, a zippered jacket and slacks and a cap; but there was no doubt the guy was edging closer, and closer. . . .

Richie slowed and let the guy get closer still . . . then dropped the groceries, gently as possible under the conditions, and whirled on the guy and smacked him in the jaw, sending him down to the sidewalk in a pile of arms and legs.

And as the fallen follower was trying to get his wits back about him, Richie's revolver moved in to stare him down, inches from his face.

"Don't shoot!" the guy blurted. "For God's sake, don't shoot me!"

Richie pressed the nose of the revolver to the man's forehead, dimpling the flesh. "Talk."

The guy blinked a bunch of times and managed, "Are . . . are you Richard Roberts? You *are* Richard Roberts. I got a subpoena for you, is all."

Richie helped the guy up, allowed himself to be served and felt a little bad for the poor son of a bitch, who had pissed himself in the process.

But not that bad.

* * *

This time, Richie and his lawyer sat next to Laurie and hers on the same side of the courtroom. Richie was in a suit and tie, and his ex-wife was conservatively dressed as well, but looking pretty enough to remind him why and how he first fell in love with her.

He leaned past Sheila and whispered to Laurie, "I'm sorry I couldn't give you the kind of life you wanted."

Her eyes went sideways to him, her expression as startled as if he'd honked his horn.

He went on: "I'm . . . I'm sorry it was never enough. You have plenty of reason to complain. But, please, don't punish me for being honest. Don't take my son out of my life."

Laurie was staring at him now—he couldn't read her face, other than the surprise there at him talking to her in the middle of all this.

Now she leaned over and her eyes went fiery and she wasn't whispering at all as she said, "You think I left you because you were *honest* and didn't take *money* like every other cop in New York? *That's* what you're saying?"

Up front, the bailiff gave them a look, but Laurie clearly didn't give a shit—she was well off the launching pad.

"Let me tell you, Richie Roberts, why you don't take money. You don't take money because in some sick, twisted way, you think that pays back you being dishonest about everything and everybody *else* in your pitiful life. And let me tell you, that is *way* worse than taking money nobody gives a damn about—drug money, gambling money, that nobody's gonna miss."

All eyes in the courtroom were on this little drama now.

And Laurie, center stage, ranted on: "I'd rather you *took* that dirty money, not because I'm greedy or want better things . . . but because maybe you'd've been honest with *me*, then. Or *don't* take that stupid money, I don't care, I don't want it; but just don't play Mr. Clean while you're cheating on *me*. Don't cheat on your kid by never being around. Don't go out getting laid by all your slutty snitches and secretaries and strippers and . . . *her*. . . ."

Laurie was indicating a stricken Sheila.

"I can tell just by looking," Laurie said with utter contempt, "*she's* one of them, too."

Sheila looked like she wanted to crawl under her pew, with so many eyes and ears in the courtroom taking this in.

But Richie, good Jewish boy that he was, accepted this punishment, knowing he deserved it.

And Laurie was winding up now: "You think you're going to heaven, 'cause you're 'honest,' do you? Well, you're not. You're a liar and a cheat and a selfish prick, and you'll be going to the same level of hell as the crooked cops you can't stand."

"*All rise,*" the bailiff said, putting a blessed end to Laurie's diatribe.

Soon they were before the same judge who'd willingly received petty paper-clipped bribes the last time Richie and his lawyer had come into this courtroom.

Sheila, on her feet next to the seated Richie, did her best, saying, "Your Honor, a lot has been said here today about how unsavory an environment Mr. Roberts offers a child. How dangerous that environment is. Well, I'm sorry, Your Honor, but the *world* is dangerous. Still, it's where we live, and yet we tell Richie and men with guns and badges like him, 'Protect us.' We give the Richie Robertses of our world that dangerous responsibility and then we say, 'Oh, but you can't bring a *child* into that—we can't trust a man like you to raise a child, we don't think you're fit for—"

"*I'm not*," Richie said, in a clear loud firm voice.

The chamber was draped in silence. The judge started reaching for his gavel, but froze instead. "Do you have something to say, Mr. Roberts?"

"I do, Your Honor," he said, getting to his feet. "But not to you, sir." He looked at Laurie, whose astonished eyes were on him. "You're right, babe. It's no place for Michael, being around me. Take him. Take him, and the farther away the better. Better for him, I mean. Just please don't remove him completely from my life, because I do love him, and would like him to grow up knowing that. . . . That's all, Your Honor."

And Richie sat back down.

And Laurie Roberts was suddenly remembering how and why she had first fallen in love with her exhusband.

21. Revenge

The snow was still white and fresh, New York not getting its chance to apply grime just yet, and the Christmas feeling in Manhattan was like everybody was living inside that old movie, *A Miracle on 34th Street*. The towering tree at Rockefeller Center had been turned on earlier that evening, its blinking red and blue and green lights casting a Yuletide glow on tourists and New Yorkers alike, who applauded as if electricity in the 20th century was still a miracle. Certainly Christmas was.

Frank Lucas did not delegate Christmas—he was still, at heart, a country boy, and the holiday meant something to him, not so much in a religious way as a time for family and friends. He had shopped at Saks Fifth Avenue for Eva, and at Macy's for his momma, his brothers and the help. By the time Doc rolled up outside Frank's penthouse, the car was piled with wrapped presents in the front and back, and though he wore not red and white but a tan cashmere topcoat, he felt just like fucking Santa Claus.

Too bad a Grinch had parked itself at the curb outside Frank's building: Detective Trupo, in the replacement Mustang the detective had bought, no doubt, with some of the proceeds from that heroin he'd helped himself to.

"Frank . . . ," Doc began.

"Yeah, I see them. Not a problem. Pull in behind."

Doc did as he was told. There was a big Christmas tree tied to the roof of the Town Car and the doorman came over to help Doc free the pine. In the meantime, Frank selected from among the presents two bottles of Crystal with festive bows choking their necks, and got out and went over to Trupo's car.

The Zapata-mustached detective was behind the wheel, and in the rider's seat was one of his partners. Frank had not bothered to learn any of the names of Trupo's team—they were insects to him.

Still, he handed in both bottles and gave the pair his friendliest smile, his breath pluming in the chill. "Here you go, boys. Merry Christmas. One of my guys will drop by your restaurant with a little green for the season, next week."

Trupo handed his bottle over to his rider for safe-keeping, then returned Frank's smile, wished Frank and his family a happy holiday, and the new Mustang rolled off into the gently snow-flecked night.

In honor of the season, Frank did not mutter anything under his breath about the evil pricks.

* * *

Half an hour later, with Christmas music playing softly on his stereo, Frank was in his vast, high-ceilinged living room on a ladder stringing lights. His old friend Charlie Williams, in sweater and slacks, was seated on a nearby sofa sipping a beer—nothing fancy for Charlie. No wonder Bumpy had loved the man so.

"It's part of the game," Charlie said philosophically, "greasing these palms. Price of doing business, Bumpy always said. Imagine how bad it would be for us if the cops *weren't* crooked assholes?"

Frank reached up to loop the string of lights around a branch; he loved the strong pine scent—that, too, brought back memories of the backwoods.

"Paying cops is one thing," Frank said. "I understand that. Hell, I been payin' 'em since I was ten—put more of their fuckin' kids through college than the National Merit Award."

"You got that right," Charlie chuckled.

"But this is different, these Special Investigation Unit dicks." He cast his eyes over his shoulder, gazing right at Charlie. "These fuckers think they *are* special."

"A badge has given a lot of small men big ideas, over history."

"That's the SIU fuzz to a tee."

Charlie shrugged rather grandly; it was his third beer. "They're just fuckin' crooks, like any other fuckin' crooks. Not cops who do their jobs and keep the streets looked after and make up for their shitty paychecks with a little gravy. No, these guys got no code of honor. These guys got the ethics of a goddamn sewer rat."

Frank was down the ladder now. He knelt and plugged in the electrical cord and the tree glowed vividly in the otherwise under-illuminated room. Rockefeller Center had nothing on the Lucas tree.

Getting to his feet, Frank said, casually, "Somebody's been following me."

"Besides cops?"

"Besides cops." He came over and sat next to his old friend, and the two men's eyes met. "I see cars where they shouldn't be. Driven by guys I don't know."

Charlie sighed. He put his beer down on a coaster on the glass-top coffee table.

"Me, too," Charlie said.

"Silent Night" by a children's choir was singing in the background as the two men chatted about the possibilities, none of which were what either wanted for Christmas, or any other day.

Frank sat and watched Eva, lovely in a dark sweater and skirt, hanging tinsel on the tree. She'd already been up on the ladder and now was doing the lower branches; when she bent over to apply the silver glittery stuff, the sight of her nicely rounded bottom made him glad to be alive.

She was everything he needed—let the other guys have their mistresses and whores. He had his personal beauty queen, right under his own roof.

Also, he had Bumpy, the German shepherd, who

Eva graciously allowed to invade the penthouse a few days a week; Bumpy was perfectly housebroken and a real gentleman, well deserving of the dog toy Frank had bought him at Macy's.

Since Frank figured the dog didn't know Christmas from Easter, he gave the animal its present early, tossing the rubber thingie to the dog, who proceeded to have the time of his life tossing it around like a dead squirrel.

Enjoying the dog's enjoyment, Frank wandered over to Eva; he was sipping a glass of eggnog with a little rum in it. "I love it here. With you."

"Me, too." She flashed a smile at him but something sad lurked within. "But it *is* nice to go out, sometimes."

"Bumpy almost never went out, after a certain point. He liked to stay in, and read, and watch TV and listen to music. Play chess. He didn't go out much."

"That sounds like prison."

"Not hardly!" He gestured around at the lavish living room. "You think *this* is prison?"

She said nothing, just applied another strand of tinsel to another branch.

Frank came over and touched her shoulder. "Bumpy *couldn't* go out without . . . something happening."

"He was more of a public figure than you, Frank."

"True."

"We can *still* go out. Even tonight."

Frank sighed, moved off a few steps, gesturing. "Where? With who? Everybody I know is under surveillance. I'm being watched these days and I don't even know who by. I can't even be with my family at Christmas."

"Why not?"

"Too obvious a target—for cops *and* business rivals."

He leaned down and played with the dog some more, tossing the damp toy, getting it back, tossing it again. Then he wandered over to a window, drew back the drape just enough to peek out at the decorative wooden Christmas angels stretched out across the street. People were out walking in the lightly falling snow; he watched them, envying them, and then took in the parked cars across the way. Idly he wondered which of them held undercover cops.

Eva's hand touched his shoulder so unexpectedly, he flinched a little.

Her head was cocked, her eyes yearning. "Why don't you just pay who you have to pay? Then maybe we'd have a little more freedom."

"Baby, I *do* pay them—I pay them all. Cops, accountants, lawyers, who *don't* I pay? *Everybody's* on my payroll—and I shell out a fortune, but it don't matter. Doesn't satisfy 'em. More you pay, the more they expect."

"That doesn't make sense, Frank. . . ."

"Of course not. Because it's like dope. You pay them off once and they can't stop coming back for more. They always want more."

The worry coloring her lovely features made him heartsick—this was his life, and his problems, that had put them in their penthouse prison.

He smiled gently at her, took her by both shoulders. "Go put on something nice."

"What?"

"We're going out."

Frank had Doc pick them up the back way, which meant going down the service elevator and exiting through a long dark hallway into an alley between garbage cans. Not an auspicious start for a nice night out—Eva had on a mink coat over her beautiful evening dress, and Frank was snappy in gray sharkskin under the cashmere topcoat, and they were a stunning-looking couple, who at the moment were acting like a couple of deadbeat tenants running out on their landlord.

When they got to Small's Paradise, things weren't any better: Nicky Barnes was in the process of climbing out of his sky-blue Bentley, in typical Superfly threads topped off by a Santa Claus cap.

"Aw shit," Frank said. "Keep going."

Doc looked at Frank in the rearview mirror. "Around back?"

"Fuck that. Sneaking out of my apartment building was bad enough. I'm not playin' backdoor man at my own damn club. . . . Just drive."

They tried several other nightspots, but some were closed Christmas Eve, and assorted reasons made the others impractical as well, so they wound up at a Chinese restaurant where nobody knew Frank from Adam and it would be an hour for a table. So they ordered takeout.

The place was a joint, no place to sit while you waited under harsh, buzzing fluorescent lighting, and steam everywhere. Eva was getting pretty steamed herself.

"Listen," she said, "I'll sit in the car."

Doc said, "Go ahead, Frank. I'll wait for the stuff."

Frank asked, "Can you carry it all? We ordered a ton."

"Sure, no problem. Go on." Doc's expression was that of a man who understood the difficulties of keeping a woman happy.

Frank slipped the big man a couple twenties, then turned to take Eva's arm, but she'd already stepped outside.

"Don't forget the hot mustard," Frank said.

"What's that, that yellow sauce?"

"Yeah, the yellow sauce."

When Frank got out the door, he saw Eva half a block down, trying to get in the car, which was locked. Snow was falling good and hard now, and he slipped a little on the sidewalk when he trotted down to her, but kept his balance.

"Damn," Frank said, not even having to search his pockets, just knowing, "Doc's got the keys. We better go back."

She shook her head, squinted; snow was dusting her mink. "I can't, Frank. Those lights give me a headache—you go."

"What, and leave you standing on the street?"

Her hands were in the pockets of the fur, and she

was hopping on her heels a little, shivering, her breath visible. "Frank, it's cold. It's just down on the corner— *go!* Get the keys."

He knew arguing with her was pointless right now, so he headed back; seemed to him the snow was coming down harder by the second. A drab-looking Chevy went by, a little too fast for the weather, catching Frank's attention. He was about to go in the restaurant when he glanced back, toward Eva, and saw the Chevy down there round the corner.

Though the vehicle had apparently moved on, something had the nape of Frank's neck tingling. He did not go in the restaurant to help Doc, who was paying and getting yellow sauce, his arms already filled with a bunch of stained sacks.

For some reason, Frank just stood out in the snow and the cold and waited, and then he saw the car coming back around that corner, and he ran, placing every step carefully so as not to slip and fall and not make it to Eva in time. He could see her standing next to the car, her expression turning curious as she saw him running toward her.

Then he had her by the wrist and she didn't have time to ask him why, as he ran with her toward that restaurant, the only door they could get into on this block. The Chevy was almost on them, gunning its engine, and then Frank pushed in through the doors with Eva, and Doc—arms full of sacks—saw his boss dive for the grimy floor and take his wife with him.

The windows shattered under an explosion of gunfire, a grease gun most likely, and patrons were screaming, and cooks and waitresses were chattering in Chinese as if gibberish could make the threat disappear.

Doc had ducked down himself, the sacks of food spilled all over the place, and had a pistol in either hand, firing out at the car through the now open window. He hit the Chevy a couple times, puckering metal, and the vehicle—which had slowed to a near stop to make the hit—screeched off.

Like a presidential bodyguard, Doc gathered Eva and Frank up off the floor and hustled them out of the decimated hole-in-the-wall and down to the car and piled them in back.

Blood had soaked through Frank's topcoat on his left shoulder, but he didn't feel anything but anger. "What the fuck was *that*?"

"Are you hit?" Doc asked.

"Just drive."

Doc did.

Christmas Eve or not, security was stepped up at Frank's penthouse, Frank's own people including his brothers as well as cops on the payroll—not SIU, of course—patrolling not just the Lucas floor but every floor of the building.

An older black doctor who had been Bumpy Johnson's medic of choice attended Frank in the master bedroom. His brothers hung around on the periphery as the doc worked on Frank's shoulder wound. Stretched out on top of the covers, Frank had been given some painkiller and felt fine, except for somebody having the fucking nerve to shoot at him . . . and to launch the hit when he was out with his goddamn wife. That was fucking low.

Upon getting back to the penthouse, Eva had disappeared, and an hour had passed before she returned bearing early editions of the papers. She'd gotten these in the lobby, from a flunky Frank had sent to gather them. Now, having made her delivery, she was perched on her side of the bed, supportive of her husband but staying out of the doctor's way.

In Frank's lap—hurting him way more than any shoulder wound—was a front page with a big nasty tabloid picture of Charlie Williams gunned down on the floor of a jazz club toilet. The only thing lower than those SIU cops, Frank figured, were the reporters who thrived on tragedies like this.

Brother Huey was pacing at the foot of the bed. "Was it Nicky did this? You think it was *Nicky*, Frank?"

Frank said nothing.

"To think I thought that guy was . . ." Huey, tears in his eyes, was trembling with fury. "I'll fuckin' *kill* that bastard, whether it *was* him or not, you tell me to. Say the word, Frank. Just say the word."

Frank said nothing.

Huey gestured with two hands, pleading. "What do you want me to *do*, Frank? Your brothers are just waiting for the word. We can't just sit here and—"

"Hitting me, I understand," Frank said, reflectively. "But *Charlie*? Who did Charlie ever hurt? And who didn't like Charlie? *Everybody* liked Charlie. . . ."

Expressions were exchanged among the brothers: *somebody didn't.* But no one said it.

Eva said, "I feel bad about Charlie, too, Frank. But what I'm wondering—who shot at *us*?"

Frank said nothing.

"You're right," Eva said, and she smiled—as icy a smile as Frank had ever seen from her. "It doesn't matter. Because we're leaving. Are you finished, Doctor?"

The doctor blinked at the woman of the house. "Yes. I can wait in the living room, to discuss medication, if you'd like some time alone with your husband. . . ."

"I would. Please leave us. Everyone?"

Frank said to Huey and the others, "Go home—go see your kids. Christmas Eve, for Christ's sake."

The brothers and bodyguards and various onlookers filed out, and Eva went over and shut the door on those loitering in the hall.

On her way to her dresser, Eva flicked a look at Frank, saying, "It doesn't *matter* who shot at us. Because we're leaving."

She yanked open a drawer and took out their passports, slapped them on the dresser; then she went to the closet and got two suitcases and began packing.

He was too weak to get out of bed, but his voice was strong: "Where did you *go*? Where have you been? You go out *alone*, after we get shot at?"

She said nothing, going to the closet again and carefully picking out items, quickly and efficiently, like a skilled shopper at a fire sale.

"Eva, what are you doing?"

"We can leave from here. Money's in the car."

Frank blinked. "What money?"

"Everything you stashed at your mother's house."

"In your *car*? The Corvette?"

"Yes. That's what I said, isn't it?"

"And where *is* your car?"

"Out front."

"With ten million dollars in it?"

She shrugged. "I guess. I didn't stop to count it."

He climbed out of bed; he was weaving, but his concern and anger fueled him. "Are you crazy, woman? We gotta get that cash back to Teaneck. Who went with you?"

"Nobody."

She was at the dresser getting stuff from drawers and he could look over her shoulder into the mirror at her—not that her eyes met his that often.

He said, "You went out driving around without security? After what went down out there? . . . Doc'll take you back."

She had one bag packed and started on another. "We're not going to Teaneck. We're going to the airport."

"The airport."

"We're leaving the country."

"To *where*? No, we are *not* leaving the country."

She turned to him and her eyes were wild. "Frank, Charlie's dead. And they tried to kill us. What *else* has to happen before you come to your senses? We have all the money we could ever—"

He took her into his arms and held her close and calmed her like a child. "Come on now, baby. Everything's gonna be fine."

She wasn't crying, but she was close; and when her

breathing slowed, he asked her, "Where are we going, anyway? Spain? China? Which fuckin' place is it to be, girl?"

Her chin got crinkly. "We can go anywhere we want. We can live anywhere."

"We can run and hide," Frank said, "is what you're saying."

"You make it sound—"

"Like something I would never under any circumstance do. Listen, baby—this is where I'm from. This is where my business is. Where my family is, my mother. This penthouse, this is *my* place, *our* place, too."

Tears pearled her eyelashes. "I'm scared, Frank."

"I know you are. I know you are. But this is *my* country, Eva. This is America. And you don't run *from* America—you run *to* America."

And he took her to bed where she slept under his good shoulder, and he tended to her as if she were the wounded one, which perhaps was right.

22. Rush

Christmas for Richie Roberts had not been half-bad. Laurie had invited him over to her folks' for Christmas Eve and he was able to spend some "quality time" (to invoke the phrase Laurie had started using lately) with Michael. His capitulation at the hearing had won him some visitation time with his son, and a personal truce with Laurie. She would never love him again, and he supposed he didn't love her anymore, either. But between them, now, was an unspoken respect for what they'd once shared, as represented by the boy they both still loved very much.

So all was right with Richie's world, on that sunny January morning, the stained glass turning everything lovely shades of brown and yellow, and even having Detective Trupo troop in as if he and his black leather topcoat owned the squad room couldn't spoil it.

Richie was at his desk and scarecrow Spearman

came over, lifting an eyebrow, saying, "Said he'll only talk to you."

"Lucky me," Richie said, and got up and joined the SIU detective off to one side of the big bullpen.

"How's it goin'?" Trupo said, not offering a hand but giving Richie a friendly nod that indicated a whole new attitude.

"It's goin'," Richie said. "Christmas okay?"

"Yeah, cool. If in-laws was illegal, I'd be a happy guy."

They moved to a nearby break table where they sat and had coffee, black.

Trupo sipped steaming hot liquid, then said casually, "Hear anything about this Lucas hit?"

Richie sipped at his own cup, then shook his head. "No. Just that whoever-it-was put Frank's wife in the line of fire, which if you don't a kill a guy can be a problem."

Trupo, nodding, lighted up a cigarette. "From what I hear, it was maybe the Corsicans."

"Yeah?"

"French Connection, Fernando Rey, the exporters Frank's put out of business."

"Makes sense." Richie was wondering what this had to do with him, and for that matter, Trupo.

Trupo told him, in a brashly conspiratorial manner: "Now, I can watch out for Frank's ass on the New York side of the bridge, but I don't wanna have to worry every time he drives over to Jersey for whatever, and somebody takes another potshot at him."

Richie was stunned that Trupo would talk this

openly about his business ties to Lucas; but he gave nothing away as he said, "Hit went down in Chinatown, what I understand. Chinatown is not Jersey, last time I looked."

"No. But now the radar's up, my side of the river, and what I need to know is, you know, that yours is up over here."

"I follow."

"Good." Trupo's mustached grin had a certain charm, but Richie had to work at it not to shudder when the detective laid a chummy hand on his shoulder. "We need to start workin' together, Richie. Need to step up, need to coordinate, our efforts. Next time whoever-the-fuck's aim could be better."

"Could," Richie admitted.

Trupo's laugh was damn near a cackle. He blew dragon smoke out his nostrils. "And, of course, we want to keep this cash cow alive, you know what I'm saying?"

"I know what you're saying."

Then, as luck would have it—bad luck—Jimmy Zee came waltzing into the squadroom through the back door; immediately the snitch caught a glimpse of Trupo, and hauled ass back out.

But Trupo had made him. "What's that nigger doing here?"

"What, Jimmy? I don't know. We had him in for questioning on some domestic beef a while back, and shook him loose. He comes in and lies to us now and then, and we pretend to believe him."

Richie hoped that would pass muster.

Trupo was a lot of things, but a fool wasn't one of them; his detective instincts were tweaked, and his eyes searched the squadroom, landing on the bulletin boards and the revised flow chart of drug criminals.

The SIU dick got up and wandered over to the bulletin boards. Richie followed. Trupo was taking a good long look at the table of criminal organization, and his eyes widened and his jaw dropped, when he saw Frank Lucas up top, in Public Enemy Number One position.

"Jesus," Trupo said. "What the fuck's *this* about? You're not actually working to *arrest* Frank Lucas? What's the matter with you, man? You fuckin' *crazy*?"

"Yeah, matter of fact I am fuckin' crazy," Richie said pleasantly. "Haven't you heard? Crazy enough to shoot somebody and make it look like an accident next time he comes over the bridge without my permission."

Trupo's shark eyes narrowed. "What are you saying, Roberts?"

"I'm saying, Trupo," Richie said, not at all pleasantly, "get the fuck out of New Jersey."

Trupo glowered at Richie for a long five seconds, and Richie looked back coldly; then the bent detective turned and went out quickly, before an accident could happen.

In Frank Lucas's penthouse, in the bedroom where he was recovering, a big television set had been brought in down at the foot of the bed, so Frank could be propped up behind pillows and relax in front of the tube.

But the tube wasn't cooperating: chaotic scenes of activity in Saigon told a story Frank did not want to hear, namely that the U.S. was pulling out of Vietnam. His pipeline in and out of the Golden Triangle was about to get seriously fucked up.

Dominic Cattano was in the process of paying Frank the rare honor of a personal visit, looking solemnly urbane in a dark suit and striped tie from Savile Row, and expressing concern about Frank's recovery.

"Are you sure you should be getting out of bed? It was just two days ago, Frank. . . ."

Frank had changed into a fresh shirt and slacks and was currently sitting on the edge of the bed, tying his shoes. "Two days in bed is plenty. Two days in bed is too much."

Cattano stayed near the doorway; he hadn't been offered a seat and the only one available besides the bed was at Mrs. Lucas's dressing table. "If there's anything I can do, Frank. . . ."

Frank, on his feet now, gave Cattano a rictus of a grin. "Anything you can do? Why, Dominic, you've already done it—you've guaranteed me peace of mind, doing business with you."

"Now, Frank . . ."

Rage barely controlled, Frank gestured to himself. "Do I *look* like a man with peace of mind to you, Dominic? They shot at my wife. Would they shoot at *your* wife, Dominic? Who *does* that?"

Cattano gave a small shrug; his expression was bland.

Frank's anger began to bleed out: "Who *was* it, Dominic, which of your people? I'll take his gun away and shove it up his ass."

Lifting a peacekeeping palm, Cattano said, "I don't know that it *was* any of them, Frank. And neither do you."

Frank came over and stood a foot away from the mob boss. "Then maybe I'll kill them all. Just to make a goddamn fuckin' point."

With a faint smile, Cattano said gently, "You want to know who it was? I can tell you."

"Who?"

"It was a junkie. Or a business rival. Or dumb-ass kids trying to make a name. Or someone who you forgot to pay off, or slighted without realizing it. Or even one of my people, unhappy with me doing business with a moolie. Or most likely? Somebody you put *out* of business by being too successful."

Frank, still agitated, said, "You can afford to be philosophical, Dominic. They didn't shoot at your ass."

"No. But my ass *has* been shot at, Frank, and more than once. You know why? Because I'm a success, and success has a lot of enemies. Your success *itself* is what took a shot at you."

Frank frowned.

"How are you gonna stop that, Frank? How you gonna kill *that*—by being *unsuccessful*?" Cattano laughed harshly. "Be a successful somebody and have enemies; be an unsuccessful nobody and have friends. It's the choice we make."

Frank said nothing.

Neither did Cattano, who had said his piece.

Then Frank sighed, grinned, and said, "Can I get you something, Dominic? Glass of vino, maybe?" He took his guest's arm. "Kind of you to stop by. . . ."

In a pay phone at the Regency Hotel, with several rolls of quarters at the ready, Frank called Nate Atkins at the Soul Brothers Bar in Bangkok.

In the comfortable alcove beyond Frank's phone booth, hotel guests were gathered around a TV watching helicopters pluck diplomats off the roof of the American Embassy in Saigon.

Half a world away, Nate's friendly baritone fought through the long-distance crackle to say, "That you, Frank? Hello?"

"I'm watching the news," Frank said. "Where the hell's everybody going?"

"Where else when a war's over? Home."

"Just like that? We're going to leave the fuckin' country to those evil communists 'cause some fuckin' *hippies* don't like it?"

"Frank—we been in Nam since '61. Enough's enough."

"Well, I ain't had *close* to enough! Before this motherfucking war ends, I want *three thousand kilos* in the air! I don't care if you have to recruit the *Flying Fucking Nun!*"

Crackly silence.

"Okay," Nate said. "When can I expect you?"

* * *

After several days of winding through the jungle, Frank and Nate and a small army of black servicemen and black thugs arrived with their pack mules at the opium farm where it had all begun.

And once again a khaki-clad Frank was seated in the bamboo hut with the hard-eyed Chinese general who had made Blue Magic possible. No one but Frank and the general was in the small room, seated at a table having tea—a table on which were stacks and stacks of banded bills, C-notes adding up to four million dollars.

"Wars end," the general said, as philosophical as Dominic Cattano, "but opium goes on. These plants are hardy enough to outlive any war—they'll still be here long after the American troops have gone. But after the last U.S. plane goes home, what will you do for transportation, Mr. Lucas? How will you import our product?"

"I'll figure something out," Frank said easily. "You'll see me again."

The general cast an openly affectionate gaze on his American business partner. At four million bucks, the old boy could afford to be friendly.

"It's not in my best interests to say this, Frank," the general said. "But getting out while you're ahead, in such a business as this? Is not the same as quitting."

"Have you been talking to my wife?"

The general chuckled. "No. And I take it you don't think she's right in her opinion?"

"I think she has a right to my opinion."

The general smiled. "Very good. I like that, Frank. I will remember that."

So the general and his American visitor drank tea, made their transaction, leaving the door to the future open.

Frank lost track of the number of mules they'd brought along—it took a lot of the animals to carry three thousand kilos of heroin in burlap bags.

The journey back was tedious and slow. Nate's Thai thugs would go ahead and take sniper positions in the trees, then the mule train would inch along below; and the process would repeat, with the snipers ready to open fire on any hostile action. The humidity and heat, the bugs and snakes, were a constant; and Frank was weak, for Frank anyway, in the aftermath of the attempted hit. He was on painkillers and antibiotics and salt tablets; his eyes were burning and his shit was runny.

After two and a half days, the mule train winding down through the jungle, Frank began to feel better— he began to feel, in fact, that they had it made.

That was when a barrage of gunfire from the trees up ahead rained down on them; their own snipers had not yet taken their new positions, so Frank's little army was vulnerable, and two of the Thais went down immediately, leaving bloody mist behind, everybody else diving for cover, to shouts of "*Vietcong!*"

As his people returned fire, Frank dropped from his mule and, with the beast between him and the attackers, shot his pistol up into the trees. Bullet-severed fronds rained down, but no bodies fell, and the onslaught continued, anonymous gunfire chewing up jungle and men.

Frank noticed the mules were taking no hits.

Nate was pinned down with the tethered train of the beasts.

"*Give them half!*" Frank yelled.

Nate couldn't make it out at first, squinting at Frank, shaking his head as slugs chewed up bark and shredded foliage.

"*Cut half of 'em loose! The mules!*"

Nate nodded, and got out his big sharp knife and cut the mule-train tether midway, then slapped at the nearest animal's ass, and the freed mules went bounding into a wall of trees.

With this the shooting subsided, then stopped altogether, as smoke rose like fog around half a dozen dead Thais and Americans, flung to the jungle floor to feed the earth with their blood.

This deadly high tariff paid, the remaining men and mules trudged on to what passed for civilization in this part of the world.

At the Soul Brothers Bar, the American entertainers were gone, just as were most of the American patrons. On stage a little Thai teenager lamely tried to sing Otis Redding's "Dock of the Bay." Pitiful and comic.

Frank, in a sportshirt and white slacks, sat at a table with a drink and a phone. He sipped the former and talked into the latter.

"Did you get that, Huey?" he asked. "Newark. Short Term Parking Lot Three."

"When do you need it?" his brother's voice asked. "Today?"

"Tomorrow will be fine."

"Short Term Lot Three. This the Mustang we're talking about?"

"No. The Camaro."

"Camaro. What's the plate number?"

"KA 760. You get that?"

"Yeah, I got it."

"You sure?"

"I got it, Frank! . . . KA 760."

Back in that other jungle called Harlem, Huey— who briefly before had been making out with a girl who wasn't his wife in the backseat of his car—had been parked near the pay phone on the corner, waiting for his brother's call.

It was nighttime and Huey's driver and cousin Jimmy Zee was standing on the sidewalk, looking like he was watching hoochie women strut by when actually he was picking up on every word of Huey's end of the conversation, watching Huey jot down the info on an old cocktail napkin.

Every jungle had its surprises.

23. Red Tape

The next morning, Jimmy Zee showed up at the squadroom, bright and early—around eleven... bright and early for Jimmy Zee.

He had a wild-eyed, incoherent story to tell, which Richie Roberts was not much enjoying, figuring a touch for a C-note would be the darkness at the end of this tunnel. Jimmy was seated in a desk chair and Richie sat on the edge of another desk nearby, with Abruzzo, Jones and Spearman encircling the snitch, prompting him, trying to get him to cough up something that made an ounce of fucking sense.

"There's no Short Term Lot Three at Newark, Jimmy," Abruzzo was saying. "They're lettered A, B, C, D—like the alphabet?"

"I don't care about the fuckin' alphabet," Jimmy insisted firmly. "I'm just tellin' you what I heard—"

"Then maybe you heard . . ." And Abruzzo leaned in and got in Jimmy's face. ". . . *wrong!*"

Jimmy's head bobbed back, as if Abruzzo's breath was bad, which may well have been the case, but Jimmy's flinch was more to avoid a possible blow.

Spearman, tired of asking Jimmy questions, tried Jones instead: "Maybe he means the time? Three o'clock maybe?"

Jones shrugged, and zeroed in on Jimmy again. "Look, Jim, this isn't a Jersey plate. Or a New York one, either . . . not with just two letters. It's three and three, *not* two and three, get it?"

Jimmy, not getting it, shook his head. "I'm just tellin' you what Huey said. You guys say keep you ears open, so I keep my ears open, and I tell you what I hear, and then you fuckin' *ride* me. . . ."

"If it's not a plate," Jones said, ignoring this outburst, "then what the fuck *is* it?"

"How the fuck should *I* know?" Jimmy blurted. "*I* ain't the detective!"

Abruzzo was shaking his head, looking like he wanted to hit somebody. Looking like he wanted to hit Jimmy, who Richic had to agree was as frustrating a snitch as he'd ever come across.

"If you're fuckin' lying," Abruzzo said menacingly. "If you're fuckin' yanking our *chain*. . . ."

"It's what Huey said. On the phone. To Frank. I'm *sure*."

"KA 760," Spearman said skeptically.

"Yes! Yes! Fucking *yes!*"

Jimmy gazed up helplessly at the cops surrounding him. The cops gazed helplessly at each other.

All except Richie, who slid off the desk and onto his feet, smiling. "None of you assholes ever been in the service?" he asked.

The three cops and the one snitch gaped at Richie.

"It's an Air Force tail number."

By early afternoon Richie and his entire staff of detectives—fifteen strong plus their big boss Toback standing next to the task force leader—were grouped along the edge of the tarmac at Newark Airport, watching a military plane with the tail number KA 760 taxi toward them.

Soon the big silver bird had rolled to its stop, and the cabin door slid up, passengers emerging, including military officers, embassy personnel and families, all looking as haggard as they did relieved to be trading Vietnam for their homeland. Richie, Toback and the squad watched with some concern as official passengers, met by a host of assistants, filed past—to Richie, everybody on that plane was a suspect, and seeing VIPs get special treatment did not thrill him.

Finally a seasoned-looking captain approached the assembly of law enforcement officers, and Richie stepped forward to meet him.

"Captain, I'm Richard Roberts, director of the Essex County Narcotics Bureau. We have reason to believe this aircraft has been used to smuggle contraband."

"Contraband."

"Heroin, sir."

" 'Reason to believe' doesn't cut it, Director Roberts."

"No, sir . . ." Richie held up the folded papers. ". . . but this warrant does."

Minutes later, the squad was turning an airport hangar into a kind of big-scale chop shop, taking the military plane apart inside and out. Within the cabin, seats were removed and inspected, carpeting yanked up, panels unscrewed, even the lavatories dismantled. Outside, engines and landing gear were disassembled, tires knifed open and searched; luggage was throughly gone through; and a nuzzle was plunged into a toilet to pump out the contents into barrels where Richie's detectives did a dirty job that somebody had to do, fishing through human waste with rubber-gloved hands.

Richie, off to one side, watched with a growing sense of panic, even despair, as his detectives and mechanics and customs agents began to peel the metal skin off the plane. In the meantime, coffins bearing fighting men who were getting out of Vietnam the hard way were being off-loaded.

By the time the search was finished, the carcass of the plane barely resembled the flying machine it had been a few hours ago—no panel had not been removed, no cavity had gone unprobed.

Toback ambled up beside him. "Rich, we've checked everything."

"Not quite," he said.

Richie was gazing at the military caskets getting

loaded onto a trunk with armed soldiers standing respectful guard. The captain was watching the process gravely.

Toback's jaw dropped; then he said, "You can't be serious?"

Richie eyed his boss. "Why, dope smugglers are going to stand on ceremony? They're gonna have a sense of right and wrong?"

"Well, keep me out of it."

Slowly Richie approached the coffins and walked up to the one next in line for lifting up onto the truck.

To the captain, Richie said, "Need to have a look inside, sir."

The captain frowned.

"Open it," Richie said.

Richie had been stared at before, by criminals including rapists and murderers and mob bosses, and by cops as honest as Toback and as crooked as Trupo, but never had colder, more contemptuous eyes settled on him than the captain's.

Richie didn't give a shit. He said, "You saw the warrant. You know it permits me to search the plane and its cargo."

"These men. They're cargo?"

"I mean no disrespect. But I do have permission."

Still the captain just stood and stared at Richie.

"Okay," Richie said, and he knelt to open the coffin himself . . .

. . . and every soldier's rifle came immediately into firing position.

Richie the target.

The captain's smile wasn't really a smile. "You don't have *my* permission."

Richie looked up and all sorts of cold eyes stared at him, some belonging to the soldiers, the others to the rifles pointed at him, those black circular eyes that could be the last ever to regard a man.

Safeties clicked off.

Fingers poised to fire.

All these soldiers needed was their captain's order to blow away this disrespectful civilian son of a bitch.

Richie glanced at the captain. "Thing is," he said, "I don't need your permission."

Having all these rifles pointed at him was no fun; but Richie did not believe this captain would kill a law enforcement officer in his line of duty, and end his own career in a court-martial.

When Richie undid them, the coffin latches popped like gun shots, and yet he managed not to jump. He lifted the lid on the long black body bag within. Sickened by what he needed to do, Richie pulled at the zipper, and the body bag parted to reveal the sad remains of a young soldier.

"That's enough!"

Richie glanced behind him and saw a very annoyed middle-aged man in a suit and tie striding toward him. The guy looked decidedly official.

Then Toback was kneeling beside Richie, whispering, "First Assistant U.S. Attorney, Richie. Do as he says."

* * *

At the Lucas family home in Teaneck, Eva was a guest. She and Frank rarely stayed at the house but—in the aftermath of the shooting, and while Frank was overseas on business—she had been installed here with Momma Lucas and several of the brothers and cousins and their families. This afternoon, however, no one was home but Eva and Momma.

Eva found Momma's presence comforting, and the house itself was lovely; today was typical of life in the upscale housing development, an idyllic world of suburban domesticity, from chirping birds and laughing kiddies to the hum of lawnmowers and the music of wind chimes.

The two women sat at the kitchen table, sipping coffee and talking and laughing, as Mrs. Lucas showed Eva family photographs of Frank as a boy. Eva was struck by the warmth of the family members, obvious in the snapshots, but also by the just as apparent abject poverty.

Eva had grown up in Puerto Rico and knew all about living poor; but even she was impressed by the squalor the Lucas clan had endured.

A tap at the kitchen doors onto the backyard startled both women. Framed there, holding up his badge, was a detective named Trupo—Eva had seen him before, several times, though she had never exchanged words with the man, and knew Frank despised this particular police officer, with whom he was forced to do business.

Other men, plainclothes officers like Trupo she assumed, were standing, chatting, in the backyard nearby. Trupo himself was handsome in a cruel way, with Apache cheekbones and a Mexican mustache and a thigh-length black-leather topcoat that probably cost as much as a small car. The German shepherd, in his fenced-in run that led into its doghouse, was barking, but nobody was paying the animal any attention.

Trupo smiled at her and waved hello.

Eva traded glances with Momma, and then went over to the door and, without opening it, asked, "Yes?"

He motioned. "Meet me around front."

Then the detective disappeared, his men trailing after.

Momma, still seated at the kitchen table, looked worried, and had a right to be. Eva said she'd deal with this and, when the front doorbell rang, was already on her way.

Trupo was on the front stoop with a cocky grin and a search warrant. Behind him were three more of his kind.

"This is for you," he said, and handed her the document and brushed past her into the residence.

The other three detectives trooped in, one of them nodding at her, another giving her a wolfish grin that gave her spine a chill.

"Listen," Eva began, but none of them listened.

Instead, the trio of detectives fanned out on the main floor, while Trupo headed upstairs, like he owned the place. Eva went quickly back to the kitchen, and sat with Mrs. Lucas, and was showing her the search warrant when one of the detectives came in, helped himself to a cup of coffee, and ransacked the kitchen, while keeping an eye on the two women.

The sound of more ransacking, upstairs, was painful

to hear, and Momma gripped one of Eva's hands in both of hers. After a very long half hour, Trupo came into the kitchen, pocketing what Eva knew to be a safe deposit key, and said to Eva, "Could use a little help."

She just looked at him.

He shrugged and took her by the arm, yanking her off the chair and practically dragging her up the stairs. The second floor was like the aftermath of a tornado. Clothes and other belongings had been thrown onto the floor from closets, and as she passed bedrooms she could see dresser drawers similarly emptied, covers off beds, mattresses gutted.

In the bedroom that was Eva's and Frank's, on the rare occasions they stayed over, Trupo gestured to the torn-apart surroundings and said, "We've done our best here, little lady, but we can use some help."

"What is this about, Detective?"

"It's about your husband's illustrious career being over. The feds are going to come in and clear everything out. Every damn cent, every damn car and toy and diamond ring. But not before I get my share. Where's the money, Mrs. Lucas?"

Eva pointed to a dresser whose drawers were on the floor along with their former contents. "There was some change and a few bills over there, but they're gone now. You must've already got it."

"Not the piddling shit, Mrs. Lucas. The *money*—the getaway stash that Frank and every other cheap gangster keeps at his house! For when the inevitable happens, and this is the inevitable, Mrs. Lucas."

Eva locked eyes with the detective. "Listen carefully, Detective."

"I'm listening."

"If you leave now, right now, there's a *chance* Frank might not kill you."

She'd barely got that out when Trupo backhanded her.

The detective had one of his men haul Eva back down to the kitchen, where Mrs. Lucas applied a cool washcloth to Eva's cheek, which was already swelling up. They could hear the search continue and escalate above them: glass breaking, panels being ripped from walls, the walls themselves splintering and crunching apart from blows by sledgehammers.

Eva had tears in her eyes, but it wasn't the pain from Trupo's slap. She was gazing at Frank's sweet loving mother, saying, "I am *so* sorry. . . ."

Periodically, the dog in the backyard would start to bark again. The invasion of the house had been going on for over an hour now, so the dog would start in, lose steam, then some particularly loud noise in the house would spur him on again.

As they stood at the sink with Momma applying the washcloth, Eva could see Detective Trupo striding across the backyard, toward the German shepherd and its elaborate doghouse. Bumpy, as Frank called the animal, was going wild at the approach of the big man in the flapping black coat.

Trupo ignored the fenced-in animal and pushed at the back of the doghouse, which seemed to give a little, as if it were levered. . . .

Eva watched through the window in horror as Trupo went over casually and removed a handgun from under his black topcoat and fired through the fence at the big dog, shooting it in the head.

The animal fell dead against the fence of its run as Trupo overturned the doghouse and revealed a dugout, insulated area underneath where stacks and stacks of banded cash had been salted away.

Eva, at the window, was comforting Momma, appalled by the execution of the poor dumb animal. Eva was heartsick, too, but as much as she liked the late Bumpy, mostly she was feeling the loss of the money that Trupo and his men were soon stuffing into black duffel bags.

In an office attached to the hangar at the Newark Airport, Richie and Toback sat in chairs opposite a desk behind which the assistant United States attorney sat. Several other official-looking gents in suits and ties were milling about, and Toback respectively identified them, in a whisper, as a deputy assistant U.S. attorney, an executive assistant U.S. attorney, and the chief counsel to the U.S. attorney.

Right now the man in charge, who had stopped Richie's efforts to search the coffins and bodybags, was hanging up after a lengthy phone conversation—most of the talking had been on the other end of the line.

The assistant U.S. attorney sighed heavily, and folded his hands. He gazed at Richie with hard eyes that blinked only occasionally, and his voice was resonant and commanding, which must have served him well in court.

"That was a military transport plane," the attorney said. "If there was heroin on board, then someone in the military would have to be involved. Which means that even as the military is busy fighting a war that has only claimed fifty thousand American lives, it was also busy smuggling narcotics."

Richie was up Shit Creek, and no paddle was in sight. The attorney was making Richie's case sound about as viable as *Alice in Wonderland*; and Toback's frozen grimace was no comfort.

The attorney glanced at the phone, indicating the conversation he'd just had. "That is how General Easton interprets these events. That someone sitting in this office right now believes the United States Army is in the drug-trafficking business . . . and is trying to prove that questionable theory by desecrating the remains of valiant young men who've given their lives in the defense of their country."

Richie sat forward. "All I know is, there are *drugs* on that plane."

"Shut the fuck up."

Richie shut the fuck up.

He shut the fuck up even though this man and his associates, who were dismissing him as a fool and even a traitor, were law enforcement professionals who had never spent a second on the street. Yet these men were obviously confident that they knew more than the street cop who'd clawed his way to being director of the Essex Country Narcotics Bureau. These men were, after all, in the unfortunately bureaucratic structure of the world Richie functioned in, his superior officers.

"Is it any wonder then," the attorney was saying, "that because of your actions, the entire federal narcotics program is now in serious jeopardy of being dismantled? Dismantled as utterly and enthusiastically as that fucking transport plane you and your people just demolished out there . . . ? Because, Director Roberts, that's what you've accomplished this afternoon, single-handedly. And that is *all* you've accomplished."

Richie, finally finding an opening, said, "I have good information that the target of my squad's investigation was smuggling dope into this country on that plane."

The attorney thought about that, giving it all of half a second. "And that target is?"

Toback winced.

Richie said, "Frank Lucas."

The attorney looked up and over at his federal colleagues. Their blank expressions and shrugs spoke volumes.

Then the attorney turned a fish-eyed gaze on Richie and said, "Really. And just who the hell is Frank Lucas?"

The attorney got no help from the various assistants around him.

"Who does he *work* for?" the attorney demanded. "What *family*?"

"He's not Italian," Richie said.

"Well, what is he?"

"Black."

A long silence followed, and you could have heard a pin drop—a grenade pin.

Finally the attorney said, "Is this supposed to be some kind of joke? Do I look like I'm easily amused, Director Roberts? Because coming from an individual like yourself, this close to the end of his career in law enforcement? Making jokes would seem ill-advised."

"No joke, sir. Our investigation indicates . . . no, *establishes* . . . that Frank Lucas is above the Mafia in the dope-trade hierarchy. We believe he is buying direct from the source in Southeast Asia, cutting out all the middlemen, and that he has been using U.S. military planes and personnel to smuggle pure No. 4 heroin into the United States."

While Richie spoke, the faces of the officials before him started out confused and then turned skeptical and finally openly derisive.

Toback sat forward. "Gentlemen, Director Roberts has plenty of experience in—"

"Plenty of experience," the attorney cut in. "Does he now? And how many arrests have you made so far, Director Roberts, in your so-called investigation?"

"I was promised when I took on this job," Richie said, "that it would be about *real* arrests. We aren't focused on pushers and—"

"Would that be *no* arrests, Director Roberts?"

"We're well on the way, building cases against most of Lucas's organization. Not him, as yet. Like all

American gangsters from Capone on, Frank Lucas is well-insulated."

"You're comparing him to Al Capone now. I see. And he has an *organization.* . . ."

"That's right."

The attorney's eyes were tight, and his voice was edged with scorn: "You're saying a single fucking nigger has accomplished what the entire American Mafia hasn't managed in one hundred fucking years."

Richie stared at the man. Then he shook his head. "Yeah, you'd *know*, right? Just sitting here. Ever been on the street? Sir?"

"Get this fucking kike out of my sight," the attorney said, with a sneer and a disgusted wave.

Richie was out of his chair and smacked the bastard, twice, the second one taking the guy right out of his desk chair and onto the floor before the others could pull Richie back.

The attorney's remarks had been out of line enough that no charges were brought against Richie; but as he and Toback walked across the hangar, Richie was already thinking about his next move.

But Toback was saying, "Rich, it's over. You're shut down."

"Right," Richie said.

Then he exited the hangar and his squad members fell in behind him as they headed toward their cars.

Behind the wheel, with Spearman in the driver's seat, Richie said, "We couldn't intercept the heroin here, well, fine. *Somebody's* got to pick it up."

"Some Country Boy or other," Spearman agreed.

"So we tail their asses, every one of them."

Richie wasn't worried about being fired. What with the federal government and their endless red tape, hell, days would go by before the team was officially disbanded.

And all he needed was the next twenty-four hours.

24. Insured for Death

When Frank Lucas saw Doc waiting for him at the baggage terminal, he knew at once from the big man's expression that something was wrong, really wrong. . . .

Doc filled him in as they headed for the Town Car, and Frank felt the rage rising in him like flames consuming a building. He sat in the back of the Lincoln and thought of a hundred ways to kill that bastard Trupo, and none of them were good enough.

Then, as he tried to shake off the rage and regain control, Frank experienced something rare for him: guilt. He should have provided better safety for Eva and his mother, made sure his brothers never left them at the house alone. The kind of people who drove by a Chinese restaurant in the middle of the night shooting up the place had seemed unlikely to invade a suburban housing development in broad daylight.

But the same could not be said for the likes of Trupo and his SIU goons.

At the penthouse, seated on the edge of their bed, Eva told him everything. She seemed bothered most about her inability to protect their getaway money.

"Ten million dollars means nothing to me, baby," he said, and slapped a clip into the butt of a nine-millimeter automatic.

"I'm sorry," she said, her eyes on the floor. "It just seems like it's getting worse, and worse. . . . We had a chance to get out, and we missed it."

Frank was too preoccupied to notice the rebuke her gentle voice delivered, that she had tried to get him to run but he had refused.

Instead he just brushed his wife's bruised face with tender fingertips and said, "*This* . . . what he did to you. *That's* his death warrant."

He kissed her forehead and, sticking the automatic into a shoulder holster under a dark suitcoat tailored not to show the bulge, stalked out.

Moving through the living room with Doc, toward the front door, Frank heard another female voice: "Frankie. . . ."

He stopped and his eyes went to his mother, who he'd brought to the penthouse for protection; she was sitting on the sofa in the living room, hands folded prayerfully in her lap. Doc had gone on and was at the door. Frank gave him a nod, indicating the driver should go on ahead and get the car—Frank would be down in a minute.

He went to his mother, stood before her and said, "Eva's in the bedroom if you need her. I have a man in the kitchen, who can cook for you. . . ."

His mother smiled but sadness made it a smile he hadn't seen for a long, long time. Not since childhood.

"I think I can cook for myself, Frankie." She patted the sofa next to her. "Sit. Please sit."

He sat.

He could feel her eyes on him in a searching way that also took him back to childhood, specifically the days when he had first started to bring home money and nice things, a boy without schooling somehow managing to make a man's living. She had been suspicious then. She was suspicious now.

She took his right hand into both of hers. Her tone was not scolding, not lecturing, rather it was matter of fact. "You do know, don't you, Frankie, that if you'd have been a preacher, your brothers would be preachers. If you'd been a soldier, why, they'd be soldiers. You do *know* that?"

He shrugged, just a little.

"They all came up north because of you," she said, and there was pride in her voice and yet a certain tinge of shame, too. "You called and they came running. They look up to you. They expect you to always know what's best."

"I hear you, Momma."

"Do you? You know they're not as smart as you. Not as accomplished. You're not just the older brother, but the father, the only father they remember. And yet even with all their foolishness, they *know* a person doesn't shoot a policeman."

Frank stared at the floor.

"Even *I* know that, and I bet you didn't think your momma knew anything that was happening in your world. But mothers know. So do wives. Eva knows you don't go around shooting policemen, no matter how much they may richly deserve such treatment. *You* seem to be the only one who *doesn't*."

"What makes you think that's where I'm off to?" Frank asked her defensively, meeting her eyes. "I might just be looking after my business interests, like any other day."

She shook her head and her eyes were slits. "I have never asked you, son, where all of this came from. Do you know why? It's not that I don't want to know, or couldn't handle it. You know where you grew up and what we all lived through. What *couldn't* I handle?"

"Not much," he admitted.

Her voice had no pleading in it—she was just telling him. "I'll tell you what I couldn't handle: you lying to me. Don't lie to me, Frank. Do what else you have to, but don't you ever lie to me about it."

He looked away. He couldn't abide her gaze. His hand in hers was a tribulation.

She said, ever so gently, "Do you really want to make things so bad for your family here up north, so bad that they'll leave you? Because they will. They'll have to. And son, so will *she. . . .*" Momma nodded toward the bedroom. "She loves you with all her heart, but she will leave you. And I *know* I will."

She released his hand.

He couldn't quite look at her.

Finally he rose, and walked over to the front door; he was halfway out when he stepped back in and shut it again, then walked slowly toward the bedroom, and Eva.

His mother had done the impossible. She had won a reprieve—at least for now—for Detective Trupo.

That night, in the basement of the U.S. Army hospital in Newark, body bags were lifted from wooden coffins and set down upon tables. The bags were unzipped, the bodies removed. A rack of clean uniforms was wheeled in by somber, matter-of-fact privates, after which morticians in white smocks began their grim ritual, dressing the deceased and applying cosmetics to ghostly gray skin.

The functional wooden coffins were replaced by a small army of white military caskets that the soldiers trundled in. Lids were removed, lifted off by gold handles, and bodies—in their fresh uniforms and make-up—were deposited on silk linings. Finally the coffin lids came down and cellophane bags containing folded flags were taped on top.

Soldiers removed the white caskets to the nearby loading dock, and set them individually, careful but efficient, into a waiting military truck. Papers were signed, copies exchanged and the truck rumbled off.

Deep in the night, two black privates on janitorial duty came into the chamber where the original plain wooden coffins had been discarded like candy wrappers. Methodically the pair removed the lids, and pried up the false bottoms, revealing four-inch cavities in each coffin—home to tightly packed bricks of Double UO Globe heroin.

Early the next morning, Sunday, a laundry truck idled in the loading dock area of the hospital. Stevie Lucas—who had traded his chance to play with the Yankees to be part of his uncle Frank's team (though he still wore a Yankee cap)—hopped down from the truck and gave the two GIs a hand, as they tossed a number of laundry bags into the back of the truck.

At the same time, in the cavernous Baptist church in Harlem where not so long ago Frank and Eva had been wed, a dignified, friendly pastor was greeting the members of his congregation as they climbed the church steps for early service. Frank, Eva, and his mother were among the flock. Soon they would be swaying in the pews in a sea of ladies' hats as the church's gospel choir praised God and Jesus, Lord Almighty.

Because no matter what was going on in Frank Lucas's complicated life, he always had time to spend Sunday morning in church with his mother and his wife. God had been good to the Lucas clan. Considering.

At the hospital, an innocent-looking laundry truck—driven by Stevie Lucas—rolled past the guard gate without inspection, leaving the base, driving past a stand of trees, which is where Richie Roberts sat waiting in an unmarked car.

Richie noticed the baseball-cap-wearing Lucas kid—Stevie wore that same Yankees lid in the surveillance photo tacked on the bulletin board in the bullpen—and took up pursuit, albeit at a discreet distance.

This was wise, because before long a beat-up van driven by a red haired black woman pulled in behind the truck, and then so did a nondescript Chevy driven by Huey Lucas. Riding with Huey was another Country Boy, likely a well-armed lad, providing security.

By the time the laundry truck approached a ramp onto the George Washington Bridge, Richie was still a couple of car lengths behind. And two more Narcotics Bureau unmarked cars had fallen in behind Richie. There was a brief moment where things could have gone wrong, as the truck kept on going, past the ramp.

Some time later, the red-haired woman's van made a right turn. Abruzzo, a car-length behind, took the same turn, but promptly slowed up as the infamous Stephen Crane Projects rose before him like a monument to poverty. The detective could see Huey's Chevy approaching the projects, too, from another direction, with Spearman tailing him. Spearman, the projects looming in his windshield as well, also slowed, and finally pulled over.

When the laundry truck's destination proved to be the same dismal towers, Richie, too, slowed to a stop outside the foreboding structures where, not so long ago, he had dealt with a corpse created by his late partner, Javy Rivera.

If the people who lived in those crumbling mammoth

tombstones knew that millions of dollars of heroin had just rolled in, Richie thought, *what a riot there would be. . . .*

And in Harlem, in the Baptist church, the gospel choir having finished their lively anthem, the minister began his sermon while Frank Lucas, nestled in his pew between the two women he loved, pretended to listen.

25. Tragic Magic

On this Sunday morning, Lou Toback—relaxing on the couch in a robe and pajama bottoms, reading the *Times*—should not have expected to hear from Richie Roberts. After all, he had disbanded Richie's team yesterday. And this *was* the Lord's Day of Rest. . . .

But he was not surprised. He carried his glass of milk with him to the phone and when Richie said, "We've got it. The full shipment."

"By 'got' it, you mean . . . in hand? Arrests have been made?"

"Well, no. We saw it delivered."

"Where to?"

There was a pause; this was apparently a reluctant admission on Richie's part. "Stephen Crane."

"The fucking *projects*?"

"The fucking projects."

"That's a war zone."

"I appreciate the briefing. Now I need a warrant."

"For the whole place?"

"No."

Toback shook his head, as if to clear cobwebs. "Where *is* the stuff?"

"Somewhere in the South Tower. Lou, it's what we've worked for, all these months. We can take Lucas down."

"You didn't see Frank himself?"

"No. Huey, though. Various other Country Boys."

Toback sighed. He allowed himself a sip of milk. Then he said, "You *know* it's there. You're *sure*."

"Positive."

Toback mulled it.

"Lou, we're ready to go in there, knowing there's a good chance we won't all be coming back out. That's what this squad is willing to put on the line. All I'm asking you to do is get me a warrant."

"How many guys you got?"

"Counting me, four of us. Lou . . . we don't exactly have a lot of time to fuck around. We're a bunch of mostly white faces hanging around outside Stephen Crane, if you catch my drift."

". . . I'll call in the warrant. I know an atheist judge I can probably catch at his country club."

"That'll do fine. But pray for us anyway."

"Pray for us all. My job'll be on the line right there next to yours, Richie. And Rich—I'm sending some backup. Don't you guys go in there before either the warrant *or* the backup gets there. Got it?"

"Got it."

Richie hung up, and left the battered pay phone

across the street from the projects to join the nearby Spearman, Jones and Abruzzo, standing outside their respective cars, waiting for the go-ahead.

"Well?" Spearman asked, lighting up a smoke.

"Toback's on board. Getting us a warrant."

Jones asked, "How long we gonna wait for it?"

"It'll be here."

On the seventeenth floor of the South Tower, five female workers were preparing for business as usual. Red Top's operation had long since outgrown the little apartment in Harlem, and this empty apartment was perfect for their purposes. First the women spread (and taped down) plastic sheeting to half a dozen card tables; then they began changing for work, which in this case meant stripping down from their street clothes to their skin.

Within minutes the naked, surgically masked quintet was at work, pharmaceutical scales balanced to their counterweights, the women cutting the heroin with quinine to the exacting standards of their absent boss, Frank Lucas. Over in the kitchenette area, Red Top put on some coffee.

The ruby-crowned former girlfriend of Frank's was, as usual, in charge, but brother Huey Lucas was supervising. He never tired of watching good-looking young naked women make Blue Magic.

The work proceeded, a paper-cutter blade slicing sheets of blue cellophane. The women at their tables, displaying the expertise of Cuban cigar makers, wrapped pieces of the blue plastic like tobacco leaves around precisely measured quarter-ounce drifts of powder.

At the same time, in the Baptist church in Harlem, Frank and his momma were joining in the Call and Response of the minister as his sermon built, though Eva just sat there, lost in her thoughts.

Barely half an hour after Richie hung up, two black-and-whites and several undercover vehicles approached, sirens off. Richie was impressed by the response time, though the other three detectives had been after him every two minutes like kids in the back-seat asking daddy how much longer. Spearman had looked at his watch so often, the action had turned into a kind of tic.

But now Toback himself was climbing out of the first unmarked car, and striding over with the warrant, handing it to Richie.

"Let the four of us go in first," Richie said, gesturing to the trio who'd become his inner circle within the squad. "An army invades Stephen Crane, and you might get a war . . . and I think you know which side the residents are gonna jump in on."

"I'll meet you halfway," Toback said. "Take three more of my men with you—then you four can lead the way."

"Done," Richie said.

"And let's get some walkies distributed. When you get the lay of the land, you call it in. No cowboy action."

Richie nodded. Then he said, "Let's leave the black-and-whites out here for now, and the uniforms. Why call attention?"

Toback went along with that, and soon three un-marked cars piled with detectives laden with weapons wormed their way through the pothole-flung lanes of the projects. Long shadows cast by these ominous tow-ers turned even the most innocuous activities into fear-inducing threats—a woman pushing a stroller, some teens shooting hoops, a couple getting in each other's face, kids laughing as they raced by on their bikes, even the old winos lounging on graffiti-obscured benches seemed to bode danger. . . .

The shipment had been loaded into the South Tower—that was all Richie and his three teammates knew. Where those laundry bags of heroin had wound up in the scarred cement monstrosity had yet to be determined. What lay ahead was both tedious and ter-rifying.

First step was Richie removing the cover plate of the elevator, cutting the wires, shutting down service. Then he, Spearman, Jones and Abruzzo—followed by three of Toback's backup dicks—ventured into the debris-strewn, graffiti-enveloped stairwell. To say it compared to Beirut would be to insult Beirut.

Floor by floor, they went, working their way up the tower, commando-style, handguns and even rifles and shotguns at the ready, which sent residents scurrying; Richie lugged a sledgehammer along—opening up doors without a key was, after all, his speciality. Some-how the higher they rose, the more squalor, decay and hopelessness they found. Cooking smells joined with scents of disinfectant and urine and feces as a sad reminder that human beings actually dwelled here. This, for many, was home.

At the seventeenth floor, as Jones who was leading the way—paused outside the fire door, a strange, creaking sound could be made out, coming closer, closer. . . .

Jones cracked the door and they all saw a little kid on a big wheel go pedaling by, the sound fading with him. The invaders grinned at each other and sighed and enjoyed one light moment, at least.

Then they returned to grim reality.

This floor was the worst yet, easily, half the apartments lacking even front doors; TVs and radios and record players echoed, a cacophony of gospel music and rock 'n' roll and preaching and cartoon voices, joined by loud arguments between men and women, and topped off by the wailing of babies.

Jones peeked around the corner.

He held up two fingers to Richie, just behind him. "Shotguns," he whispered. "I'll go."

The black detective in blue denim was the natural emissary—it wasn't like Richie was wearing an Afro.

Richie risked a peek as Jones confidently strode up to the two guys seated on folding chairs outside one of the apartments that still had its door—a closed door; both watchdogs had sawed-off shotguns in their laps.

"Huey in there?" Jones asked with casual authority. "I gotta talk to the man."

"Get the fuck out of here," said the one nearest Richie's position.

Jones leaned in, irritated and unimpressed. "What the fuck kinda mouth is that? I got business with Huey, which is none of *your* fuckin' business except to get off your dead ass and knock on the fuckin' door and *get* him!"

The guy got to his feet, pumped his shotgun, and Jones latched onto the weapon and brought it up hard against the guard's throat, then whipped behind him and used the barrel of the weapon like a garrote to force the bastard to his knees. The shotgun went off, but didn't hit anybody, though plaster and pellets showered all over the place, as Spearman and Abruzzo came around quick and a rifle and a handgun were in the other guard's face before he could blink away the plaster spray.

The second guard put down the sawed-off, held up his hands in surrender, and Spearman cuffed him and tossed him on the floor like a filled garbage bag.

At the same time, Richie was swinging his sledge-hammer, turning the door into splinters.

And when Richie shouldered in, tossing the sledge, getting out his revolver, the room was already in chaos, naked women in surgical masks screaming and bumping into one another, almost comically, knocking over tables, sending packets of Blue Magic to the floor and knocking piles of heroin off onto the floor with stray powder getting into the air to offer a top-dollar contact high.

"Get *down*!" Richie yelled to the girls, and Abruzzo was behind him, giving the same order.

Then a shot came from somewhere, ringing off the walls, winging Abruzzo, and Richie hit the deck, other detectives entering the apartment to do the same, getting on their bellies to crawl like infantrymen taking a beachhead.

As he'd burst through the door, Richie had glimpsed somebody running toward another room, a male, probably Huey, and as no other gunfire had as yet followed, he got to his feet and ran in that direction, down a hallway.

Revolver in hand, he edged into a darkened bedroom, but found no Huey or anybody else—just a big tapestry of a tiger almost covering a wall.

Instinct told him to tear the tapestry down, which he did, exposing a humongous hole knocked through the wall, probably with a sledgehammer like his, connecting the bedroom with the next apartment. He climbed through into another darkened space, a living room (he soon realized) with light from the hallway slanting in through an open door.

Richie rushed out into the hallway and saw no one, but he could hear footsteps echoing down the metal stairs of the nearby stairwell. He and his revolver followed, and he started down the steps one at time, then two at a time, and finally five at a time, two flights worth.

It was Huey, all right, down there on the next landing, yanking open the door and exiting the stairwell onto the fifteenth floor. Huey had a pretty good lead on Richie, who followed him down the corridor, watching him duck into a doorless apartment.

Through that open portal he saw Huey step through to an exterior balcony and run, left. Instead of cutting through the apartment, Richie ran down the hallway, staying parallel to Huey, seeing him through other open apartment doors as his prey hustled along. And Richie smiled as he saw Huey tripping over some toys in his path; the balcony was enclosed with chain-link, and with hanging wash and assorted crap in the way, Huey had picked a hell of a cluttered escape route.

So Richie put on the steam and got ahead of Huey, and cut through into another doorless apartment; but access to the balcony was boarded shut! His strategy failing him, Richie saw Huey through the window, running by, and, impulsively, the detective grabbed a tiny portable TV off a nearby counter and hurled it like a baseball, shattering the glass . . .

. . . and knocking Huey alongside his head.

By the time Huey was back on his feet, Richie had found his way to the balcony, and was standing there facing Huey.

"Give it up, Huey."

Huey, dazed, somehow shook it off and charged into Richie, pummeling him with blows. Richie, tired of fucking around, kicked out once, hard, breaking Huey's femur.

This time Huey went down and didn't come back up, being busy howling in agony.

"You have the right to remain silent," Richie advised him.

But Huey didn't seem to be listening.

* * *

Over the next twenty-four hours, the Lucas brothers and their cousins would all be arrested—Dexter at his dry-cleaning establishment, Melvin at his metal works, Turner at his tire service, Terrence at his electrical shop—cuffed and led to patrol cars and driven away.

But on Sunday, barely half an hour after he had broken Huey Lucas's leg, Richie went out of his way to make the most satisfying arrest of all. He was hardly dressed for church, and was by any reasonable assessment a sweaty, rank mess, when he pulled up to the Baptist church in Harlem. He'd used the siren to make good time and Toback had called ahead, so half the police in New Jersey were already waiting, having surrounded the church as if it were a gangster's hideout.

And wasn't it?

Frank Lucas, his wife and his mother were among the surprised members of the congregation who exited the service and started down the steps only to realize police and police cars were everywhere. Frank's driver, Doc, had already been cuffed and taken into custody.

And all of the many shotguns, revolvers and automatics were pointed at Frank, making two things clear: he was their target, and he wasn't going anywhere. . . .

Through the crowd, Richie moved—a rumpled guy in street clothes approaching an impeccably groomed and dressed drug kingpin.

For the first time, Richie Roberts and Frank Lucas faced each other, Richie standing one step down from Frank, whose aloof manner spoke of more than just a single church step separating him from the detective.

"Richard Roberts, director of the Essex County Narcotics Bureau," he said and held up his ID. "You're under arrest, Mr. Lucas."

"Was it really necessary to—"

"Yes. Turn around, Frank."

Frank sighed, shook his head, took his time, but he turned around. And he even put his hands behind his back, for the cuffs, without being told to.

"You think you got Frank Lucas," he said, with a cold over-the-shoulder glance at his captor, "but you got nothing."

"There's a difference?" Richie asked.

And hauled him away.

26. Official Correct

At his apartment, Richie Roberts looked at himself in the long mirror inside his closet door, thinking that the new gray suit had seemed to fit better at the discount clothing store. Too late to get another, and anyway he'd already cut the tags off.

So he cut the tags off his blue striped necktie, too, and put it on; took only four tries to get a decent knot, and the thing looked pretty good against the pale blue of his shirt. The man in the mirror appeared professional enough, confident, ready for the big day at the courthouse.

Of course, once at the courthouse, the big day really began with Richie upchucking his breakfast in a men's room stall. And the guy looking back at him in the mirror over the sink had a kind of sickly, even deathly pallor. He decided the fluorescent lights were to blame, but splashed some water on his mug just the same.

Gathering himself, he went out to do battle somewhere much scarier than the streets: a courtroom.

Richie and a single assistant at the prosecutor's table were grossly outnumbered by the battery of expensive legal hired guns at the defendant's table.

And when Frank Lucas came bursting through the courtroom doors, a celebrity had arrived, a handsome, charismatic figure in a tailored suit worth three months of Richie's rent, escorted sans handcuffs by an amiable federal marshal who seemed to be getting a kick out of the accused's company.

The celebrity defendant was greeted by a gallery of other celebrities, smiling, fawning, over this pope of dope. Hands reached out to Lucas, to pat him on the shoulder or back, and beautiful women, black and white alike, leaned out with their lovely lipsticked mouths offering kisses and words of encouragement. Joe Louis—who was scheduled as a character witness for this benevolent community leader—was allowed to hug Lucas, in front of God, the judge, the jury and everybody.

Maybe, Richie thought, *I should just toss it in now. . . .*

All Richie had to offer up to counter these famous friends and assorted community leaders were three evidence tables piled with cash, weapons, bonds, property deeds, photographs of Lucas's real-estate holdings and samples of heroin in their distinctive blue cellophane.

Lucas's gray-haired old mother embraced him warmly, and the accused's coolly confident eyes swept the courtroom, taking in his phalanx of attorneys, the jury itself and finally landing on Richie in his off-the-rack suit at the prosecutor's table.

The two men's eyes locked, and Lucas smiled, just a little, almost cocky but not quite, as if to say, *Can't you see what you're up against, little man?*

Finally at the end of his receiving line, Lucas brushed by the seated Richie and, over on the other side of the room, other side of the world, the defendant disappeared from view within the fortress of his multi-million-dollar legal team.

"*Mr. Roberts . . .*"

The omniscient voice almost made Richie jump. Somehow he got to his feet and out from around the table and turned to the jury, who were studying him like his new cheap suit was all the evidence they needed, and managed to speak without squawking.

"Thank you, Your Honor," Richie said. "Ladies and gentlemen . . ."

And he told them the story that he'd been living these many months.

After that first day of opening statements, Richie was led into the County Jail visiting room for a meeting he hadn't expected to get. At a table not unlike the one in front of the bulletin boards in the squad bullpen, Frank Lucas sat across from his battalion of lawyers.

Lucas looked above half a dozen expensive haircuts to see Richie waiting behind wire-mesh. To no particular one of the lawyers, Lucas said, "Here he is. . . . Let me talk to him alone."

There was some muffled discussion on this point—which Lucas did not participate in, his eyes gazing coolly Richie's way—and finally the pack of legal wolves took their briefcases and went.

Within seconds, Richie was seated across from Lucas. Finally the prosecutor's new suit trumped Lucas's jailhouse threads of T-shirt and brown trousers.

Richie, stone-faced, sat there letting Lucas look him over, the prisoner smiling that same knowing smile he'd worn in the courtroom.

Finally Lucas said, "I just heard something. I said I didn't believe it. Couldn't be true. Just some crazy-ass story from the street."

Richie said nothing.

The half-smile dug a deep dimple in Lucas's cheek. "You didn't *really* turn in a million dollars you found in the trunk of a car, did you?"

Richie said nothing.

Lucas searched Richie's face for a clue. Then he grinned. "I'll tell you what happened to that money you were too pure of heart to take—it wound up in a buncha cops' pockets."

Richie shrugged. "Maybe."

"Maybe my ass. No, it did." Lucas flipped a hand. "And all you did was give all that bread to them, for no good reason. For nothin' in return."

Richie said nothing.

Lucas shifted in his chair. "No, I take that back—you *did* get something in return—their everlasting, motherfucking contempt."

Richie said nothing.

"So why did you *do* this crazy thing? Why give these other assholes all that money? What, you're trying to prove you're *better* than them? Hell, you're not better than them. You *are* them."

"I'm sure these philosophical ramblings would be of interest to somebody," Richie said. "Just not me. You may have heard, I'm in the middle of a big case, so I have neither the time nor the interest to—"

"You turned that dough in because it was the right thing. That's all. You're a good boy and your momma raised you right. Why can't you say that? Why's that so hard for you?" Lucas's grin widened but his eyes narrowed. "Question is, would you do it *again*? . . . I mean, that was a long *time* ago, my man."

Richie said nothing.

Lucas shrugged, and his voice became damn near a purr as he said, "It'd be very easy to find out. Just tell me you'd like to participate in that little experiment, you know, give me an address, and a new car will be waiting for you . . . trunk loaded."

"No thanks."

"You think I'm fucking *kidding*?"

"No."

The cool prisoner suddenly boiled over, eyes and nostrils flaring. "Who the *fuck* are *you* to say *no* to *that*? What, you think that *impresses* me?"

A guard had gotten to his feet, but Richie wasn't reacting—the outburst was clearly over—and the guard sat back down.

And Richie remained impassive.

A few seconds ticked by before Lucas said, "Let me

ask you something. Do you think by putting my ass in jail, things'll change? You think you're gonna stop even one junkie from dying? Because you won't. And if it isn't me, it'll be someone else, probably some brutal prick who won't be so goddamn nice and professional. . . . With me or without me, nothing's gonna change, except maybe for the worse."

"I'll just have to live with that," Richie said.

Lucas's eyebrows tensed. "You have *any* sort of case? Or just that idiot drives for my goddamn brother. Is *Jimmy* your case? 'Cause if Jimmy's your case, him and that powder you confiscated? It's not enough."

Richie smiled, just a little. "Well, then. You got nothing to worry about."

But Lucas was worried, clearly worried. The drug kingpin was not used to sitting across from a cop who didn't want his money, on the one hand, and on the other refused to be one iota intimidated by the fabled Frank Lucas presence.

"My brothers won't talk to you," Lucas said, matter of fact. "My cousins'll stay zipped. My whole family's a bunch of deaf mutes, you'll find. No one's gonna get chatty but that motherfucking driver, and he's an unreliable dope addict."

"You think that's all I have, Frank?"

"Yeah, I think that's all you have."

Now it was Richie's turn to smile smugly. "Frank, I got a line of people stretches around the block and out the door wants to testify against you."

"You're talking bullshit."

"Am I? Any of these names ring a bell? Tony the Bug. Benny Two-Socks. Carmine Camanetti."

Lucas grunted a laugh. "Who are they? Buncha spaghetti-spinners I don't do no business with. Don't know them, they don't know me."

"Sure they know you, Frank. They're the guys you all but put out of business. They sell dope for the Mazzano family, only not so much dope after you put your foot in their trade."

Lucas was shaking his head. "*This* is who you got to stand up against me? Guys who don't *know* me? Who got nothing to *do* with me?"

"They have everything to do with you, Frank. They hate you. The only thing they hate more is what you represent."

"I don't represent a goddamn thing."

"Really? A black businessman like you? You think the Italians like to have black guys put them out of business? Make them look bad, make them look stupid?"

"They were born stupid."

"Maybe. But they know, once your ass is in the slammer, their world can get back to normal. Things can return to how they were."

Lucas was clenching his fists. His voice was softly menacing. "Look at me, chump. You looking? Can you *tell* by looking that it would mean nothing to me tomorrow if you turned up dead?"

"It *might* mean something to you. But if that was a threat? You better get in line . . . chump. That one stretches around the block, too."

Lucas's frustration was palpable. Richie understood

why: Frank Lucas was used to buying people, and he was used to outmaneuvering people, and outthinking them. The druglord obviously wanted to work out something with Richie, but could not find a way in.

And Richie wasn't about to give him one.

Finally Frank said, "What can we do?"

Richie's voice had no self-satisfaction, in fact it even carried a certain compassion when he said, "You know what you have to do."

Lucas did know. He didn't like it, but he knew. *The only way to improve his future was to flip.*

"I could give you cops," Lucas said quietly, "but that's not who you want, right? You want the Organized Crime names."

"I'll take the cops, too. I want all these bastards."

Lucas seemed confused. "You'll take the cops, *too*? You'd go after cops, like those SIU pricks?"

"Especially those SIU pricks."

"You'd do that? Go after your own kind?"

Richie's upper lip twitched. "They're not my kind. Not the bent bastards you've been doing business with. They're not my kind any more than the Italians you put up with are yours."

The two men sat and studied each other in silence.

Then Lucas asked, "What can you give me?"

"Only my promise that if you lie to me about one name, you'll never get out of prison. Lie about one dollar in one offshore account, and the only time you'll see daylight is in the exercise yard. You can live rich in jail, rest of your life . . . or poor outside it. That's what I can promise."

"You're not saying I could *walk* . . . ?"

"No. But you won't be an old man when you get out."

Lucas sat thinking. Richie let him.

Finally, Lucas said, "You know, I don't care if you feds take all my buildings, my stocks, my offshore accounts. Take it all, I don't give a shit—use it to build battleships or paint bridges or whatever the fuck. Fight another pointless war, far as I care."

Lucas leaned forward, fire in his eyes.

"But, Roberts, those other motherfuckers . . . those prick cops . . . they put *my* money in *their* pockets. We're talking *millions.*"

"I believe you."

Lucas got a distant look, still debating with himself over whether to step off this particular cliff. . . .

"I'll want to know everyone you've met for the last twenty years," Richie said. "Everyone you sold to. Every cop you ever paid off. Everybody who ever cheated or stole or shorted you. Every one you can remember."

Lucas chuckled. "Oh, nobody ever said Frank Lucas don't have a good memory. Hell, I remember them all, every damn name, every ugly face. That's not the problem."

Richie blinked. "What is?"

"You ain't got jails big enough."

Frank Lucas's trial was still under way when Richie sicced his squad on their new target.

Surveillance photos were again gathered, but this

time the subjects were not players in the dope game, rather cops receiving envelopes of money on 116th Street and other drops on the New York side of the river. The new table of criminal organization that went up was strictly cops—crooked cops.

And right up at the top of the chart went a surveillance photo of Detective Trupo, Richie finally deciding the son of a bitch *was* special. . . .

Trupo's special moment came at his house, over his morning coffee. Two squad cars pulled into his driveway, blocking him in and embarrassing him with the neighbors. He and his associates had, over the months, watched many of their brethren getting hauled off in cuffs, praying that as the Princes of the City, they breathed air too rarified for them to be taken down.

They were wrong.

Trupo fled to his backyard, but unlike the Lucas place, no buried treasure was waiting, unless you counted the self-administered bullet in the bent cop's brain.

Indictments handed down by the Manhattan DA's office, working in concert with Richard Roberts's narcotics task force, numbered fifty-three NYPD and SIU detectives. By 1977, out of the seventy officers who'd worked the SIU, fifty-two were either under indictment or in jail.

Frank Lucas was convicted of conspiracy to distribute narcotics and sentenced to seventy years. Federal authorities confiscated over 250 million dollars in real estate, equities and cash in domestic and foreign banks.

The day after he convicted Frank Lucas (and thirty Country Boy relatives), Richard Roberts borrowed four hundred bucks from his credit union for a three-day vacation to the Bahamas.

He figured he'd earned it.

And six months later, he quit the Prosecutor's Office to become a defense attorney. He had been a lost cause long enough himself to have developed a rooting interest in other lost causes.

First among his new clients was one Frank Lucas.

With his attorney's help, Frank got out of stir, after fifteen years.

27. Joint

On a bright sunshiny day in 1990, a graying Frank Lucas stepped out of a federal prison, free-at-last-Great-God-Almighty-free-at-last, but also broke as hell—owning nothing more, in fact, than the small cardboard box of odds and ends he'd filled in his cell not long ago.

Frank blinked at the sun—God, it seemed blinding out here. But he was not complaining. His gaze stretched across the parking lot, looking to see if his ride was here.

Richie Roberts, standing by a couple-year-old Pontiac, raised his hand like a kid wanting a teacher to recognize him. Long-haired as ever, Richie was in a black sportcoat over a black T-shirt and black slacks, while Frank wore the gray suit he'd worn into the prison fifteen years before, but no tie.

"You know," Frank said, ambling up with his cardboard box, "a lawyer billing a guy for driving him around could run into dough."

"You don't have any dough."

"Keep that in mind."

Frank set the box on the car's trunk and the two men shook hands, then embraced.

"Where to?" Richie asked.

"Where else? Gotta see it—116th Street."

Pretty soon the two men—who by now had been friends much longer than they'd been adversaries—stood on the sidewalk near Richie's parked car. The street sign Frank was looking up at said: 116TH STREET AND FREDERICK DOUGLASS BOULEVARD.

"Frederick Douglass Boulevard?" Frank asked, dumbfounded. "What was wrong with just plain Eighth Avenue?"

Richie chuckled. "You don't have a sense of history, Frank."

"Bull *shit*. I got too much sense of history, is my problem. Look at this street. Everything Bumpy predicted, a hundred years ago, has come true—corner groceries are gone now. Chain stores everywhere."

"It's a franchise world," Richie said.

But without Blue Magic, Frank thought.

Frank shook his head and grinned. "I used to sit here in my old beater car, with Eva? She hated it, but I liked it 'cause I could be invisible, and watch my street, watch everything goin' down. But it's not my street anymore. And I don't even have a car."

Or Eva.

Right across the street was where Frank had shot Tango Black, a lifetime or two ago. This memory he didn't share with his attorney. The fruit stand he'd shot Tango in front of, it was gone. And his favorite diner.

In the sign of a store labeled NIKE was a huge painting of basketball star Michael Jordan, and a big sign saying JUST DO IT.

"Just do *what*?" Frank asked.

"What?"

"What the fuck is that? Just do what?"

Richie smiled. "Sneakers. Expensive ones. People get killed over them."

"Over *shoes?* Who the fuck would buy those ugly things, much less shoot somebody over 'em?"

"You need a better lawyer than me to come up with an argument for that."

A car booming with subwoofer bass came rumbling by, bleeding rap. Frank stared at the vehicle with a pained look, and suddenly he remembered Bumpy staring at that electronics-emporium window, the day the great man dropped dead on the street.

Casually, maybe too casually, Richie asked, "Your brothers know you're out?"

"Haven't talked to them in years. Better that way— for them. I don't know where they are. Went back home to Greensboro, I guess, when they got out. Hope they're leading straight lives."

Richie nodded.

Frank was taking in the strange storefronts. "What the hell am I gonna do now? Be a janitor or some shit? What do *I* know how to do on this strange fuckin' planet? How am I gonna live?"

"I told you," Richie said, "I wouldn't let you starve. I got legwork needs doing."

"Yeah, you told me, but you can barely take care of yourself, 'cause of all your, what-you-call-it, pro boner shit." Frank nodded toward a pay phone down on the corner. "One little phone call, Richie, I could be back in business."

"You'd need a different lawyer."

"I *won't*. I'm just saying I *could*."

"And I could go to the cops and help put your evil ass back in jail."

"Uh-oh—look out."

Richie swivelled to see what Frank was looking at: a trio of young hoods swaggering up the sidewalk like they owned it and everything around it, baggy pants, bandanas tied around their heads, dripping with what they were calling *bling bling* these days.

Frank was right in their way, but he didn't move, which forced one kid to squeeze between him and a parking meter. The kid glared back, obviously about to say something or maybe even *do* something . . .

. . . but something about the expressionless expression on Frank's old-school face made the kid think better.

One of his pals said, "What?"

But the kid who'd squeezed past Frank had the good sense to let it go. "Nothin'," he mumbled.

And they bounced on.

Frank glanced at Richie. "Hell. Every idiot gets to be young once."

"You think?"

The man who once owned 116th Street had no idea what lay ahead, but he knew one thing: he was alive today when he should have been dead and buried, a hundred times over. So he was ahead of the game.

"Let's get out of here," Frank said.

"Where to?"

"I don't care. Just some other direction."

As Richie was getting behind the wheel, Frank said, "Tell me the truth, Rich—when you were first investigating me, you couldn't believe I'd pulled off that Southeast Asia connection, could you? An uneducated black man, come up with a slick smuggling operation like that? You just couldn't buy it. I mean, man, in my own twisted way, I really did something. Admit it."

"You really did," Richie granted. "In your own twisted way."

And the two friends drove out of Harlem.

A TIP OF THE FEATHERED FEDORA

Although this novel is based on the screenplay by
Steven Zaillian, I am also indebted to the original basic
source material, Mark Jacobson's fascinating August
14, 2000, *New York* magazine article, "The Return of
Superfly."

As you may have gathered from a passage in the
text, the somewhat cryptic chapter titles make use of
"brand names" of heroin in Harlem in the early '70s
(listed in the *New York* magazine article).

Despite its basis in fact, Mr. Zaillian's fine screenplay is a fictionalized take on events in the lives of
Richard Roberts and Frank Lucas. This novel takes
further liberties with this fact-based tale, and the
"Richie Roberts" and "Frank Lucas" in these pages
must be viewed as highly fictionalized characteriza-
tions (as should "Nicky Barnes"). In interviews, for
example, Mr. Roberts has made clear that his depiction
as a womanizer during his first marriage was a fiction
created for the film to make him seem "less vanilla."

My thanks to Cindy Chang of Universal Pictures
for providing stills and other materials throughout the
writing of this novel; and to Tor editor Jim Frenkel,

who was always available for help and support. Thanks also to my agent and friend, Dominick Abel.

As usual my wife, writer Barbara Collins, was my first reader and editor, and I appreciate her help and encouragement, which began long before I ever knew I'd be writing this novel, specifically on our honeymoon in Chicago, when I took her to see *Cotton Comes to Harlem*.

ABOUT THE AUTHOR

MAX ALLAN COLLINS was hailed in 2004 by *Publishers Weekly* as "a new breed of writer." A frequent Mystery Writers of America Edgar nominee, he has earned an unprecedented fourteen Private Eye Writers of America Shamus nominations for his historical thrillers, winning for his Nathan Heller novels *True Detective* (1983) and *Stolen Away* (1991).

His graphic novel *Road to Perdition* is the basis of the Academy Award-winning film starring Tom Hanks, directed by Sam Mendes. His many comics credits include the syndicated strip *Dick Tracy,* his own *Ms. Tree, Batman,* and *CSI: Crime Scene Investigation,* based on the hit TV series for which he has also written video games, jigsaw puzzles, and a *USA Today* best-selling series of novels.

An independent filmmaker in the midwest, he wrote and directed the Lifetime movie *Mommy* (1996) and a sequel, *Mommy's Day* (1997). He wrote *The Expert,* a 1995 HBO World Premiere, and wrote and directed the innovative made-for-DVD feature *Real Time: Siege at Lucas Street Market* (2000). *Shades of Noir* (2004), an anthology of his short films, includes his award-winning documentary *Mike Hammer's Mickey Spillane,* featured in a collection of his films, *Black Box*. His most recent feature, *Eliot Ness: An Untouchable Life* (2006), based on his Edgar-nominated play, has won two film festivals and is also available on DVD.

His other credits include film criticism, short fiction, songwriting, trading-card sets, and movie/TV tie-in novels, including the *New York Times* bestseller *Saving Private Ryan*.

Collins lives in Muscatine, Iowa, with his wife, writer Barbara Collins. Their son, Nathan, a recent University of Iowa graduate, has completed a year of post-grad studies in Japan.

BOOKS BY MAX ALLAN COLLINS

THE ROAD TO PERDITION SAGA

Road to Perdition (graphic novel)
Road to Perdition (movie tie-in novel)
Road to Perdition 2: On the Road (graphic novel)
Road to Purgatory
Road to Paradise

THE MEMOIRS OF NATHAN HELLER

True Detective
True Crime
The Million-Dollar Wound
Neon Mirage
Stolen Away
Dying in the Post-War World
Carnal Hours
Blood and Thunder
Damned in Paradise
Flying Blind
Majic Man
Angel in Black
Kisses of Death
Chicago Confidential

RECENT NOVELS

Deadly Beloved (Ms. Tree)
A Killing in Comics (Jack and Maggie Starr)
Black Hats (as Patrick Culhane)
The Last Quarry (Quarry)
Antiques Roadkill (with Barbara Collins, as Barbara Allan)
Antiques Maul (with Barbara Collins, as Barbara Allan)